SUPER GIRL

Books 4 – 6

John Zakour & Katrina Kahler

Table of Contents

Book 4 - The Expanding World 3

Book 5 - Out of this World 115

Book 6 - Saving the World! 223

Book 4

The Expanding World

Road Trip

I sat in the high-speed hover plane that belongs to my dad's company, pondering over how much my life has changed this year. When the year started, I was a normal everyday kid living with her mom. I hadn't seen my dad in years. I had learned to deal with that by mostly not thinking about it. Plus, Mom and I had a good life together, and we were a team.

Then I hit the big one-three, thirteen, the teen years. Little did I know at the time that meant I had absorbed enough energy from the sun to become Super Teen. Yep, me…nice normal, Lia Strong, suddenly became a superhero. I'm so strong that a whiff of my feet can knock out a mall. I can lift a building without breaking a sweat. I can jump super high and far. I've been practicing hovering, and I have heat vision and super breath. I can, with practice, even use my scent to make people do what I want them to do. Pretty much, I am a one girl army. Yet the thing that is most different in my life, is that my dad is back.

Turns out, my dad is the head man of BM Science. It's a huge company that invents all sorts of nifty inventions, like this hover plane I'm flying in. Now that I'm super, my dad wants to help me use my powers for good deeds. He and my mom have been great trainers for me. Mom teaches me how to act like a super person, while Dad uses his company to help me use my powers where they are really needed.

That's why right now we hovered over Africa. Until today I had never been more than 100 miles away from my home town of Star Light City. And I now found myself sitting in the passenger seat of a really sweet plane next to my best buddy Jason.

Jason knows everything about superheroes, so he has become my official consultant.

In front of us sat Dad and his beautiful assistant, Hana. From the way Dad looked at Hana, I could tell he thought of her as more than an assistant. I could almost see the hearts in his eyes. I tried not to think about the fact that Hana was an android Dad had made. Yep, my dad had made his own beautiful assistant who he now had a crush on.

"Doctor Strong, we will be over the drop site in two minutes," one of the pilots informed my father.

Dad swiveled his chair to face me. "You've got this, honey!"

Jason could barely sit still. "Your first mission outside of the country! I'm so excited, Lia!!"

I smiled at him. "I just hope I can handle this."

Jason patted me on the shoulder. "You've so got this, girl! Fifty rhino poachers don't have a chance against Super Teen!"

"I hope so…" I said.

Jason looked me in the eyes. "I know so! I may not be super like you, but I do know super when I see it!" His eyes popped open. "You know, I've been thinking about another defensive ability for you. I'm betting you could hypnotize people."

"I have the pheromone thing going on with my sweat that can make people do what I want, kind of," I said slowly.

Jason grinned. "Yeah, I know, but that's almost impossible for you to control."

"I'm working on it!" I said defensively.

Jason leaned back and held up a hand. "Yes, I understand, but even at best, that's a power that will blast everybody. I think you can do a more controlled one. What about getting a person or animal to focus on your finger moving really fast while using a commanding super voice."

I looked at him. "That sounds pretty comic-book-like…"

"You do have super farts, and you've knocked people and animals out with morning breath…" Jason laughed.

"Good point," I sighed. I lifted up a finger and put it in front of Jason's eyes. I moved my finger rapidly back and forth and said in my most commanding voice, "Follow my finger."

Jason's eyes locked on my finger, following right and left, left and right. I saw Jason's eyelids start to droop. "You will cluck like a chicken!" I ordered.

"Cluck! Cluck!" Jason said, even using his arms for wings.

He squatted down.

"You're Jason again!" I said quickly before he tried to lay an egg.

Jason shook his head. His eyes popped open. "Did it work?"

I smirked.

Dad came over to me. "Okay, honey, we're almost over the drop site."

"Tell me again why we're doing this," I said to Dad.

Hana smiled. "The government of this country wants to stop these poachers, but they don't have the resources. Your father volunteered our services. Once you take out the small army of bad guys, the government will come in and take them away."

"We're over the drop site, sir!" one of the pilots announced.

I stood up. "Mac, activate my suit!" I told my computer assistant that Dad had built for me. I think of Mac as a really smart watch.

"Roger!" Mac said. "I am so excited."

I saw my holographic mask appear in front of my face. My nano clothing morphed into a really pretty light green, sleeveless body suit. The side door to the hover plane popped open. I leaped out and started falling to the ground.

"Since you are immune to sunburn, I thought the sleeveless look would be a nice touch!" Mac said as I fell through the air.

"It is," I agreed.

I took a deep breath. I held out my arms and my legs. My fall slowed to a glide. I smiled. My body rippled with joy! I felt amazing as I slowly descended towards the ground with the wind in my face.

All of a sudden, I spotted my target. It was a campsite of canvas tents surrounding a bunch of men with big guns and bigger trucks, sitting and standing around a table. They looked like they were getting ready to move. To the north, I spotted a majestic herd of rhinos. No way would I allow those men to hurt the rhinos.

I steered myself towards the camp. I kicked my legs. I'm not really sure why, but it seemed to help. My super hearing picked up the voices of the men making plans.

"Okay we will circle the rhinos and then open fire on my count," one of them said.

I had heard enough. I straightened my arms and legs into the diving position. I dove into the ground and landed right in the midst of the group. I hit the hard surface with concussion force that sent the men sprawling.

Leaping to a standing position, I quickly dusted myself off.

Pointing at the men, I announced firmly. "I'll give you guys one chance to surrender!"

They drew their weapons.

"Why should we surrender? We have you outnumbered 50 to one!" a man holding a pair of binoculars smirked.

I took a deep breath to clear my head and calm my nerves. I knew I had this, but that still didn't stop me from being nervous. After all, I had never done anything like this before. I pointed up to the sky. "Look, dudes, I just dropped from the sky." I pointed to the crater caused by my landing. "The ground took way more of a beating than I did." I paused to let that sink in. "Now, unless you guys want me to do to you what I did to the ground, you'll just give up."

The lead man shrugged. “We have weapons.”

I shrugged back. “I am not impressed. But in the interest of fair play, I will give you guys first shot.”

I stared down the barrels of the biggest guns I had ever seen. I had done the practice simulations in dad’s lab. I felt pretty certain these guns couldn’t hurt me. Dad says I am pretty close to being completely invulnerable. I'm not quite sure if that meant I could deflect bullets from 50 guns. Pretty sure it did.

The boss poacher, who looked more like a soldier than a hunter, smiled. “You’re nervous, I can tell.”

I nodded. “Yep, I’m nervous about hurting you all too much.”

The boss shrugged. “Look, we don’t want to fight you. Leave now and we’ll let you go!”

I shook my head. “Not going to happen!” I stomped my foot on the ground.

The force of my stomped ripped through the ground and sent them all reeling backward.

"Tell you, what, I'll make you guys the same offer. Swear you'll never hurt rhinos and run away now. Then I'll let you go!"

A couple of the smarter guys tossed down their guns and ran away. But most of them stumbled back to their feet and stood their ground. The boss glared at me. "Neat trick. Let's see if you're bulletproof!" he said. "Fire!" he shouted.

I heard the sound of about forty high-powered weapons firing at me. I saw the bullets coming towards me. I could trace the path of each one and dodge them if I wanted. While that would certainly be impressive, I figured it would be more sensational to let the bullets bounce off me instead.

I held my breath. I stood there as each bullet hit me then fell harmlessly to the ground. Truthfully, I kind of impressed myself with that.

I rubbed my hands together. "O-kay, you can't say I didn't give you jerks a chance!"

I shot forward at super speed. I decided to save the boss for last. I grabbed the second nearest bad guy's gun. I bent it in half. Then I tapped him on the forehead. He fell over, out cold before he even knew what had hit him. I grabbed the two guys next to him. I smashed them together like cymbals, and let them drop to the ground. I raced at the next four or five men at super speed. Each time I took their guns, tied them in knots, then tapped each man on the forehead, knocking each one out. After dealing with the first ten or so, I stopped for a moment, just to take in how the other bad guys were reacting.

They all started to panic and aimed their weapons aimlessly. If I had let them fire, they would have all shot each other. Instead, I inhaled then exhaled, hitting them all with super breath. I hadn't eaten for a while so I figured my breath probably wasn't very pleasant.

The force of my breath knocked them over and the less than pleasant smell knocked them all out.

"Sorry, I forgot my breath mints," I told their unconscious bodies.

Turning my attention to the boss, I smiled as I walked towards him. "I thought I'd save the worst for last."

He instantly dropped to his knees, reaching into his back pocket and pulling out a wad of money that was thicker than a deck of cards. He then waved it at me. "Look, I have a lot of money! It's all yours if you just fly away now!"

I placed one finger under his chin and lifted him off the ground. "That's the problem with people like you, all you care about is money! I don't want your stinking money! I want to do the right thing!" Then I smiled. "And I think I can help you do the right thing!"

The man shrugged and shook his head. "Nah, kid, I'm a pretty bad dude. I don't think there's anything you can do to change that. Just knock me out and turn me over to the authorities, then be done with it."

"I appreciate your honesty!" I told him.

He pulled a knife from his sleeve and plunged it into my neck. The knife snapped. I shook my head. "If bullets don't hurt me, why do you think a knife would work?"

He shrugged. "Like I said, I'm a bad guy. Didn't say I was overly bright. Just brighter than my men..."

I shook my finger in front of his eyes. I noticed how he followed my finger and waved it in front of his eyes very quickly. "Follow my finger," I ordered in my most commanding voice.

The man did as he was asked. His eyes darted back and forth, all the while locked on my finger.

"You are getting sleepy!" I ordered.

"I am getting sleepy..." he repeated slowly.

"Sleep!" I ordered.

His eyes shut and his head dropped forward. I smiled.

"When you wake up you will become a rhino activist. You will do whatever you can to help rhinos," I ordered.

"But I'll be in jail..." the man muttered.

"Well, you can work over the internet while you're in jail!" I replied.

"I obey!" the man said.

I let him drop.

"Man, that felt good!" I said to Mac.

"Yes, nice use of super hypnosis," Mac said. "You did such a good job that I'm almost afraid to mention this."

"Ah, Mac! Mention what?" I said, looking at my watch interface.

"All those bullets spooked that heard of rhinos. They are now charging a nearby village."

"Oh, that is so not good..." I gulped.

"Agreed! I estimate they will reach the village in three minutes."

"Which way are they going?" I asked frantically.

"East!" he said.

"I'm going to need more help than that." A little arrow pointing left appeared in the watch face and I leaped up into the air.

Dear Diary: Why is it that even when I do something right, I do something wrong? You would think being super would be easier than this!

Rhinos

I jumped into the air towards the charging heard of rhinos. My super vision locked in on the pack. I saw a dozen large gray rhinos running in fear, their stomping caused a giant dust cloud. I could have spotted them even without super vision. Further in the distance, I saw the little town that was directly in the path of the stampeding rhinos. The homes were small wooden shacks and there was no way that those homes could stand up to a rhino.

"Okay Mac, any suggestions on how I can stop a herd of charging rhinos?" I asked.

"I'm calculating right now," Mac replied.

"Well," he continued slowly. "You could release a super fart over them. That will stop them cold in their tracks. The trick is calculating wind direction and speed. You will also drop the town you are trying to protect. But knocking them all out is better than having the villagers stomped on."

Mac was right. I had to use one of my super farts. I squinted my eyes and tried to force my butt cheeks to let one rip. Nothing. Nada. Zilch. Of course, it was one of the few times in my life that I actually wanted to fart in public and I wasn't able to.

"Anytime now…" Mac instructed impatiently.

I squinted harder, pushed harder and squeezed my fists. Not sure why I thought that would help.

I shook my head. "I don't have it in me," I sighed for a moment, then crashed to the ground just a few yards in front of the charging pack.

Shooting back up to my feet, I lifted my arm up in the air to halt the rhinos. With nothing better to do, I shouted, "Stop!"

Yeah, I knew rhinos couldn't understand English, but I thought maybe the force of my voice would have an impact.

The lead rhino stopped in its tracks. Could my voice have worked? The rhino abruptly turned blue.

Then, without warning, it rolled over with its legs up in the air. And one by one, each rhino stopped, gasped, and then flipped over.

"That works too," Mac said.

It took me a moment to figure out what happened. I sniffed my raised underarm. Woo, that had a kick to it. I think it even made my eyes spin. Yep, the pressure of fighting fifty armed bad guys and then stopping a charging herd of rhinos had burnt through my deodorant.

"I suggest you put your arm down unless you want these poor rhinos to wilt and never recover," Mac added.

I quickly thrust down my arm and walked towards the lead rhino. His stomach was rising and falling and I breathed a sigh of relief. I was fairly certain he and the others would wake up in a few hours.

"Do you think I need to drag them all away from the village?" I asked Mac.

"I don't believe so," Mac told me. "When these rhinos regain consciousness, they won't have the energy to do much except wander back to their field. You did it, Lia! You saved the day!"

I smiled weakly. "Yep, I guess so."

"Your dad says...great job! Now, report to the hovercraft so that he can get you home in time for dinner. After all, tomorrow is the first day of school!" Mac stated firmly.

"Oh great," I said. "I can hardly wait!"

Dear Diary: Wow, my first road trip mission was a pretty big success. I'm amazed by how much my power is growing. A whiff of my underarm stress sweat can drop a heard of rhinos. Part of me thinks, 'WOW, that's so cool'. Another part thinks, 'YIKES! I could be really dangerous.'

The Plane

With the job done and both the poachers and the rhinos dealt with, I figured it was time to get home. I leaped up towards the plane, keeping my right arm extended to steer me into the open door. I knew I'd have to lock my arm to my side the moment I entered, or else my scent would quickly overpower everybody on the plane.

The plan was simple…get on the plane, then hit the shower ASAP.

I entered through the open doorway and the door whirled shut behind me. I forced my arm to my side. But when I turned, I saw Jason, my dad, and the two pilots instantly go limp.

"Oops, I must smell worse than I thought…" I said.

"Stress sweat can pack quite the punch," Mac replied. "I hold myself partially to blame since I gave you a sleeveless suit. If only I hadn't been such a slave to fashion, then I could have added sleeves and the nano anti-smell bots might have been able to keep up with you..." Mac computed for a second more. "Of course, if I had done that, you might not have stopped the rhinos, so I now conclude that I did the right thing."

The plane shook, then started dropping towards the ground.

"Okay, maybe not," I said.

"Hmmm, one of the unconscious pilots must have their head on the descend switch," Hana said, standing up. She calmly walked towards the cockpit. "It's a good thing I have no need to breathe and I can fly this plane. Otherwise, all the regular humans on board would be in big trouble."

Hana walked into the cockpit and pushed the lead pilot off his seat. She sat down in front of the controls.

I felt the plane lift upwards and then hold steady. Hana looked over her shoulder. "Now you go take a nice refreshing shower, Lia. We'll talk girl to simulated girl when you're finished."

The second the cooling water from the shower head hit my head and I felt myself tingle. Ah, I had no idea how much dirt, grime and sweat my body had covering it, but it felt so good to wash it all off. Although, I guess I did know how much sweat there had been, since a whiff of me, even with my arms down, overpowered all the regular people on our aircraft.

"Make sure you wash extra-long under your arms," Hana told me over the intercom. "It's nice that all the men are napping now, but we do want them to wake up before the trip is over."

"I understand," I grumbled back. Though truthfully, I was upset that Hana thought she needed to remind me of that.

"Sorry if I am being over-cautious and telling you the obvious," Hana continued, "it is just what I do."

I added a bit of extra soap under my arms and scrubbed a bit. I then lifted them so the spray could rinse them off. I took it as a good sign that the spray head didn't melt when I pointed my underarm at it. It's a weird feeling of power when your underarms can melt a showerhead. Luckily, that only happened once.

I finished showering, dried off, and then used my super deodorant generously under each arm. I headed to the front of the plane. Hana sat in the pilot seat, using the pilot as a footrest.

She looked at me, saw my expression and shrugged. "Your father made me shorter than I would like, so I'm using the pilot to prop my legs up. Don't worry, I took off my shoes, and my feet aren't stinky at all." Hana motioned to the co-pilot's seat. She had moved the co-pilot to the floor next to the seat, so I stepped over him and sat down.

"I'm glad we have this little time alone," Hana said slowly.

"Ah, me too," I said even slower. "But what's going on?"

She smiled at me.

I pointed at her. "Look you're not going to challenge me to a fight like your previous model did! That didn't work out too well for her as I reduced her to scrap metal."

Hana laughed. "We're not made of metal."

"Well, scrap, or whatever," I said.

Hana leaned towards me. "I just want to have some girl talk..."

Sitting in the co-pilots chair. I looked down at the white fluffy clouds below us. It felt funny to be flying so high especially with an android pilot who wanted to chat. But, pretty much everything about my life felt weird these days. "So, what do you want to talk about?" I asked.

"Your father," Hana said quickly.

"Ah, okay. He's a cool guy. A little on the nerdy mad scientist side, but I know he means well. I mean, if he insulted you or something, I'm sure it was a misunderstanding. Human interaction isn't his strong point."

Hana laughed. "How true, which is why I am glad I'm not human. And it's also why I would like to ask your father out."

"Excuse me?" I said. For some reason, I felt my face blushing.

Hana looked me in the eyes. "I find your father interesting, and funny, and I enjoy being around him. I want to see more of him..."

"By more of him, you mean?"

Hana giggled. "I want to see him out of the office. I want to go bowling with him. Watch Netflix with him. Go out to dinner with him!"

"Do you even eat?" I asked. Yes, I know that shouldn't have been my main concern just then but I wanted to know.

"I have no need to eat, but I can eat for fun. My e-stomach acids can dissolve food into energy much like humans do. Except I have no need to poop or pee."

"Too much information, Hana. Too much information!"

"Right! Sorry. It's my job to give information. I forget that with you humans, it's possible to give too much information for your little brains," Hana replied.

"Okay, let's get back on topic, please. Does my dad know about this?"

Hana grinned. "No, when it comes to matters of the heart or e-heart, your dad is pretty clueless."

"So, Dad didn't make you want to be his date?"

Hana laughed. Her laugh somehow sounded like birds chirping. "Of course not, your dad made me only to be a tool. A tool that can grow. That's what I am doing."

"Okay, if Dad made you only as a tool then why did he make you so…."

"Hot?" she asked.

"I was going to say built like a supermodel."

Hana grinned. "Oh, please. The average super model weighs 110 pounds, and I weigh 120 pounds."

"So, the answer is no then?" I said.

Hana shook her head. "Nope, you father has no idea I am thinking this way. He will be surprised, but hopefully pleasantly surprised. I'm sure at first he may go out with me simply as an experiment to see how I will react."

I nodded. "Yeah, he can be a big nerd. The first time he came back into my life, he attacked me with a drone."

"Yes, I heard." Hana's eyes opened wide. "But it is my hope that he will grow to see me as more than an invention. I hope he will learn to love me."

"Wait…love?" I stammered. "Are you able to love?"

Hana's eyes widened even more. "I hope we will all find out soon enough. Even though I know you can't hurry love."

"So you're asking for my permission to date my dad?" I asked.

"I thought it would only be proper," Hana nodded.

"And if I say no?" I shot her a curious look.

Hana's eyes became smaller. "I will be sad. But I will still ask him out once I win you over. I just compute it will be easier on all of us if you agree."

"Then go for it!" I said. "I hope you and my dad will be happy together. But I'm definitely not calling you, Mom!"

"How about mother-2.0?" Hana asked.

"Nope. Definitely not!!!"

Dear Diary: Just when I think life can't get any stranger, my dad's android assistant asks me for my permission to date him. Yeah, sure it's strange, but I just want my dad to be happy. Just because he and my mom didn't work out, doesn't mean he doesn't deserve happiness. I hope it works out for him.

Back in the USA

By the time the hover plane landed, Jason, my dad, and the pilots had all regained consciousness. And I actually made it home before Mom did, which was kind of weird. Mom is never out past 9 PM, so I texted her:

LIA>Mom u ok?

MOM>B home soon honey.

'Well, that was cryptic', I thought to myself.

My ever faithful dog, Shep, walked over and I gave him a nice scratch behind the ears. I think he enjoyed that so much, he might have even purred. Since I still felt pretty fresh from my hover plane shower, I kicked my shoes off. I wanted to spend my last night before school as comfy as possible.

"Hopefully a whiff of my shoes won't knock you out!" I told Shep.

He didn't fall over instantly which was a good sign. Still, for some reason, Shep always needed to take a good sniff of my shoes. Apparently, he wasn't as smart as I had always thought. Shep walked towards the spot where my shoes had landed.

"I wouldn't do that if I were you," I warned. "My feet may have been cleaned from the shower but those shoes had been through a lot today." Shep stuck his big nose right into the shoe then pulled his nose out.

"Phew, I guess they've aired out enough," I said.

His knees began to wobble and he rolled over onto the ground.

"Oops, I guess they haven't aired enough after all," I shook my head at Shep. "I did warn you!"

I heard the front door open. Mom walked in wearing a red dress, a very short red dress.

Mom pointed at Shep. "That dog will never learn!" she smiled.

I stood up. "Wow, Mom!" was all I could say.

She opened her arms and spun around.

"Did you have an event at the hospital?" I asked.

She leaped over and sat on the couch, then kicked off her red high-heeled shoes and wrinkled her nose. "Phew! If Shep wasn't knocked out by your shoes, mine would certainly put him down. I could sedate patients with those. Heck, I could sedate the entire hospital." She looked up at me and grinned, "Guess I was nervous."

I finally put two and two together, and my face lit up. I shot over next to her. "Wait, you were on a date?"

She looked at me and smiled. "Yes. I hope you don't mind."

"Of course I don't mind! You deserve to be happy!" I said, taking her arm. "Who's the lucky guy?"

Mom didn't answer. She turned away smirking.

"Come on Mom, spill."

"I met him at the hospital…" she replied slowly.

"You're dating a patient?"

She shook her head and laughed. It felt good to hear my mom laugh. "No, he was putting together a news story on what makes medicine work!" she said.

"So he's a reporter? I didn't think they had newspaper reporters in this town? Is he from out of town?"

"He is a reporter and he is from this town, but he works for the TV station. It's Oscar Oranga!" mom said.

"You mean the Oscar Oranga who is always reporting on Super Teen? The man who has made it his mission to discover who Super Teen is?"

Mom nodded. "Yes, I'm afraid so. He's very dedicated and also very nice."

"But Mom! He's like my arch nemesis!" I said, admittedly being overly dramatic.

Mom smiled. "Don't be silly. He's just doing his job. You don't have an arch nemesis. You're a teenage girl, not a comic book character. Besides, if you did have a nemesis, it would be Wendi Long!"

"Good point," I added.

I thought carefully about what to say next. After all, I did want Mom to be happy. I just couldn't be sure we could trust Oscar Oranga. "Do you think he might suspect that I could be Super Teen? Do you think he might be dating you to get information? Reporters can be tricky when going after a story."

Mom looked at me with raised eyebrows. "What your mom can't get a man on her own? I'm a doctor, and I'm still pretty fine looking if I do say so myself."

I put my hand on her arm. "Mom, you know I think you're beautiful. But this seems awfully suspicious. I mean the man is always asking, 'Who is Super Teen?' Now he's dating Super Teen's mom.

She smiled at me. I knew that smile meant - *Honey, I'm not nearly as dense as you think I am*. Then she spoke the words but they weren't exactly what I was expecting to hear. "Honey, I thought the same thing. So when he asked me out I put him under."

"You did what?"

"I used my hypnotic voice on him," Mom said.

"Hey, that's cool, I just used mine today!" I said, getting slightly off topic.

"Yes, it's a handy power, but one I don't like to use too much, or else I might make everybody around me just roll over and be quiet for a while."

I nodded. "I know the feeling."

Mom put a finger under my chin and lifted my head up gently. "These powers of ours are a blessing. We can do a lot of good in the world, either openly or behind the scenes. Still, we have to be careful not to become dependent on them or abuse them. That would be very bad..."

I put my hand on her shoulder. "I know, Mom. I'm careful."

She grinned. "I don't like using the hypnotic command voice, but when it comes to my daughter's safety I will. So, I questioned Oscar, and he really only wants to go out with me because he finds me smart and also very attractive. Her grin grew. "His words not mine." She put a hand on my shoulder. "You are always first in my book."

I leaned in and kissed her on the cheek. "Love you, Mom."

"Love you too, my girl."

"So how was the date?"

She leaned back in the chair and smiled. "Let's just say there will be a second date!"

"Good for you Mom!" I truly was happy for her. Now both my parents would be dating. What a coincidence!

"How was your trip?" Mom asked, changing the subject.

"You know me, same old, same old. I took out a small army of rhino hunters, accidentally knocked out a heard of rhinos, and then knocked out everyone on the hover plane with my nervous sweat. All in all, mostly successful."

She laughed. "Yes, nervous sweat can have quite the kick. I think it's part of our superhuman defense mechanism. It's painless for people we put to sleep and lets us get on with our job."

Mom and I spent the rest of the evening chatting. I didn't mention that Dad's android assistant wanted to date him. I figured it was best to see where that went before mentioning it.

After all, Mom and Dad were friends now, so there was no use tossing more information out just in case nothing came of it. But even so, it was a huge coincidence that the dating thing was happening in both their lives at exactly the same time.

Dear Diary: Wow, my mom and dad are both possibly dating other people. Well good for them. Maybe with a new year starting at school, something will click for me as well. Who knows? Maybe Brandon will finally see that Wendi isn't good enough for him. Or maybe I will meet somebody new! But then, there's always Jason. Yeah, he's my BFF but sometimes I still wonder if maybe, just maybe, there might be more between us. He knows me so well. But there is no need to rush. I'm not old like Mom and Dad. I have plenty of time to sort this all out, and I'm sure the right boy for me is out there.

I just wonder who it will be.

Schooling

The next morning Jason and I walked to school, just like we had done every day since we were six. I liked our walk time together. It felt warm and reassuring, like a nice snuggly blanket. Plus, it gave us a chance to talk about life.

"So, I thought the mission went well yesterday," Jason told me.

"Me too, but sorry about knocking you out."

Jason chuckled. "Ah, I'm used to it now."

"It's just amazing how much our lives have changed in the last year," he continued. "Wow, I'm best buddies with Super Teen. Your dad is back in your life. We know other super people. It's all so cool."

"Yeah, it's pretty amazing!" I agreed as we passed by Ms. Jewel's house.

Sure enough, her mean dog, 'Cuddles' started barking and running towards the fence that surrounded the house. Cuddles happened to be the worst named dog in the world. Nothing sweet about this dog! He rushed towards us until he either saw or sniffed it was me then he stopped dead in his tracks and rolled over with his legs up in the air.

"It's nice Cuddles has learned he's no match for you," Jason grinned.

I smiled back, "Yep, it does save time."

We walked by Felipe's and Tomas's house. Normally Felipe would come out to greet us. But not today.

"That's weird. No Felipe," I said to Jason.

Jason shrugged. "Maybe he's sleeping in. After all, he is getting older."

I looked at their house. "Funny, I don't sense them in there."

Jason pulled me along. "They could be on vacation or out shopping. Even half-vampires need to eat and shop and relax."

"Good point," I nodded, as we continued on our way.

Even though I hadn't been too keen to go back to school, now that we were on our way, I was eager to get there. It was always fun arriving for the first day. The school was still as ugly as ever, but it was clean and smelled fresh. Janitor Jan always did a great job preparing the place. I always wondered how one woman could clean such a big school until I learned she was a sorceress. That made perfect sense in this new world of mine.

As soon as we arrived, my good friend, Krista rushed over to me. She had her hair curled and it looked great.

"Big news! Brandon isn't running for class president because he wants to concentrate on his grades and his LAX," she said in one breath.

"How is that great news?" I asked.

"Because Wendi is running!" Krista said hurriedly.

I shook my head. "Krista, I'm still not hearing the good news part..."

"I have to agree," Jason said.

Krista took a deep breath. "Well, I didn't want Wendi to run unopposed because, well, she's Wendi. She's on enough of a power trip already!"

"So you're running against her?" I asked.

Krista laughed. "No, I could never beat Wendi. I nominated you! Steve Mann seconded it. And then Marie thirded it."

"Ah..." I said. I felt honored but also a bit overwhelmed. I had a lot on my plate. Plus, I knew the candidates for class president would have to give a speech in front of the entire class. I hate giving speeches. My knees were shaking just thinking about it.

"Of course, Mr. Ohm, our class advisor says none of this matters until you agree. So do you agree?" Krista asked me, her eyes batting away.

Before I could respond Wendi sauntered over. "So, Strong, I heard a rumor that you think you can beat me for class president," she sniggered. "I'm a better LAX player than you. I'm smarter than you. I'm prettier than you. I'm more popular than you."

"Yeah, well..." I stuttered.

"Oh, good comeback!" Wendi replied. "Yep, you have what it takes to run the class," she snorted.

I fought the massive urge to blast Wendi with heat vision. Or, maybe use super voice to make her think she's a chicken or my pet poodle. But no, that's not how good guys do it. We do it the right way. We let the people pick their leaders.

"Well, Wendi," I said, slowly locking my eyes with her perfect blue ones. "Guess we'll let our classmates decide because I'm definitely running against you!"

Krista jumped up and down applauding until Wendi stopped her with a glare.

Wendi held out a hand. "Well then, may the best girl win!"

I shook her hand.

Yeah, I can stop a small army of bad guys. I can drop a charging pack of rhinos. However, something told me this would be my toughest test yet. I knew I could do it. At least I hoped I could do it.

Wendi walked away with her posse. Jason and I headed to my locker so I could store my jacket.

Standing next to my locker was a short stocky kid with braces and glasses. His name was Steve Mann.

"Ah, ah, hi Lia," he said slowly like he had trouble thinking of the words.

"Oh hi, Steve."

He looked at me and then began tapping his foot. Glancing shyly away, he murmured, "Ah, you know I seconded your nomination for class president."

"Thanks, Steve."

Jason came straight in, "I would have done it if I had been here." "Only my BFF and I were still walking into school together like we always do!"

Interesting. I got the impression Jason was hinting to Steve to stay away. Although Steve didn't seem to pick up on that.

"You know Lia, the school has a dance this year," he stared directly towards me.

"Yep. They have one every year. Though it's more of a listen to music, talk and stand around..."

"I'd love it if you'd go with me!" Steve blurted suddenly.

"Steve, the dance isn't for like six months!" I replied.

Steve nodded. "Yeah, I know." He looked down. "Has somebody else already asked you?"

"No of course not, because the dance is still six months away," I repeated.

His eyes popped open. "Great! So you don't have a date?" He looked at me eagerly, like a puppy expecting a treat.

I really didn't want to go to the dance with Steve Mann. I didn't mind that he was a bit of a nerd. It's just that he happened to be shorter than me. Plus, to be honest, I had never really even said three words to Steve before this. I had no idea why he was so keen for me to go with him.

"Look, Steve, let me think about it for a few months," I said slowly.

"That's not a no!" Steve said, his voice cracking.

"No, it's not a no...," I said even slower.

Jason leaned past me. "But it's not a yes either!" he told Steve.

Steve smiled and turned and walked away humming. "I have a chance! I have a chance!"

I sniffed my underarm. Had I forgotten my deodorant? Had my pheromones been firing extra hard? Nope, I smelled like spring flowers. Certainly not my natural scent.

Jason locked his eyes on Steve's back. "That kid bugs me. Always talking about how his computer is so fast, how he has a cool drone, how he's going to go to MIT and will invent the next Google."

He looked at me, "You're not *seriously* thinking about going to the dance with him, are you?"

I'd never seen this side of Jason before. I do believe he was jealous. "No, I just didn't want to hurt his feelings," I replied.

Jason breathed a little sigh of relief. Then the bell rang and we headed to class.

"Of course, if he is going to invent the next Google, I'd be crazy not to at least consider him!" I added, walking into Mr. Ohm's homeroom, a wide grin attached to my face.

The amazing thing is that the rest of my day went pretty smoothly. Sure, I had to listen to a bunch of teachers telling me how their subject was the most important subject in the world. Sure, they would each pile on homework like they were the only teachers in the school. Of course, the hot food in the cafeteria was cold, and the cold food somehow hot. But I went through the whole process with my friends and teammates, and that made everything more fun. Besides, while I would never admit this out loud, I liked learning. Oh, and I'm pretty sure I caught Brandon smiling at me.

After classes, I hit the school weight room with a few girls from the team. Obviously being Super Teen, I didn't need to train in that particular weight room. In fact, I could easily carry all the weights in that room with one hand. My dad's company had a set up a special gym and a weight room for me to train in, along with the other super girls, Tanya, Lori, Marie, and Jess. The company weight room has special ultra-mega weights that weighed tons and I could lift them easily. I only came here to keep up appearances and to bond with my teammates.

Since the weights here also meant nothing to Lori (with her bionics), she and I ran around the room while the other girls used the weights.

Marie worked on the bench press while Cindy Love and Michelle Row spotted her up front. Luke Lewis was also there. Usually, the boys don't lift when the girls do, but Luke was recovering from an injury. I think he has a crush on Marie.

Marie was going for a record bench press for her, 100 pounds. Impressive, considering that I don't think Marie weighed 100 pounds soaking wet. Lori and I stopped our running and moved next to the bench to cheer Marie on.

Marie pulled the weight from the rack. She took a deep breath.

"You can do it, Marie!" I said.

"You got this girl!" Lori told her.

Marie guided the bar slowly down to her chest. She took a deep breath. She pushed up. The weight moved up. She let out a breath. She straightened her arms. She locked the weight back in the rack. She sat up. "I did it!" she shouted.

Marie shook her head and beads of sweat bounced off her short dark hair. One of the droplets hit Cindy and she turned to gold. Another drop of sweat hit Michelle and she too froze into gold. A couple of drops hit Luke, who became gold as well. Lori and I spotted beads of sweat coming towards us but managed to dodge them. The sweat hit the ground, turning the floor beneath us into gold.

"Oops," Marie said. "This is bad."

Lori looked at the golden kids and the golden floor. "Marie you could be so rich if you wanted to be!"

"Oh my, this is not good...." Marie said. "I really didn't want to do this."

Tanya Cane walked into the room. "Oh, now I see why Janitor Jan sent me down here. She thought my time control power might be helpful. I see she was right."

Packed

Tanya looked over the situation. "Wow, Marie! That is a cool power!" She tapped Michelle and Cindy. "They are truly solid gold."

I glanced at Tanya. "Can you reverse time to before the accident happened?"

"Maybe," Tanya replied. "But time is very particular. It likes to happen the way it's supposed to happen. So, my guess is if I did it right, Marie would just turn them into gold again. And, if I did it wrong and went back too far, I might turn them all into babies. Which might not be much better. In fact, it could be really messy. Plus, if I do it really wrong, EVERYBODY could turn into babies!" She shook her head. "My power can be tricky to control. That's why I usually just slow down time… It's simpler. I've already slowed down the school so nobody comes in here and sees this."

"Oh my gosh, this would be so hard to explain," Lori said.

I walked over to Marie and put my hands on her shoulders. I let out a little sigh of relief when I didn't turn to gold. "Marie you did this, and you can undo this," I told her.

Mac spoke up from the interface I wore on my wrist. "I've spoken to your father. He says he'll send a relief team if needed. They can move the golden kids to the lab and work on them there."

"Tell Dad 'thanks', but not necessary just yet. I know Marie can turn them back."

Mac paused for a moment and then informed us, "Your father says he will keep the team on standby."

I locked my attention on Marie. "You've undone this before, Marie. You can undo it again."

"But that was just one person, now it's three of them."

I nodded in agreement. "That is true, but it's still the same concept. I know you've been working on this with Dad's people. You can create a field with your power. You should be able to turn all three of them back at once."

Lori pointed to the floor. "Why don't you practice on the floor?" she smiled encouragingly.

"Lia and I will move the statues close to each other to make it easier for you."

Tanya walked Marie over to the golden spots on the floor. "You can do this Marie!" I called over as I picked up the now solid Luke and moved him next to the two girl statues.

MAC spoke up, "Your father reminds you that you all have a power training session tomorrow. He says that things like this are the reason why we have these weekend sessions."

"We'll be there," I said.

"All of you?" Mac said.

Tanya and Lori both nodded. Marie groaned and said, "Of course I'll be there! I don't want stuff like this to keep happening."

"I noticed from the school records, Jessica is absent today," Mac said. "Do you know if she will be coming?"

I shrugged. "Jess takes her power seriously, so if she's around I'm sure she'll be there. But, let's stick to the problem at hand. We need Marie to turn these kids back!"

I thought about the situation. The last time Marie's power misfired she had been thinking about money for college. Maybe it was the same now. "Marie," I said slowly walking towards her, "Have you been worrying about money again?"

Marie looked at me. Her eyes popped open. "Yeah, I have," she admitted. "I was thinking that I need to get stronger and better so I can get a LAX scholarship to college!"

I touched her gently on the shoulder. "That's the key to your power misfiring. When you worry about money you tend to turn things into gold."

"That certainly would help with the money problem," Lori said with a grin.

"This isn't funny, Lori," Marie scolded. "I'm dangerous like this! I'm worried that if I sneeze or fart you'll all turn to gold! Plus, what about having a boyfriend someday? What if I get nervous and turn him into gold?"

"You might have the perfect boyfriend then," Tanya snickered. "He'd be worth a lot of money and he wouldn't talk a lot. Plus, he'd always smell good!"

Marie turned to her. "Tanya, don't even kid like that!" she said, poking Tanya on the hand. Tanya's hand instantly turned to gold. The gold then began to streak up her arm.

Marie threw her hand over her mouth. "Oh no!"

Tanya stayed calm. She waved her non-golden hand over the golden one. The skin instantly stopped transforming into gold.

"Whoa!" Tanya said slowly. "This is a weird feeling. I've slowed time around my arm but not sure how long I can hold this."

Marie put her hands on top of her head. "Yikes! I didn't mean to do that. You see, I am dangerous!"

I looked Marie in the eyes. "Marie, you are one of the kindest people I know. You're not dangerous. You just need to learn to control your emotions, which will allow you to control your power."

She stared back at me and her body relaxed.

"Take a deep breath and let it out," I said.

"I'm afraid my breath will turn you into gold!" Marie frowned.

I shook my head. "No, it won't, because you can control this. You can control your power."

She took a deep breath and let it out. I felt her breath hit my face and then an instant relief when I didn't turn to gold.

"See? I am still flesh and blood!" I told her. "You can control this! Just don't worry about money. Marie, you're a strong player and smart. I'm sure you will get a college scholarship!" I patted her on the shoulder.

Marie smiled. She bent down and touched the gold spots on the floor. They turned back into whatever gray substance weight room floors are made of. Her smile grew. She stood up and tapped Tanya on the hand. Tanya's hand slowly transformed back from solid gold to flesh.

Tanya flexed her hand. "Much better. I know they say being golden is good, but nope, it is not."

I smiled at Marie. "See, easy peasy."

I led Tanya and Marie to the three golden statues. Marie looked at the glistening bodies. "I can do this!" she said. She leaned forward to touch Luke, and then stopped, her hand in mid-air. "Wait, if I turn one person back, how do we explain to them why the others are golden statues?"

"Good point," I told her. "I guess this means you'll have to turn them all back at once."

"You did turn them all into gold at once," Lori added.

Marie leaned back a little. "I can do this. Everything is going to be fine," she said softly to herself. The only reason I heard her was because of my super hearing.

She took a deep breath and exhaled on Cindy, Michelle, and Luke, her breath covering all three. Instantly each of them transformed, and we watched the gold coating fade into normal skin.

"How'd we get over here?" Luke asked, a puzzled expression on his face.

"Yeah, we were spotting Marie over there," Michelle said, pointing to the bench.

Marie laughed a bit nervously. "I made the lift, and then we all came over to this side of the room to try some different equipment. Don't you remember?"

I moved forward, focusing on the three of them. "Yes, that was what happened!" I said, in my most forceful command super voice.

The three nodded. "Yes, that was what happened!" they repeated.

Lori then led the three out of the weight room. "Okay girls, let's get going. We'll see you all on Monday."

We all breathed a little sigh of relief.

MAC chimed in. "See, your father is correct! This is why your weekend training sessions are so important."

We all nodded in agreement.

Dear Diary: Wow, that situation could have become really ugly, but luckily my friends and I kept it under control. I'm amazed by the power we each have. I now truly understand the saying, ***with great power, comes great responsibility****. I also figured out that the way to control our powers is through practice and understanding of our powers. We can all be dangerous if we don't learn to control the powers we have. But I have faith in myself and my friends.*

I guess I should be thankful that Wendi didn't come down to check on us. Of course, maybe if she was there, Marie would have turned her into gold as well.

Now, that would have been fun! Wendi would make such a great lawn ornament or scarecrow!

Okay, Lia, wipe those thoughts from your mind.

Practice makes Better

By the time Jason and I got to BM Science the next morning, Lori, Marie, and Tanya were already there. Hana met us at the gate and drove us into the test building. Yep, BMS had made an entire building just for us.

Dad and Hana had Marie working with their team of mind experts. They'd arranged for her to do meditation and yoga to keep her powers under control. We saw Marie in a small white room standing on her head and going "Ooohhm". She seemed content.

Next, we walked past a room filled with weights. Lori had two heavy ton weights over her head, as a trainer looked on giving her encouragement. A couple of people dressed in white lab coats were observing Lori's progress. One had a stethoscope around her neck to check Lori's heart rate, and she seemed very surprised at what Lori was capable of.

The other person was holding an iPad to keep track of Lori's results.

"So, what will I be doing?" I asked Hana.

Hana grinned. "We want you and Tanya to have a friendly sparring match. The goal is for each of you to simply stop the other one any way you can."

"Me versus Tanya," I smiled. "I think I can power through her time control and take her down," I said confidently.

Jason looked at me with a frown.

"What?" I asked him.

"Lia, don't get overly confident. You have awesome raw power. All the abilities you have makes you super-duper-uber powerful," he said slowly. I could see he was choosing his words carefully.

"Your point?"

He hesitated. "Tanya is older. She's had her power longer and her power...wow... she can control time. That's pretty cool too! If she concentrates her power on you, she can certainly slow you down!"

Hana grinned. "That's an excellent point, Jason, that's why we have you as a consultant."

We entered a room shaped like an octagon. The walls were all covered with mirrors. The floor was padded.

Tanya stood in the room dressed in a pretty blue top, white shorts and electric blue canvas sneakers. She smiled at me. "I see it's you versus me in a friendly little fight."

"I guess so," I said. I had to admit I was a bit put off by her calmness. After all, I am Super Teen. Nothing she could really do could hurt me. Yet she stood there so steady.

Hana motioned us both to the middle of the room. "Now, Doctor Strong, Jason and I will be watching from the observation room. The room will flash red and then you two can begin. Remember this is only practice. The winner will be the one who knocks out the other."

"Wait, I thought we only had to stop each other?" I asked.

Hana looked at me. "I changed the rules to make it more challenging. After all, in a real fight, the rules change all the time." She took Jason by the hand. "Come."

Tanya and I glanced at each other.

"This should be interesting," Tanya said. "I've been working on new ways to use my power."

"Good," I said with a nod. "I'm always trying to improve myself too."

"Have you seen Jess?" Tanya asked.

"Nope, I'm getting a little worried about her."

Tanya shrugged. "She's a witch, she'll be fine."

A red light flashed. I figured I'd take out Tanya fast and easy: dart forward at super speed, a quick nerve pinch, and game over. But I felt myself slowing down. It was like the gravity around me had become so strong, each step felt like my legs weighed a few tons. I gave Tanya credit, she had slowed time fast. Still, that wouldn't be enough to stop me. I kept creeping towards her, even though each step felt heavier than the last.

Tanya moved closer. "I know you're tough and not much can hurt you, but even you have to breathe." She popped a shoe off one foot. "I really feel sorry for you about this. While I can't totally stop you in time, I can slow you down enough." She placed her shoe over my nose. Wow! If my head could have jerked back it would have. "My shoes get nasty if I don't wear socks. I know a quick whiff of this wouldn't normally hurt you. But I am speeding up time around your nose, making it seem as though you've been breathing in nothing but my shoes for a year!"

Tanya removed her shoe away from my nose. She snapped her finger. "Okay, time around you is back to normal."

The room spun around me. My eyes felt so heavy, it was like elephants were trying to force them to close. But I refused to fall. Tanya walked up to me. She tapped me on the head with her little finger. I hit the floor.

"Sweet dreams," were the last words I heard.

I came to in a bed in a white room, with a doctor looking over me. Dad and Jason were also there. "You okay, honey?" Dad asked.

"Yeah, only my ego took a beating."

"All superheroes have some weakness. Yours is that you have to breathe."

"Hopefully, now you've learned you're vulnerable to gas attacks. The good news is, I am sure if you're prepared for a gas attack, you can hold your breath for a great deal of time!" Dad commented.

Tanya patted me on the shoulder, "Once again, sorry I had to do that. But your dad and Hana thought of it. I'm glad to see you're alright now."

Jason gave me a thumbs up. "Yeah, the MMA Fighter, Samurai and Ninjas that Tanya practiced on last week are all still recovering! Two of them haven't stopped sucking their thumbs. The third drops to the ground and rolls over when she sees Tanya."

"I do leave quite the impression," Tanya grinned.

All of a sudden, red lights began flashing. Sirens started blaring. A voice over the intercom said, "Alert! This is not a drill!"

Dad looked up to the ceiling, "Mac, show us the security feed!"

A TV monitor dropped from the ceiling to the middle of the room for us to see. There in the monitor, we saw Jessica storming into the building. A couple of guards rushed towards her. Jessica pointed at them. The guards instantly began to cluck like chickens.

"What have you done with Felipe and Tomas?" she shouted at one of the security guards. She waved her fist into the camera. "You'd better give them back or else!"

"Oh, this could be trouble…" Dad said.

Dear Diary: Ouch, I finally lost a fight. Sure, I've had my close matches before. But this marks the first time I actually got knocked out cold. I guess it's good that I do have a weakness. It keeps me humble. ☺

Tanya packs a lot of wallop. Her ability to slow time is powerful and her feet pack almost the same punch as mine. I wonder if having natural super powers give you naturally super stinky feet? Whatever...I now know for sure that I can be taken down, especially if I don't plan before a fight. My brain is as useful as any of my powers!

I just hope we can sort out the issue with Jessica!

Angry Witch = Big Trouble

I sat up in bed. "Dad, what's Jessica talking about?"

Dad took a few steps back. He scratched his head. "I have no idea..."

Standing up, I looked at Hana, "Is there something going on here that Dad doesn't know about?"

Hana grinned. "My dear Lia, there are many things going on here that your dad doesn't know about. We have become a huge organization. One single human cannot track them all. But luckily, I am not human, and I am close to your dad at all times. I also can track them all. We have done nothing with Tomas and that adorable little Felipe."

"We did invite them to train," Dad said slowly. "But they turned us down. So that was that."

"Apparently not," Jason said.

Hana's nose started to twitch. Her mouth locked into a wide grin and her eyes sprung open, with her pupils dilating until the whites of her eyes disappeared.

"Ah, what's going on with Hana?" I asked dad.

He glanced at her. "She's doing a deep search. It's so cute!"

I let that comment slide. I had bigger fish to fry than to worry about my dad thinking his *cute* android.

Hana's nose stopped twitching. Her eyes blinked again and the wide grin disappeared from her face. "Doctor Donna Dangerfield recently started her own company, Bio Augmented Diversified, and they are doing work like ours. They refer to themselves as "BAD". Their motto is, "Making You a Better You!"

"Where are they located?" I asked.

Hana's nose twitched. It stopped. "No idea. It's very hush, hush."

Looking up at the monitor, I could see that Jess had moved deep into the building and anybody she came in contact with instantly dropped to the ground and began clucking. "Okay, we stop Jess first. We need to explain to her what's going on. Then we find out more about this BAD!"

I looked at Tanya. "You ready for this?"

"You're asking me to take on one of our best friends who is an angry powerful witch? Of course, I am!"

We raced out the door then stopped at the weight room to grab Lori, who had been watching the situation unfold. "This is going to be tough!" Lori said. "Jess has a lot of magical power, but if I can sneak behind her I think I can take her out."

"Let's try to talk her down first," I said. "Nobody wins if we go up against Jess."

We stopped at the lab to get Marie. Both the scientists working with her had been turned to big yellow cheese statues. Marie came over, "Sorry, guys I was hungry and got a little nervous watching Jess."

"Marie you stay here and turn these guys back. We'll use you as our backup plan against Jess if needed."

Marie nodded. "Sounds like a good idea."

Mac used the building guidance system to lead us through the halls towards Jess. The walls of the building were all electronic, so he could display arrows showing us the way to go. He also gave us a constant feed to let us see Jess's actions exactly. The good news is that so far she hadn't vanished anybody. Plus, she hadn't completely turned anybody into a chicken yet. That made me hope we could reason with her.

We met up with Jess who was approaching a big lab filled with scientists who were busy at work, completely unaware of what was going on around them.

As soon as Jess spotted us, she turned towards the scientists who immediately dropped to the floor and began to cluck like chickens. A few of the robot security drones tried to stop Jess but she instantly reduced them to piles of melted metal.

She then glared at each of us. Her gaze made us all shiver.

I took a deep breath. "Jess we need to talk," I said slowly but firmly.

"Tomas, cute little Felipe, and his mom are all missing!" Jess replied.

"Yeah we've heard," I said. "My dad and Hana insist they don't have them."

Jess raised an eyebrow, "You trust your dad? The man who wanted nothing to do with you until you had superpowers and a robot to look out for you?"

Jess hit a nerve there. She had a solid point, but now wasn't the time to think about my relationship with my dad.

"Hana's an android," I said, realizing that Jason was rubbing off on me. "But yes, you make a good point."

Jess stood there tapping her foot impatiently. "So now what?" She raised her arms over her head.

"If you're trying to knock us out with super BO, it's not working," Lori said.

I held my breath just to be on the safe side, but I felt pretty sure that wasn't what Jess was up to. She wasn't a super BO kind of girl. Sadly, that was one of my moves.

"No, I'm putting a magical invisible shield around me so you can't attack me!"

"We'll see about that!" Lori yelled, leaping across the room at Jess.

Jess stood there, arms crossed. Lori flew towards her then bounced off harmlessly. She rolled into a bunch of scientist chickens, knocking them over like bowling pins.

Lori sat up, "Nope, she's not bluffing."

Tanya whispered to me, "I may be able to freeze her in time, even in that shield. But if I can't, we might both end up as chickens. Actually, once I saw her turn two guys who whistled at her into turnips..."

"I have a better idea," I told Tanya.

I looked Jess in the eyes. "Let's all go talk to my dad and Hana. I'm sure we'll get the truth out of Dad, at least. If they aren't involved, which I'm pretty sure they aren't, they can help us find out who has Felipe and Tomas."

Jess dropped her arms. "Deal."

She sniffed herself. "Good timing, my deodorant was about to wear off!"

Dear Diary: I hate to admit this, but Jess really had a point about Dad. I want to trust him. I need to trust him. But man, oh man, I haven't seen Dad for about ten years, then all of a sudden I'm super, and he shows up at my door. As well as that, it turns out he runs a giant scientific research company that is interested in super beings. Plus, the man built himself a girlfriend, which, I'm sorry, is totally weird. Hopefully, though, he was telling the truth. But I need to find out for sure!

Planning for Action

We all gathered in one of BM Science's lush conference rooms. The room had a long polished oak table surrounded by the most comfortable leather chairs ever. I assured Dad and his people that Jess wouldn't turn any of them into something weird, as long as they told the truth.

Dad sat at the head of the table with Hana positioned next to him. A fierce-looking security guard stood behind him at the ready.

Though I knew that if Jess lost her temper, there would be nothing that any security personnel would be able to do to stop her, regardless of how fierce or tough he was. Just as that thought entered my head, three more security people walked into the room. These ones all wore red body armor and helmets. By the mechanical sounds they made when they moved, I knew the armor must have been enhanced.

"Jess, I assure you that my company has nothing to do with the disappearance of Felipe and Tomas," Dad told her.

Jess pointed at the guards. "Then why all the security people in the room."

Hana answered for Dad, "My dear girl, you have reduced half of our staff to mindless chickens. I have called for extra security to be cautious. Mr. Strong's brain is our company's biggest asset. It is my job to protect it."

Jess glared. She snapped her fingers. The red-shirted guards turned into tomatoes. The bionic-enhanced guards turned into toy soldiers. "Just to be clear, no amount of guards will help you if I find out that you are behind the disappearance of Tomas and Felipe."

I believe I saw Dad gulp. Hana, though, stood her ground. "Impressive use of power."

Jess nodded. "When I am angry, my power flows freely. That's why I usually try to control it. People don't like me when I'm angry."

Hana grinned. "Good point, but you see my dear, I'm not people." Hana pointed at Jess. A bolt of electricity ripped into Jess. Jess jerked back and forth in her chair. She collapsed.

A team in white medical suits rushed in. They gave Jess a shot in the arm.

I leaped up. "Dad, Hana, what are you doing?"

Hana answered again, "Just protecting my man, honey. Jess is fine. We'll simply keep her sedated until the rest of you figure out who's behind this."

"So it's not you guys?" Lori asked.

Dad stood up and answered, "No, it is not us. We would never do anything like this." He looked at Hana.

"I do not approve of you doing that to Jessica! She was scared and reacted. She was defending her loved ones."

"As was I," Hana replied.

Dad pointed at Jess. "Wake her up!" he ordered the medical team. "I have truth on my side. I don't need protection."

One of the docs gave dad an, '*Are you sure about this*?' look.

"Do it now!" Dad ordered.

I'd never seen this forceful side of him before. I think I liked it. Looking at the smile on Hana's face I knew she liked it too.

The medic leaned in and gave Jess another shot.

Jess slowly started to move. Her eyes shot open. "What the?" she said.

I placed an arm over Jess, preventing her from standing. "Jess, calm down, it's a misunderstanding."

Jess shook her head. "My brain feels scrambled. I can't concentrate enough to use my powers…"

"That will wear off soon," Hana told her.

Dad shot Hana a look.

Hana lowered her head. "I'm sorry if I overreacted."

"Let's all get to talking now," I said slowly but forcefully. "We're stronger when we all work together. What do you know about this BAD company?"

"They are very new. Doctor Donna Dangerfield started them just a couple of months ago. According to their web page, their goal is to make the world a better place for everybody," Hana explained.

"Okay, if they have a web page, they must have an address," Marie commented logically.

Jason answered. "They do, but the address is only a PO Box in Moon City."

"So they are somewhere in Moon City?" Jess asked.

"Possibly," Dad said. "I'll have one of our 'fly on the wall' drones head straight there and keep an eye on their PO Box."

"Fly drones?" Tanya asked.

Dad beamed. "Drones that look like flies. They are amazing!"

"They are!" Jason added.

"So that's all we have?" Lori shook her head in disgust.

"For now," Dad said. "But I promise you, we will get to the bottom of this."

I turned to Jess. I put my hand on her shoulder and looked her in the eyes. "I trust him and so should you."

Jess didn't blink. "I'll give him a couple of days."

Well, that actually went better than I thought.

Dear Diary: Okay, life never gets easier. But I guess learning how to cope is part of growing up. I had to trust my dad would get this done, especially since he had Jason helping. My relationship with Dad might have been shaky for a while (most of my life) but Jason had never let me down. Plus, I knew dad was trying to make things right. I just hoped we could find a solution before Jess went ballistic!

Date

I got home to find a note on the dining room table: "Out on a date. Buy a pizza, on me." Well, at least Shep greeted me with a lick. I bent down and patted him. "Looks like it's just you and me tonight, big guy."

He woofed.

"Actually, I don't mind at all, Shep. We'll enjoy the pizza together!"

My phone started to explode with beeps. I picked it up.

LORI: Turn on TV.

MARIE: Yikes!

TANYA: Turn on TV.

JASON: Yikes!

I turned on the television. I saw Oscar Oranga hiding behind a table. "This is Oscar Oranga reporting from Casa De Amor restaurant where I had my date rudely interrupted."

The camera scanned the restaurant. Everybody there lay on the ground stiff and pale. They were all breathing, but slowly. I saw Mom laying there, quite still. I hoped she was faking so as not to expose herself.

A girl dressed in black, with a black mask, boots, and cape, grabbed the mic from Oscar. She shook her fist at the screen, "Super Teen…I, Glare Girl, challenge you!"

I leaped out the door. I knew where Case De Amor was. Not because I had ever been there, after all, my love life was less than zero, but I had always dreamed of eating there. I was glad mom got to. Even if she did have to face a super bad girl. I leaped into the air. I finally might have an arch-rival, one besides Wendi. I guess I should be happy in a way.

"Should I call the rest of the team?" Mac asked.

"No," I said. "I need them as a backup just in case I lose," I replied.

"Tanya says she's glad she's not out in the open as a superhero!" Mac told me.

"Yeah, it's not a life for everybody," I grunted with a shake of my head.

Arriving at the restaurant, I found Glare Girl sitting with her boots up on a table. Her hands were behind her head and her hair was as dark as her black costume. "Well, well, you're braver than I thought," she commented, still not bothering to stand up.

The restaurant looked amazing: silk table cloths, flowers, and candles on every table. A band was set up in the corner. But of course, they were on the ground now. All the unconscious waiters were dressed as Matadors. The place smelled of sweet onions.

I forced myself to concentrate on Glare Girl. "What's your deal, girl?" I said.

Glare Girl snickered. "You're just so sweet and wholesome all the time, and I thought the world needed balance. I'm the balance. Not so sweet, not so wholesome. I'm just a hot girl out for fun!" She looked around the restaurant. "Nice place you folks have here in Starlight City! Of course, the people are all a little stiff," she giggled.

I pointed at the people stiff on the floor. "This is how you have fun, terrorizing people?"

Glare Girl nodded. "It is. Besides, at least when I take out a room of people, I do it on purpose, not with super foot odor or a fart. No class or style there."

I stopped walking towards her. "Those were accidents."

Glare Girl snickered. "That makes it worse." She stood up. "Now are we going to give each other manicures, or are we going to fight?"

I flew at her. She focused her glare on me. The pressure of that glare made me feel like I had a hundred-ton weight smacking me in the face. The air around me heated up, making me feel like I was in a sauna set on NUKE. It slowed me down but didn't stop me. I grabbed Glare Girl and lifted her in the air.

"Is that all you got?" I asked.

A flick of my wrist and I tossed her across the room. She tumbled to the floor. I watched her pause briefly before staggering to her feet.

"How impolite, you never let me answer you!" she said, wiping a bit of blood from her lips. She smiled. I did not like the look of that smile.

Glare Girl stood up. She cracked her neck then reached into a pocket she had under her arm. She pulled out a tiny, little, red-headed girl. And when I say tiny, I mean she had to be one inch tall.

"About time," the tiny girl said. "Whoa, you might want to consider switching deodorants!"

Glare Girl let the small girl float to the floor. "Please, I don't use deodorants. When you're a bad girl you enjoy your own natural scent!"

"Gross!" the tiny girl said.

The tiny girl abruptly grew to normal kid size and I eyed her pink and yellow jumpsuit. Her mask was shaped like an S, for a cool look. She waved to me. "Hi, Super Teen, I'm Ellie Mae...I mean Shrink Girl."

"You seem like a nice kid. Why are you working with the princess of black?" I asked.

Shrink Girl shrugged. "We're cousins. Like they say, you can't pick your family. So if you let us teleport away now, everybody will be happy. We both have a cool video we can show on YouTube. All the people get to recover. My cousin has had her fun."

I walked towards them slowly. "I can't let her keep hurting people."

Glare Girl laughed. "Nobody is really hurt. I didn't wilt anybody. I just wanted to test you. I'm helping you be a better you."

"I hate tests! Especially on Sundays!" I said, darting towards them.

I saw Shrink Girl point at me and then take her index finger and thumb and squeeze them together. Suddenly I found myself looking up at Glare Girl who now towered over me.

"Sorry, I had to do that!" Shrink Girl said. "It will wear off soon."

I leaped up into the air and clobbered Glare Girl with a flying uppercut to the jaw. My blow jolted her head back, knocking her to the ground.

"Even small, I still pack quite a punch!" I told Shrink Girl as I hovered in her face.

"Yikes!" she shouted. She turned and quickly made a circular motion with her hand.

"She's tougher than the doc said," Glare Girl whispered to her little cousin. "Get us home!"

"I'm still getting used to this porting power," she whispered back. "I can only go a few miles."

"That will get us home!"

A glowing sphere of silver energy appeared next to Glare Girl. Shrink Girl shrank down again. She darted over to Glare Girl and grabbed her. They both disappeared into the ball of energy.

"We mean you no harm!" Shrink Girl's voice echoed from the energy ball. "Oh and I can teleport too!" she added, her voice echoing like it was in a tunnel. The ball of energy sizzled, then faded away.

"Yeah, I kind of figured out the teleporting part," I said, feeling my body return to normal size. For a second I considered chasing them, but I realized I had no idea where they had gone.

Mom stood up and came to my side. "Come on Super Teen, help me get all these people back on their feet."

Dear Diary: Well, I guess I've finally made it as a superhero now that I have an arch-rival or nemesis. As powerful and mean as Glare Girl is, I still somehow find her more likable than Wendi Long. Ha, I guess you don't need superpowers to be super annoying. Certainly, this Glare Girl wanted to be a pain in my behind but I really didn't get the feeling that she hated me. She just wanted to see what I could do and what I could take. I think I gave her a pretty good idea of that. Sure, her glare stung, but it wasn't anything I couldn't handle. Sure, her little cousin Shrink Girl succeeded in miniaturizing me, but that didn't slow me down much at all. Honestly, the girl's teleporting powers seem more impressive to me. Man, that certainly means she would be hard to find.

Dad and Hana *told me they guessed these two came from BAD. I trusted them, maybe I shouldn't have, but I did. Plus, Glare Girl did mention a doctor. Could that be Doctor Dangerfield? Could BAD be making their own super people? Now, that would be bad. It couldn't have been a coincidence that these two popped up around the same time I was learning about BAD. I had faith I would get to the bottom of this and also rescue Felipe and Tomas. I needed to do it fast though before Jess lost her cool. Plus, I had an election at school to win. Well, if not win, then at least not embarrass myself. The thought of giving a speech made my stomach gurgle. Man, if I farted in the middle of a speech that would be bad on so many levels. Wow, being super can make life super complicated!*

My Other Arch Enemy

On Monday, I walked to school in my usual way, alongside Jason. That seemed to be the constant in my life. The one thing I really needed.

"That fight you had yesterday was weird," Jason told me.

I nodded. "Yeah, I know. Being blasted by some sort of glare vision then shrunk down to a tiny size wasn't my idea of a relaxing Sunday evening."

"Have you seen what people think about the battle?"

"Nah, I'm taking some time off Facebook. It's just a place for people to go and say stuff they wouldn't say face to face with anybody. It's just not worth worrying about or wasting my time on..."

"Well, Wendi thinks it was staged to make you look better."

"Of course," I sighed.

"But most people are really thankful you showed up to save the day," Jason added.

"That's nice. I do like to help. But what's your point, buddy?"

"I think this was a test of their powers and your powers. To see how they stack up to you."

"So do you think these two were made super?" I asked.

Jason nodded. "I do. One was older than you. The other was younger. Yet they were cousins. So they probably have some trait that makes them easier to turn super. I'm pretty sure BAD is making super people."

"They were from our town," I said.

Mac chimed in. "I've given the recording of your fight to your father's people for analysis. They noticed that both the girls had slight scars on their necks. Which means…"

"They had implants," Jason answered.

"Exactly," Mac said.

"I just thought of something!" I broke in quickly, unable to mask the excitement in my voice. "The Shrink Girl slipped for a second and called herself Ellie Mae. I figure she has to be nine or ten. If we search nearby areas for a girl with that name, we can talk to her and get a clue. She seemed nice. My super hearing picked up the fact that she can only teleport a limited distance."

"I'll alert your dad's people," Mac said. "I'm sure they will come up with something."

"Great!" I said.

"Until your dad's company finds some information for us, I suggest you concentrate on more normal but just as challenging problems," Jason said. "Have you thought about your campaign yet?" he asked.

I shot him a look. I fought back the urge to hit him with a bit of heat vision. "When would I have had time?" I asked.

Jason grinned. "Good point." He turned and pulled some rolled up papers out of his backpack. "That's why I've done some work for you!"

He unrolled one the papers and showed it to me:

VOTE FOR LIA!

SHE'S JUST LIKE YOU!

There was an American flag and also our school flag (which I didn't even know we had), under the text. It looked pretty cool.

"It's nice. You know I'm not like anybody else in the school though. Even Tanya, Jess, Marie and Lori aren't bulletproof and super strong. I'm like really super. Heck, I could fart and be the only one left standing in the school!"

Jason laughed. He put an arm around me. "Lia, those are your powers, those aren't you. You are the person who worries about knocking out the entire school."

"Yeah, that would be bad..." I said.

Jason continued. "You are the person who tries to use those powers to help the world become a better place."

"Yeah, I do."

"You are a person who is constantly trying to figure out what the right thing to do is."

"Yep, that's me."

"You worry about little things like your breath not smelling fresh," Jason added.

"When your morning breath drops your dog, you learn to worry about these things," I told him.

"You have all these cool super powers that others don't have."

I nodded as we neared the school. "Yep, that's kind of my point. You're making my point for me."

Jason stopped walking and turned me to face him. "But you also still have to worry about...homework, who your parents are dating, what other kids think of you and most importantly what your place in this world is going to be." He paused to let that sink in. "Your super powers are great and they let you do fantastic feats, but they come with problems too. They make you different from the rest of us. And that's any kid's greatest fear...being so different they can't find a way to fit in. Which makes you worry about fitting in with the rest of us. That makes you just like the rest of us!" Jason explained. "In fact, you're an inspiration, you're learning how to take your differences and make them work for not only you but also the world. You're fitting in by helping others." Jason stopped talking, out of breath.

"Wow, Jason I've never heard you talk so much."

"It's because you're an important person to me. Watching you inspires me to be a better me. I know you can do that for others as Super Teen but more importantly as Lia."

We walked into the school grounds which seemed very quiet for that time of morning. Usually there were heaps of kids milling around the front entrance. I wondered where everyone was.

But then I considered what Jason had just said. I felt better about myself than I had for a long time. I felt like I was glowing. I turned to Jason. "I'm not glowing am I?"

He smiled. "Nope, but you're floating a bit."

"Oops," I said forcing myself back down to the ground.

We headed inside the building and out of nowhere, Wendi appeared. I watched her strut over towards us. So much for me feeling good about myself. "I see my worthy opponent has finally entered the school," she said, almost choking on the word worthy.

Looking around I noticed the walls already lined with posters that featured Wendi's perfect face with the caption.

Vote for Perfection!

Vote Wendi!

Dear Diary: Jason helped me to feel so good about myself today. And then I saw Wendi's posters. How am I going to compete with those?

Jason went to work putting up my signs next to hers. Of course, my signs were much smaller and not as flashy. Wendi looked at them with disdain. I'm surprised she didn't put a finger in her throat and pretend to throw up. Instead, she laughed. She turned to her new BFF, Maggie Carr, a tall, athletic looking girl with red hair. "Can you believe that I have to compete against this?" Wendi whispered to her, still loud enough for everybody to hear.

Maggie nodded. "Sure I can. Those are the rules," Maggie replied confidently.

Wendi gave Maggie a look that said, "Duh".

Maggie fumbled with her words for a second or two, trying to figure out the best way to keep her BFF happy. "But your posters are SO much better. And they're bigger too!" she added.

She then thought for a second. You could tell when Maggie was thinking because she would tap her foot and roll her eyes like she wanted to force herself to think faster. "I think I read on Facebook that the biggest signs always win!"

Patti Queen, a small girl with short brown hair, darted over to Wendi. Patti had a roll of tape in her hand. She saluted. "I've posted all your posters," she told Wendi. Then she half looked at me. "Oh hi," she said as if I should be honored that she'd noticed me.

The three girls turned and walked away. No other words were said. Although Maggie did give a small goodbye wave and a curt smile.

I shrugged and headed to my locker. Of course, Steve Mann stood there leaning against it. "Hi, Lia! What a nice surprise to see you here!" he said.

I pointed to my locker. "Ah, this is my locker."

"I knew that," he said stepping away from it and standing in front of Jason's locker. "Nice day isn't it?"

"Yeah, it is," I said.

"Man, that Wendi is something else, isn't she!" he commented, leaning casually against Jason's locker. He began to slip then steadied himself. "I mean, sure she's good looking if you like that sort of thing. But I like you..."

I stared back at him and frowned.

Before he had a chance to say anything else, Jess came over. "You! Get lost!" she ordered.

Steve's eyes glazed over. He turned and started walking towards the school doors.

Jess groaned. "Ugh, he's being too obedient. He probably will get lost somewhere," she sighed.

"Jess, stop him," I said.

She looked at me. "Well, it would stop him from annoying you!"

"Jess!"

"Yo nerd, I meant go to homeroom!" she ordered.

Steve stopped walking towards the door. He turned and headed towards his homeroom. Jason and a few other kids had their eyes glazed over as well. They too stopped talking, and turned and walked like zombies to their classrooms.

Jess grinned. "When I talk, people listen, whether I want them to or not."

"What's going on Jess?" I whispered.

"Any progress in finding Tomas, Felipe, and Felipe's mom?" she asked me.

"You sure his mom's missing too?" I asked.

Jess nodded. "Yes, I've been checking their house daily. They're all missing. But all their stuff is still there. They were certainly taken."

"We have a lead on BAD. My dad's people are finding the address of one of their test subjects. Then I'll go talk to her," I explained.

"Good! When they get her address, I'll go with you," she replied anxiously. "When will they have it?"

"Not sure," I said. "But I'd better go alone, to begin with."

"Why, Lia? Don't you trust me?"

"Actually Jess, when you're in this mood, I don't. The girl's just a kid. She seems like a sweet kid. Plus, she can't talk if she's a turnip."

Jess dipped her head. She took a deep breath. "You may have a point." She looked at me and thrust a finger in my face. "But as soon as you have BAD's address, you text me! I want to rip that place apart with you."

"I promise," I said. "After all, we're all part of a team. Right?"

She turned to walk away.

"Right, Jess?"

She stopped. "Yes, we're a team," she sighed.

I placed my hand gently on her shoulder. "Good to hear you say that. We're stronger as a team."

She looked down and away from me.

"You know it's true, Jess," I said forcefully, trying to will the words into her mind.

She looked up at me. "I know it's true. But it's hard for me to accept that I need help. Bad for my cool, loner image."

I patted her on the shoulder. "Don't worry, you're still cool!"

Her eyes lit up. "For sure." She turned and headed towards the door.

"Ah Jess, we have school."

She shook her head. "I can't think of school on days like this. It's hard to concentrate. I might slip up and turn my classmates into toads."

I reached out and grabbed her by the arm. "Nope, as being part of that team, I can't let you wander off; school's important. Not just for the learning stuff, but for the social interaction."

She tilted her head. "You don't look like a nerd but you sure talk like one."

"Thanks!" I told her.

The bell rang.

I pointed up. "They're playing our song."

"Nerd," Jess laughed walking towards her homeroom.

I let out a little sigh of relief and raced into my own classroom.

The rest of my school day went pretty average for me. First off, in English, I realized that I'd forgotten to write a paragraph explaining my plans for the year. Luckily, I was able to use my super speed to write it in class. I told Mrs. Dexter that writing it by hand made it more personal. She accepted that. I didn't feel bad about using super speed. I hadn't written the paper on Sunday night because I'd been battling a super kid teleporting girl, and a nasty Glare Girl, who broke up my mom's date with a reporter who was trying to learn my secret identity.

In history and political science, Mr. P asked me what my platform for class president would be. I told him that it was to be a good person and to treat people fairly. A few of the kids laughed, but a few more nodded their heads. I noticed Brandon was one of them. In fact, Brandon even talked to me after class.

He told me he had to vote for Wendi since she was his girlfriend, but he truly wished me the best of luck. That was both sweet and frustrating at the same time.

In gym class, Coach Blue spent much of the class explaining the importance of hygiene to us. Then she made us do push-ups and sit-ups for the rest of the class. Joy.

But I could handle that. What got to me was that after class, I heard a couple of girls (Lori and Patti) snickering about the hair stubble under my arms. They compared my armpit to a jungle. It looked like I needed to shave.

Dear Diary: I think I'd rather deal with deadly drones, robots, and androids than with some of the mean girls in my class. My body may be invulnerable but my feelings certainly aren't.

The Pits

At the end of the school day, I fought the urge to leap home in one bound. I have no idea why I let Wendi and Patti get to me so much. But they did. All I could think about were the mean things they said, especially about my underarms. Man, it would have been so good to give them a blast of super underarm odor. That would have made them nice and quiet. Of course, it probably would have also made a lot of other people nice and quiet too. People who didn't deserve to get blasted, just because of two mean girls.

Jason noticed that I was moving at a quicker pace than normal. "Ah, why are we walking so fast, is there something wrong?" he asked, a worried look appearing on his face.

"Or do we have a lead on who that girl is?" he added hopefully.

"No," Mac answered for me. "Lia is upset that Wendi and Patti made fun of the hair growing under her arms."

"Oh right," Jason said, his eyes popping open. "That explains why you're keeping your arms so close to your sides."

I turned to him without slowing down. In fact, I picked up the pace. "It made me feel bad, okay?"

Jason began to jog so he could keep up with me. "Of course. You may be super, but your feelings are regular human." His face turned slightly red and he slowed his pace. "Ah, have you shaved since you've become super?" he asked, chewing his lip with embarrassment.

I shook my head and sped up more. "Nope. But now's the time. I know it's weird, but that's all I can think about now...like how gross my armpits must look. It's ridiculous how I hadn't even thought about this until I heard them laughing. Now it's all I can think about."

"Okay, well, don't you think you should wait for your mom...for like tips and stuff..."

I shook my head. "Nope, can't wait. I've seen her do it. How hard can it be?"

"Ah, well...your mom isn't as invulnerable as you are..."

We stopped in front of my home. "Thanks for your support, buddy. You're a good friend. I'll be back to normal once I get rid of this hair!" I raced into the house at super speed.

Leaving Jason on the pavement to continue alone to his house, I shot inside and gave Shep a quick pat. Then I zoomed upstairs into my mom's bathroom. Tossing open the cabinet, I scanned for razors. Funnily enough, I only saw one pink one sitting in the corner on the top shelf. I grabbed hold of it and could see that it looked unused. I knew my mom wouldn't mind me using it.

I raced into my bathroom. I turned on the water and ran the razor under it. I lifted my arm. I put the razor on my armpit. I thought about the process. I mean this wasn't rocket science. You move the razor down the underarm, lift it up and repeat the process.

I lifted my arm. I got a whiff of myself. Ouch. I'd have to shower after this. I ran the razor down my underarm. I looked at my underarm. The hair was still untouched. I repeated the process pressing harder. I looked at it once more. It was still covered with hair. I looked at the razor. Maybe there wasn't a blade. The razor now looked crinkled and bent. It shook and wobbled like it was made of putty.

Yep, the razor met my underarm and lost. My underarms had wilted a razor. This was such a feeling of power but also absolute horror. Would I be forced to have hairy under arms and legs forever? OMG, people would call me Wookie!

Wait, wait, no. Mom's legs and armpits are smooth. She'll know what to do. I pulled out my phone.

LIA>MOM OMG I JUST TRIED 2 SHAVE MY UNDERARMS!

MOM>HONEY ABOUT TO GO IN 2 SURGERY TALK AFTER. LUV

That was it. I took a deep breath. Okay, fine, surgery could only last a few hours. I could wait this out for a few hours. Hopefully, there would be no crimes I had to stop, or leads on who the teleporting shrinking girl was. My phone beeped.

JASON>Ah, how's it going?

LIA>Why do u ask?

There was a pause.

JASON>This is kind of awkward but I'm guessing you can't shave…

LIA>OMG how do you know?

JASON>Lia, you're super. Bullets can't hurt you, no way a razor can.

LIA>(POOP) OMG! (POOP)

JASON>Use UR heat vision.

LIA>Huh?

JASON>Think about it. Please don't make me say more about this. It's pretty embarrassing.

LIA>OK

I put the phone down. I dropped the razor (well what was left of it) into the trash. I lifted my arm. I locked my vision on the hair. I concentrated and sent out my heat vision. A beam of energy sparked from my eyes. The beam hit the hair, the hair burnt off. It took about three seconds until my underarm was nice and smooth. But way warm. I thought about ice cubes. I blew a little puff of super cool breath on my armpits. Ah, now that felt better. I lifted my other arm. I repeated the process. Yep, I was right. This certainly wasn't rocket science. I lifted up my underarms and checked them out in the mirror. Smooth as glass!

I figured that while I was at it, I may as well do my legs. My legs were actually a little easier since I had a nice clear view of them. I smiled. Now a quick shower and I would be ready for whatever the world threw at me next.

Dear Diary: When you are super, it's amazing how the littlest, simplest, almost silly task can become quite the chore. Who would have thought being invulnerable would make it impossible for me to shave like a normal girl? My BFF Jason, that's who! Not only did he realize I had that problem, but he knew an ingenious way to solve the problem. All that comic reading he does sure comes in handy. My lesson from all of this…no matter how powerful you are, you still need friends.

Cat's Out

The next couple of days were pretty normal. Wendi and her gang made their usual taunts, and mocked my chances of winning the election. Wendi constantly pointed out that she was better than me in everything, which to her meant, LAX and being pretty. Okay, she also had slightly better grades. That was only because I got a B- in gym class last year. And that was only because I'd been getting used to my powers. So I took it slow in gym class to make sure I didn't accidentally hurt anyone.

Jason discussed my campaign strategy with me. My strategy was simple. While Wendi talked about being perfect, I talked about being just a normal kid who can relate to other kids. Ha, me normal, now that was something. Although, as Jason had said, I really am normal. I'm just normal with super powers.

Sadly, there was still no progress finding Tomas and Felipe. I knew we had to do something fast before Jess turned the entire town into turnips. Dad's company still hadn't been able to find Shrink Girl, Ellie Mae. I started to think that maybe we had the wrong name.

But then while walking home on Thursday, Mac came to life. "Finally, finally!" Mac exclaimed.

"They've found Ellie Mae?" I asked, almost panting.

"They did. Her full name is Ellie Mae OPAL. She lives at 1111 Side Street, in Moon City," Mac told me. "The name and address were encrypted, but we broke through."

"Excellent! I'm good as there now!" I said.

Jason grabbed my arm. "Wait, don't you find it a little weird that after days of searching, she suddenly pops up at such a strange address?"

I stopped. "Maybe..." I admitted.

"Don't you think this could be a trap?" Jason added.

"Maybe," I groaned.

"Shouldn't we tell the rest of the team?" Jason asked.

I answered without really thinking, "No, not yet. The others don't even have costumes. It would be weird if these girls from Starlight City just showed up in Moon City. Besides I'm scared of what Jess might do."

Jason nodded. "Good point. Then take me with you instead."

I shook my head. "No way! If it's a trap, I don't want you getting caught or being in danger."

"I can take care of myself," Jason replied. "I've been training with Hana. She says I have natural moves."

My first thought was…is there no man in my life who doesn't have Hana in their life now? I fought back that thought because it wasn't useful. Plus, being jealous of an android was just plain silly.

I looked Jason in the eyes. "If this is a trap. I'll need you and the rest of the team to save me and take out BAD." I told him.

Jason gave me a weak grin. "Got it…"

I activated my costume and leaped into the air. "Ah, Lia, not to chill your cool vibe," Mac said. "But you leaped the wrong direction. Moon City is the other way." A flashing arrow pointing behind me appeared on the screen.

"Oh okay, right," I said.

I landed and turned around. I leaped up in the right direction. I figured four or five super leaps and I should be there. I needed to make a quick decision. Did I want to approach this girl as Lia Strong or Super Teen? I figured Super Teen might be a bit too much. I didn't need to tip her off or scare her off. I wanted this to be a girl to girl talk, not a super to super talk.

I landed on the outskirts of Moon City and walked the rest of the way. Truthfully, it reminded me a lot of Star Light City.

Maybe the houses were painted in slightly darker colors than the houses in Star Light City, but apart from that, it screamed average middle sized town.

With Mac's GPS, I found 1111 Side Street, a small dead-end street just off Main Street. There were only three houses on the street: 1111, 1110, and 0111. I thought the numbers were a bit strange.

1111 Side Street was a single story, dark green house. It looked very modern with big tinted windows and solar panels on the roof. In fact, it looked a lot like the other houses on the street. The front yard had two big oak trees in it. I don't know much about trees but I did know that these particular trees had to be older than the house. I walked along a neatly trimmed pavement and up the steps onto the front patio that led to a dark wooden door. I pressed the doorbell. I heard a beep.

"Coming," a young girl's voice called from behind the door. I noticed a camera on the ceiling next to the door. The camera turned to me.

The door popped open. The young girl smiled at me. "Hi!" she said. "We don't get a lot of visitors down this street. Kind of funny. So, I am guessing you are Super Teen, and you want to talk."

I laughed nervously and took a step backward. "ME?" I said pointing to myself, my eyes popping open. "SUPER TEEN? I'm so honored that you would think that." I shook my head and rolled my eyes. "Nope, I'm just simple Lia Smith, from Starlight City. I'm here doing a book report on our neighbor city."

The girl looked at me. "Ah, sure... Lying isn't nice. Did you come to join BAD?"

I laughed again. "Ellie, I assure you I'm not lying. And why would I join anything called BAD."

Ellie's eyes popped open. She leaned on the door. "Cause BAD is good. They help people get better. They cure sick and injured people."

She paused. "Wait, if you know my name is Ellie, you must be Super Teen. Right?"

"Lucky guess?"

Ellie looked up at me. "You're a great superhero but a terrible liar!"

Okay, time for a bit of truth. "Actually, I'm a teen reporter for the Sun City paper and blog. A couple of our teens are missing. Rumor has it BAD has them."

Ellie shook her head. "No, BAD wouldn't do something like that."

We both heard a cat crying from above. Ellie walked out the door past me. She looked up in one of the oak trees. Sure enough, we spotted a striped ginger cat up on one of the top branches.

Ellie looked around. She smiled. "I got this." Ellie started growing, and not normal growth, mind you. She grew to the size of the tree. The now giant Ellie put the cat in her palm and lowered her palm to the ground. The cat hopped off her palm and stretched.

Ellie shrank back to normal size.

"So much for being Shrink Girl," I said.

She laughed. "Well even when I grow, I have to shrink again, I can only stay big for a little bit. It really tires me out."

The cat looked at me. The cat opened its mouth. A net flew out of the mouth. The net fell on top of me. Electricity shot through the net burning the ground beneath my feet. I ripped the net off me and tore it into pieces.

"So much for you NOT being Super Teen!" Ellie demanded.

"So much for BAD being good," I replied.

She looked at me. She looked at the cat. "I'm sure it was just trying to protect me. Down kitty!"

The cat stood up, closed one eye and arched its back.

It showed me its claws.

"Not impressed," I told the cat.

The cat crinkled its neck. Its body started to expand. The cat grew to the size of a really large lion.

"Still not impressed!" I said.

The big cat dropped back onto its back paws. You didn't need to be a cat expert to know what its next move would be. The cat pounced at me, three-inch claws out and glistening in the sunlight. I caught it by the paws before they could hit me.

"Bad kitty!" I said, pinning its claws up in the air and keeping the big cat on two legs. "Give up now!" I said. "I really don't want to hurt you!"

I saw the cat inhale. I did the same thing. It breathed a green smog at me. I held my breath. The smog passed over me. My eyes actually burnt a little. Ellie sighed and fell to the ground. I flung the cat up in the air away from me. The cat thing sprouted wings and hovered above me. It made a hissing sound. It showed me its claws.

I blasted one of its paws with my heat vision. The cat screamed, then flew off.

I lowered myself down to Ellie. I gave her a little shake. I used super breath to blow away the green yuck that still surrounded us. I waved my hand over Ellie. Her eyes popped open.

"They told me you'd come and that they just wanted to talk to you. Ah, okay, maybe BAD isn't so good after all," she said. "I will help you find your friends."

Dear Diary: I think it's safe to say BAD is pretty rotten. They took a nice normal cat and turned it into something that wasn't normal at all. They even tricked Ellie into thinking they were good. At least now I had Ellie on my side. Yeah, I know this could be a trap. Ellie may be pretending to be on my side to get my guard down, but I don't think so. My gut says no, and my brain says listen to my gut.

Oh, I'm also pretty darn pleased with myself that I did learn from my loss to Tanya. As soon as I figured the cat thing might use a breath weapon on me, I prepared. Yes, I may need to breathe like everybody else, but I can hold my breath for a long time. In this case, certainly long enough to get rid of the green toxic gas that spurted out of that cat's mouth. Life lessons can actually be rewarding.

New Friend

"What's your plan?" Ellie asked me?

I looked at her. "I need to get into BAD'S research lab. You know the address, correct?"

Ellie nodded her head. "It's just outside of town, underground. But I can teleport you in. I can even shrink you so they don't find you. But you have to promise not to hurt anybody."

"I just want to save my friends and get out of there with them," I said.

Ellie looked at me. "I really haven't seen your friends, but there are levels in the lab I'm not allowed in."

"Then that's where I have to go."

"Little cousin, what the heck are you doing?" we heard from behind us.

Turning, I saw Glare Girl standing there with her hands on her hips.

"Oh hi, Martha, I mean Glare Girl," Ellie said. "Why are you here?"

Glare Girl moved towards us. "Does your mom know you're hanging out with people like this?"

"Actually, she does," a voice called from beside us.

We turned to see a short woman with curly dark hair standing on the porch. She had a smile on her face. "I've been listening to the conversation intently. I agree with Ellie and Super Teen."

Glare Girl slammed a foot on the ground. "Oh, Aunt Jeanie! You would take their side! BAD has been good to us. They've cured us and made us super."

"Huh?" I asked.

"I had a gluten allergy," Ellie told me. "The people at BAD made it go away. Plus, I get these cool super powers!"

"I had acne that wouldn't quit; until I met BAD. Now my skin is perfect. And I'm super."

Jeanie walked off the porch. "I did some legal work for BAD so I know they aren't all bad." She took a deep breath. "Still, if your friends are missing, I understand the need to check them out."

I didn't know this Jeanie woman but I had a good feeling about her. I thought I could trust her. I knew the trick here would be getting Glare Girl on our side.

"Look, I don't want them to take away my treatment! I DON'T want acne again!"

Ellie looked up at her, eyes open wide. "I mean, I don't want to have a gluten allergy again either, but I don't want people hurt because of me."

Jeanie put her arm around Ellie. "That's my girl!"

Glare Girl shook her head. "Look, I appreciate your problem, I really do. But that's YOUR problem, not mine. I refuse to go against the people who made me, me."

"As long as you don't get in our way," I said.

Glare Girl shook her head. "I'll try, but I can't lie. If they call me in to help. I am there. I'm not biting the hand that feeds me. I want action, but I'm not stupid."

Time to think this through. I didn't need Glare Girl as an enemy but I also didn't need her coming to fight me, especially when I might be surrounded by security. Plus, I couldn't let my friends down. I couldn't let anybody stand in my way.

"Okay Glare Girl, you're either with me or against me. And as powerful as BAD may be, trust me, you don't want me as your enemy." I made a fist. "You really don't want to go against me."

Glare Girl took a step back. She squeezed both her fists together. "Well then, I do believe all heroes need an arch-rival." She leaned forward and focused her eyes on me. She squinted.

I felt my body heating up. In fact, my hair started to crackle with energy.

"Martha, stop!" Ellie pleaded.

"Come on girls, we can work this out," Jeanie said slowly. "Let's all take a step back and collect our breath."

Glare Girl took another step backward. "Why should I stop? I'm winning!"

I took a step back too. I took a slow breath. "You should have taken your aunt's advice."

I thought of the polar ice caps and frozen drinks. I exhaled on Glare Girl. My breath encased her in a block of ice.

"Ha, I've put her on ice!" I laughed.

"Ah, I wouldn't bet on that," Ellie said, pointing at Glare Girl.

Sure enough, her ice block turned red and started to shake. The ice crumpled off her. Heat from her eyes slammed into my shoulder, knocking me down. The glare did pack quite a punch. I leaped up to my feet. I flew through the air and landed on top of Glare Girl, driving her to the ground. She tried to focus her eyes. I covered her eyes with my hand. My hand shook with the pain, but I kept my left hand locked over her eyes. With my right hand, I gave Glare Girl a pinch on the neck. The pressure on my hand stopped, Glare Girl went limp.

I turned to Ellie and her mom. "She shouldn't be a problem now. We should be in and out before she wakes up." I smiled. "Now I just need a good way in. You said you could teleport me in?"

"If you're okay with being shrunk," Ellie said.

"I'm cool with that. I trust you."

Jeanie stepped forward. "You still have a problem. Ellie Mae just can't show up at BAD for no reason. They always call her; she doesn't call them."

"What if I go to visit Dad?" Ellie asked.

Jeanie looked at me. "Her dad, my husband Don, works for their R&D department."

"So he'll know about my friends?"

Jeanie shook her head. "No, he's only involved in the legitimate stuff. He would never condone holding people against their will. Believe me, honey, most of what BAD does is for good. Doctor Dangerfield really wants to help people."

"So, she is in charge?" I asked.

"Yes, very much so."

"Then why is she so secretive?" I asked. "If she's helping people?"

"She claims her experiments are in the very early stages. She doesn't want to go public until she is sure the experiments work for the masses. She also says she's afraid people will try to steal her technology and misuse it. That's why the company is mostly underground," Jeanie laughed. "Most people in this city don't even know BAD exists. If they ask me or my husband, we just tell them we work for a think tank. Which is true."

"How do you get me in there then?" I asked.

"In my purse. While Ellie May can't go there on a whim, we can certainly stop in for a family dinner. Like I said, most of what they do, in fact, everything we see them do, is legitimate and legal, but they do make their staff work long hours. Luckily they encourage family picnics."

Okay, that certainly didn't sound very evil to me. Still, I had to get in there to see what was up.

"Let's make this so!" I said. I pointed at Glare Girl.

"Great!" Ellie Mae smiled. "I love a picnic, and seeing my dad." She pointed at Glare Girl. "But what do we do about her? I love my cousin but she does have a temper. And she's already waking up from that nerve pinch."

Sure enough, Glare Girl was starting to stir. "Both of you hold your breath!" I said. I raced over to Glare Girl. I popped my foot out of my shoe.

She started to push herself up off the ground. I wiggled my toes under her nose. She stopped moving upwards. "OMG!" she sighed. Her eyes rolled to the back of her head. She rolled over holding her throat.

"You didn't kill her, did you?" Ellie asked.

"Nah, she'll just sleep for the rest of the day." I quickly popped my foot back into my shoe before I actually did kill her. I picked her up and carried her into the house.

As I plopped her down on the couch, I got a text from Mom.

MOM>Hey, where r u?

LIA>Chatting with a new friend and her mom.

MOM> Oh, I'm going on another date tonight. Hope ur ok with that?

LIA>NP Mom…I want you to be happy.

MOM>I hope u won't have to save us tonight.

LIA>Ah something tells me Glare Girl won't b a problem 2nght.

Dear Diary: First off, it is amazing how my foot odor is still my most potent weapon. I try not to think too much about that. But, man, when I'm nervous, my feet just sweat, and it's certainly not a sweet sweat. Oh well, Jason tells me it's my body's way of defending itself. I like to think he's right, and it's not that I'm gross.

My fate, and perhaps the fate of Thomas and cute little Felipe, is now in the hands of two people I've just met. I have to hope this isn't a trap. Actually, I know it isn't. I may have just met Ellie Mae Opal and her mom, but I can sense they're good people. I trust my senses. Of course, even with them on my side, I'll still be going into BAD against long odds. Luckily, I'm pretty sure this is nothing Super Teen can't handle.

Now, as for my mom dating a reporter who is trying to discover the identity of Super Teen, and my dad dating his android assistant, that's something Lia Strong is going to have to learn to handle. I'm not a kid anymore. Heck, I'm most likely the strongest person in the world. My parents deserve to be happy even if their choices are weird.

Can They Be Trusted?

As Jeanie packed a nice picnic dinner, I made plans with Ellie.

"I'll shrink you so you fit into our picnic basket," Ellie explained to me.

"They don't check the baskets on the way in?" I asked.

"No," Jeanie answered from the kitchen. "Like I said, BAD is really trusting. As long as you don't wander into the restricted areas."

"You don't find all of that suspicious?" I frowned.

"A lot of companies have restricted areas. BAD says it's because of chemical use and radiation. Until now, I've had no reason to doubt them. Like I said, they have always been good to my family."

I had to think again about whether I was doing the right thing. I was pretty much just putting my fate into the hands of two strangers. Sure, they seemed like very nice people, but they also seemed to really trust BAD. That couldn't be good.

Jeanie walked into the living room carrying the picnic basket. "You look concerned," she said to me.

"BAD has been good to you," I said.

"They have," Jeanie said. "And so now you're worried that we might be bringing you into a trap."

"I'd never do that!" Ellie said.

I put my hand on her shoulder. "I know, Ellie."

"But she can't be totally sure she trusts me," Jeanie said. "After all, I am a lawyer for BAD."

"I want to trust you," I said, looking Jeanie in the eyes.

"Look Super Teen, trust me or not, but I'm your best chance to get into BAD. Sure, Ellie Mae could teleport you in, but security would notice you fairly quickly. Sure, you might be able to take them on, but if your friends are there, they could move them elsewhere pretty quickly. You may not trust me, but I'm still your best chance," Jeanie's eyes were locked on mine.

"She has a valid point," Mac said from my wrist. "Besides, I have been doing a voice analysis of her and she appears to be telling the truth. Either she is being truthful, or she is a fantastic liar!"

Jeanie's eyes jumped open. She pointed at my wrist. "Wow, talk about smart watches."

I glared at Mac. "Yep, he's smart but a bit annoying at times."

"I just speak the truth!" Mac said.

Jeanie put her hand on my shoulder and looked at me again. "Trust me Super Teen, if BAD is holding people against their will, I will do everything I can to help you free them!"

"They did do a lot to help your daughter and niece," I said.

Jeanie grinned. "Yes, they did, and I am so grateful. But not so grateful that I would let them hurt other innocent people. I would never allow that. Never!"

"Okay," I said with a weak smile.

"You ready to get shrunk?" Ellie Mae Opal asked me.

I nodded.

Ellie Mae pointed at me. She squeezed her fingers together. I felt myself shrinking to miniature size.

"Okay, I don't think I'll ever get used to this," I said.

Jeanie leaned over and picked me up. She placed me gently in the basket. "There's some fried chicken for you in there!" she told me.

"Mom, should we drive or teleport there?" Ellie asked.

"Driving is so slow and normal," Jeanie laughed. "Besides, you know the location well!"

A brief moment later, far inside the wonderful smelling picnic basket, I heard Jeanie talking to whom I assume were BAD security people.

"Yes, we're here to have a nice picnic dinner with my husband, Don Opal."

"Have a wonderful evening," I heard the guard say.

I felt myself moving for the first time since I'd been put into the picnic basket. Man, my life was weird. We walked for a bit. I heard an electronic beeping. I assumed it was a code to a door or something. I believe I heard a door slide open.

A man's voice said, "What a pleasant surprise!"

I heard a kiss. Ah, how sweet! The lid to the basket popped open. Jeanie looked in. "You can get out now," she told me.

I leaped out and found myself staring at the surprised face of Ellie's dad.

"Super Teen," Don said. "What's going on here? Is this another training mission like the one in Starlight City? I didn't agree with that... but Doctor Dangerfield insisted no one would get hurt and that it would also be a good experience for Super Teen. Having an arch-rival will inspire her."

"It did kind of inspire me to be better," I admitted.

Ellie pointed at me. I felt myself stretching back to normal size.

"Daddy, she's here to find her friends," Ellie told him. "She says BAD was bad and that they took her friends away."

Don shook his head. "No, BAD wouldn't do that. All the people they recruit are asked to take part in our research. Nobody is forced."

"I'm sure you believe that, but I need to search the place myself, especially the restricted areas!" I said.

The door to the lab opened. In walked Doctor Dangerfield with a couple of security people behind her. The security personnel wore blue body armor.

"Super Teen, if you wanted to visit my lab, all you had to do was ask." Doctor Dangerfield said. She turned to Jeanie. "We scan all packages that come into the complex. We noticed your picnic basket had something special inside of it."

"You can't do that!" Jeanie protested.

"Actually, this is private secure property. We can do it and we certainly do," Doctor Dangerfield said to Jeanie. Doctor Dangerfield turned her attention to me. "Super Teen, my staff and I will gladly give you a tour of our facility. All you have to do is ask."

'"I want to see the restricted area!" I insisted.

Doctor Dangerfield smiled. "I assure you we have no restricted areas here."

"I've seen them," Ellie protested.

Doctor Dangerfield put a hand to her ear, listening to a headpiece. "My aides assure me those were just for a test simulation they were running. There are no restricted areas here."

Ellie touched me on the shoulder. "Well, one way to make sure…"

A shimmering sphere appeared in front of me. The shimmer cleared to reveal a long black hallway. Ellie grabbed my hand and said, "Come."

We passed into the sphere. We came out in the long black hallway. Red lights lining the hallway started blinking. A robot voice said, "You have entered a restricted area. Please wait to be detained and escorted out."

Four silver hover drones dropped from the ceiling, they looked like electronic beetles. Red dots appeared on both Ellie's shoulders and mine as well. The two front drones fired beams of energy at us from their eyes. A beam hit Ellie, she fell to the ground. A beam hit me. It bounced off me.

"My turn!" I told the four hovering drones.

I leaned forward and focused my heat vision on the drones. They all shattered into pieces. I bent down and picked up Ellie.

"I'm okay," she told me. "She pointed down the hallway. Leave me, they won't hurt me. Check the door at the end of the hall."

I shot down the hallway at super speed. A couple of laser turrets appeared from the walls. They fired at me but I easily dodged their shots. I noticed a patch of yellow ick on the floor, right before the door. I leaped over it and smashed through the door. I rolled into a huge room with a dome ceiling and just three beds in it. One of the beds held Felipe, another held Tomas, the third held an older woman who I figured had to be Felipe's mom.

The three of them had weird rings with diodes on their heads. The diodes were connected to some sort of computer and a big glowing tube. The tube seemed to be filling with golden energy. The three of them laid there unconsciously. I rushed over. I looked over the computer and the tube. Oh my, this went way beyond my eighth-grade science level.

I wanted to just pull off the diodes but I was afraid that would do more harm. I heard footsteps behind me. Doctor Dangerfield was there along with her security team. The big surprise was Doctor Dangerfield looked as shocked as I did. "What in the name of Newton is this?" she asked.

I took a step forward while pointing at my friends. "You call this volunteering?"

Doctor Dangerfield put her hand on her chest. "Super Teen, you have to believe me... I had no idea what was going on here."

I shook my head. "I find that very hard to believe," I said.

"You can believe her," a voice very much like Doctor Dangerfield's said from behind her.

Another Doctor Dangerfield walked into the room. She was followed by two other Doctor Dangerfields. I'm not sure who looked more shocked, me, the security people or the original Doc Dangerfield.

"C1, are you behind this!" Doctor Dangerfield said, pointing at my friends.

The copy of Doctor Dangerfield grinned. I did not like that grin. "I'm C2," she said.

Doctor Dangerfield shook her head. "You all look alike to me!"

"Doctor Dangerfield, what's going here?" I asked.

Doctor Dangerfield turned to me. "I'm a busy, busy woman. I have a lot to do and quite frankly, I love my research but hate the day-to-day details that go into running a company, so I cloned myself," she said calmly.

"Oh, of course you did, that sounds SO logical," I said.

"Well, they aren't straight clones of me, they each have bio augment devices in them to help them do even more."

"Oh, that makes it so much better..." I groaned.

Doctor Dangerfield shook her head. "You would not believe the pressure I'm under doing all this. Trying to make the world a better place is hard! With a surprisingly large amount of paper work involved!"

One of the clones tapped each of the guards on their shoulders. The guards fell to the ground. "That's okay, Doctor," the clone said, "we're now relieving you of all the pressure."

Dear Diary: I'm sure that somehow, some way, there may someday be a use for clones. But man, for a smart woman, Doctor Dangerfield sure did a dumb thing cloning herself. Sure, at times I guess I think it might be cool to have two of me, one to do the homework and regular girl stuff, the other to fight crime or maybe see Brandon. But then I realize it wouldn't be wise to split myself like that. The homework, the boys, the saving the world, the whole package is what makes me me. There are no shortcuts to a complete life, even when you are super. Looks like Doctor D had to learn this the hard way.

Doctor Dangerfield held up her arms. "Wait, you three were only supposed to do the boring stuff I didn't want to do!"

The lead clone laughed. "Sorry, Doc, we've decided to take over. Not just this lab, but eventually everything. We can use these naturally super beings here to super charge our biodevices, making them even stronger. Soon, everybody in the world will want one of our implants!"

"That sounds so wrong…" I said.

The lead clone cackled. "How is it wrong to make everybody better? They will all be faster, stronger, and immune to most diseases…"

"I do not laugh like that!" Doctor Dangerfield insisted.

"Doc, stick with the program," I said. I looked at the lead clone. "Okay, what's the catch?"

"Why do you think there's a catch?" the lead clone snickered.

"I do not talk like that!" Doctor Dangerfield insisted. She turned to me. "They want to be able to control the biodevice users."

"Oh that IS so, so wrong," I said.

"And not anything I wanted," Doc Dangerfield sighed.

The lead clone chuckled. "Ha, you non-bio enhanced non-clones think so small!"

The second clone stepped forward. "You wanted to make the world a better place and that's what we will be doing. Everybody will be better and under control."

Doc Dangerfield shook her head. "That's not what I wanted…"

The third clone moved towards her. "Sorry, boring original version of us, you have no say in this matter."

"I created you all!" Doc Dangerfield shouted.

"Yes. But now we have surpassed you. Actually, you should be proud," all three clones said at once. "But since you seem to disagree with our planned course of action, we will put you on ice…" the first clone said. She pointed her hand at Doctor Dangerfield. A thick beam of blue frost hit Doctor Dangerfield. She instantly froze in place, covered in ice.

The clone aimed her hand at me. "Now for you!"

I saw the frozen blue beam coming at me. I jumped up over the beam, diving at the freezing clone. The clone reacted far faster than a normal person, she fired at me again. This time the beam of frost hit me face first. I felt a chill ripple down my entire body, coating me in ice. I spun and spun around like a mini tornado. The ice went flying off me. I crashed down on top of the clone, driving her to ground.

"It will take more than ice to stop me!" I shouted.

The clone smiled up at me. "You certainly are impressive."

"Thank you," I said.

"But you do know we are not alone. Right?"

"I know there are three of you, but I can handle three super clones!" I said bravely.

The clone pointed behind her. "But you might want to look over there."

Looking up, I saw the other two clones smiling. Behind them, I saw about a hundred floating drones that looked like winged metallic crabs, complete with metal claws that glistened to show how razor sharp they were. Each of the drone crabs also had mini-missiles on their backs.

"Those claws can also generate energy beams," the clone told me.

Before I could react, the drones blasted me with a barrage of missiles and energy beams. The attacks sent me flying backward, slamming into the wall across the room. I slinked down the wall to the floor. My uniform smoked from the firepower they had hit me with.

I got up.

"Not bad," I told the clones and the drones.

The lead clone jumped back to her feet. "Look Super Teen, you are an amazing piece of genetic work. We don't want to hurt you. But you are way outnumbered. Just join our team."

I leaned forward and let the crab drones have it with a full wide blast of heat vision. It felt good to let my powers rip again. It felt even better watching the drones crumble into piles of metallic dust.

"So much for being way outnumbered," I said.

The lead clone held up a finger. "Wait for it."

Each pile of dust started to shimmer. The dust specs began clotting together and growing like metallic blobs of silly putty. Claws and legs sprung out of each blob. The blobs continued their morphing back into metallic drones.

"The drones are made of self-replicating nanobots," the lead clone said. "You can melt them down or freeze them. They will rebuild. They also don't get tired. See, you are outnumbered!"

"She may be outnumbered but she has powerful friends," I heard a familiar voice say.

There, standing behind the clones were Tanya, Jessie, Lori, Marie and Ellie Mae Opal. "I thought you could use your friends," Ellie Mae said.

The lead clone turned towards my team. She thrust a finger at them. "Get them, drones!"

The flying drone crabs turned towards my friends. They started humming with anticipation.

"Take them...

Everything froze in place.

Tanya stood there with her arms outstretched. "Take these things out fast, ladies. I'm not sure how long I can keep that area slowed in time before things start to get dangerous!"

Marie darted forward past Tanya. She concentrated on the mass of killer crab drones. Her chest rose as she took an extra deep breath. She exhaled, aiming her head left and right. As Marie's breath hit each drone, it reduced from shiny metal to dull yellow cheese.

The cheese crab drones plopped to the ground with a squishy splat.

"I'm way hungry," Marie said.

The three clones looked at each other, hands clenched into fists. "Can the nanobots adapt from this?" one of the clones asked.

"Maybe…" the other two said. "Depends on how deeply that girl's power changed them."

Jess walked up towards the clones. "Sorry, they won't get a chance." She looked at me. "Can I vanish these?"

I grinned. "Yes please."

Jess turned to a corner of the room and clasped her hands together. She slowly separated her hands. A rift appeared across the room seeming to cut into reality itself. The rift slowly rolled open, revealing a deep black emptiness. Jess pointed at the cheese drones and then waved towards the rift. The drones floated off the ground and flew into the dark emptiness. Jess clapped her hands closed. The rift slammed shut as if it wasn't ever there.

The three clones exchanged worried glances. "What do we do now?" one of them asked. "We were prepared for Super Teen, but not all of these Super Teens."

Lori sprang forward on her bionic legs, landing between the three clones.

"What you do now is you all go to sleep!" Lori said. She walloped the lead clone in the jaw. The bionic punch sent the clone staggering backward, her head popping back.

The clone spat out a tooth. "Not bad, but it will take more than that to stop us. You and your friends have impressive power, but I'm guessing the time controller, the witch, and the molecular controller are all worn out from using their powers! And they are no match now for the three of us super clones!"

"Ha!" Lori said with a stomp of her foot. "My friends are just warming up!"

"Actually, I'm beat," Marie said. "Turning everything to cheese is hard!"

"I might be able to slow time a bit, but that trick also drained a lot of me," Tanya admitted.

"I still have power to spare!" Jessie said, she raised her arms over her head. Her hands crackled with yellow energy. The energy sizzled then fizzled out with a puff of smoke. Jessie dropped her arms to her sides. "Okay, maybe not..." she said slowly. She sniffed herself and curled her nose. "But I did manage to burn out my deodorant."

"See, I told you!" the lead clone said, pointing to her head. "We are really smart."

Lori took a fighting stance. "I will take you all out myself then."

The three clones snickered. "You don't stand a chance!"

Doc Dangerfield jumped between the clones and Lori. She held her arms up. "Wait, I made you so you could help make the world better!"

The lead clone shrugged. "We are; it is just that our idea of "better" differs from yours."

Doc Dangerfield dropped down into a fighting stance. "Then you must fight me too!"

The clone sighed. "Original us, you are in great shape for a non-enhanced being, but no match for us!"

"Ha, but you're my clone, I programmed you so you can't hurt me!" the good doctor smiled.

The clone nodded. "True," she pointed at the other two clones. "But they aren't your clones, they are my clones. They can hurt you."

The two others nodded readily in agreement.

"Oops, loophole," Doctor D said.

I stomped my foot on the floor, sending a shock wave rippling through the surface that knocked over everybody else in the room.

"You probably shouldn't forget me. You know...Super Teen."

The three clones jumped back to their feet. "Yes, our niece Wendi is right. She has such an ego."

"She's my niece, not yours!" Doc Dangerfield said.

I rolled my eyes. "Please, she is so wro- "

The three clones leaped across the room at me. "See, my fellow clones? I knew talking about our niece would distract her!"

They landed on top of me, pushing me to the ground. They were right. They did make me mad talking about Wendi like that. I filled with anger. And when I got angry, I tended to burn through my deodorant. I grabbed two of the clones and stuck their noses right under my arms. The two struggled for a bit. They fought to break my grip, my scent was too strong. Heck, I could smell it myself. I actually thought it had the aroma of a pleasant cheese. I guess the clones didn't agree. The two clones, with their noses locked in my armpit, sighed then went limp. The third clone, the leader, leapt up off me.

"You won't put me down that easily, Super Teen!" she said.

Lori tapped the clone on her shoulder, and the clone turned. Lori hit her with a jab to her jaw. The clone stumbled towards me. I rolled the other two clones off me and jumped to my feet. I caught the stumbling clone.

I tapped her on the forehead. She fell over stiff. I blew on my finger.

Doc Dangerfield ran up to me. "Super Teen, I am so sorry. I never meant for any of this to happen! I only wanted clones to help with the workload, not to take over the world."

I pointed to Felipe, his mom, and Tomas laying on the strange beds. "Yeah, well, we all make mistakes. If my friends are okay, I guess there's no real harm done."

"Right, I'll wake them up now!"

I watched as Doctor D went over and removed Felipe, his mom and Tomas from the devices they had attached to them. Felipe hugged me. Tomas hugged Jess. Doctor D promised us that with the help of her security people, she would keep the clones on ice so they couldn't cause any more trouble. All was good with the world. We had stopped three crazy clones from taking over. It felt good to be me. Once I saw Felipe, Tomas, and Felipe's mom were all okay, I thanked my team and we all headed home.

When I got home I got a text from Jason.

JASON> I heard u did great.

LIA>Thanks.

JASON>Wish I could have been there but ur dad said it would be too dangerous for me.

LIA>Sorry bud. I missed u but I do need to be able to fight super bad guys without u. Just so I learn.

JASON>Well I did my share by helping for tmw.

LIA>Tmw?

JASON>Ur speech in front of the entire school.

LIA>NO!!!!!!! I so forgot.

JASON>Yeah u were busy saving the world and all.

LIA>OMG!!! I just took a shower and I'm sweating again! It might knock out the block!

JASON>Don't worry u'll be great. U just need to let the other kids know ur a nice normal person who has their best interests at heart.

LIA>Really? Me normal?

JASON>Lia, we've been through this, mentally ur as normal as they come. Though, I think u better go take another shower. I just noticed all the birds in the trees between our houses have passed out!

Dear Diary: I try not think too hard about the fact that my scent can overpower super-powered clones. Or, for that matter, knock out all the birds in the area. I consider it just another weapon I can use to stop crime. It's amazing that despite all my powers, the thing in this world that still bothers me the most is Wendi Long. Oh well, I guess it's nice to be super, but still, have to deal with regular problems. If I am going to win this election, it will be because I am mostly normal.

Speech Morning

The next morning, I found Mom and Dad both there to greet me at the breakfast table. Now, I'd always had breakfast with Mom, it was our thing, but Dad being there was new.

"What's the matter? Did Grandma Betsy get hurt or something?" I asked.

Mom shook her head and motioned for me to sit at the table. "No all is fine."

I sat down in front of a breakfast of pancakes with blueberries, fried potatoes, fresh pineapple and raspberries, and bacon, lots of bacon. (One of the cool things about being super, is that I do burn a lot of calories throughout the day.)

"Wait, why are all my favorite foods here?" I asked.

"You had a big day yesterday," Dad said. "Taking out the clones and the drones."

"I had help," I said. "My team kicked it up."

"True," Dad acknowledged. "But you're still the leader and the face of the team. You're the only one who has gone public with their powers."

"I don't mind," I said, nibbling on nice crispy bacon. "I was born to be a hero. All my women ancestors have been super. I mean, Lori and Marie were made super by experiments that they didn't even really agree to. Tanya and her little sister are super because of a nuclear accident. Cute little Ella Mae Opal was altered to be super. And Jessie, well she's just different."

"That's what's really super about you," Dad smiled. "How you live up to being super."

"Plus, we want to talk to you about love lives," Mom said slowly.

"Oh, so gross mom. I'm eating here!"

"I mean, it can't be that easy for you, me dating a reporter who wants to learn your secret identity, and your dad dating a woman that he literally made."

"Hey, what's wrong with that?" Dad asked turning to Mom.

"So many things," Mom sighed.

"Look, guys, any kid thinks the idea of their parents dating is weird, no matter who they are dating. It's just how life goes. But really, all I care about is you guys being happy!" I told them.

"Thanks," Mom said, putting her hand on my arm. "You're a great kid!"

"I appreciate it too, and so does Hana," Dad said. "And to repeat, I don't see anything strange about me dating an android who is human in almost every way."

"Actually Dad, the only really strange thing is that she seems to get human nature better than you do," I snickered. It was kind of a joke, but also not a joke.

Dad looked at me. He slumped back in his chair. "Yeah, I get that, but I'm trying."

I put my hand on dad's arm. "Thanks, Dad, I appreciate the effort."

"Plus," Mom said, even slower, "you have a big event at school today."

I turned away. "Oh do I? I have hardly thought of it."

Suddenly I had a hiccup. And when I say a hiccup, I really meant the up part. The hiccup forced me up into the air, I banged into the ceiling, putting a huge dent in it. I dropped to the ground, smashing the wooden chair I'd been sitting on into pieces.

"What the heck—" Another hiccup sent me flying up and down again, putting another hole in the ceiling and grinding the wooden chair to dust.

"Honey, take a deep breath," Mom said.

"Those are nervous hiccups, you had them when you were younger," Dad said.

Mom turned to Dad. "I'm surprised you remember?"

"Look, I know I wasn't the world's greatest dad, but I remember things."

"Guys," I quivered. "Help me before I destroy the kitchen."

Mom put her hand on my back. "Like I said honey, breathe in."

I took a deep breath in.

"Now let it out!"

I exhaled, sending Dad flying across the kitchen. He crashed into the wall. He fell to the floor. He laid there out cold.

"Oops," I said.

Mom started to laugh harder than I had ever seen her laugh before. She actually doubled over with laughter. "Oh honey, I can't believe you did that, but I am so glad you did."

Mom paused for a second and wiped a tear out of her eye. "I obviously still have issues with your dad. I mean, come on, the man is dating an android."

"I know it's weird Mom, but he's happy. Plus, she keeps him grounded."

Mom bent down and hugged me. "That's why I love you. Your spirit is as strong as any of your powers."

I noticed the hiccups were gone. "I'm hiccup-free!" I said.

Mom nodded. "Yeah, they're a nervous reaction, and you're not nervous any longer." Mom looked me in the eyes. "Trust me, honey, you're going to be fine."

Dear Diary: Wow! Just when I thought I'd run out of embarrassing super powers, I discovered super destructive hiccups. Man, those aren't fun. I just need to stay relaxed, and I will be fine. Who would have thought that my dad dating an android would be one of the more normal events of my life?

Speech Time

The day flew by. Pretty much the next thing I knew, I was sitting up on stage in the school auditorium. Jason, as my campaign manager, sat beside me. School Vice Principal Macadoo stood at a podium in the middle of the stage and he was going on and on about the importance of elections in our society. I didn't mind because the more he talked, the more time I had to wait.

Across from me sat Wendi and her campaign manager Patti. Wendi looked so smug wearing a red dress with a red jacket on top of it. She had a flag pin on her collar. I swore her dress had to be extra short. That Wendi would do anything to get a vote. I couldn't blame her; she did have really good legs! Wendi sat there looking at VP Macadoo and smiling.

That's when it hit me again. I knew I was about to experience another super hiccup attack. I stood up.

"Where are you going?" Jason asked me.

"I've got a personal problem…" I said hurriedly. I started off the stage, hoping nobody would notice.

"Ms. Strong, where are you going?" VP Macadoo asked.

"Sorry sir, nature calls!" I said.

The entire school student body laughed.

I streaked off the stage. Once I got out of the view, I ran at super speed into the girls' bathroom. If I was going to have a super hiccup attack, I'd do it out of sight. Luckily, the entire school was at the speeches. Well, not so lucky, since they all now were laughing at me.

I raced into the bathroom so fast I almost ran into Janitor Jan who was wiping some writing off of one of the stalls.

Good thing Jan saw me coming, so she levitated out of the way. Jan dropped back to the floor.

"Lia, what are doing in here? You should be giving a speech now."

"Sorry, Jan, I had a nervous attack. I had to get out of there before I did something bad."

"What?" Jan said.

"HICCUP!" I shot up to the ceiling, cracking it. I fell back down on the floor, denting the floor.

"That..." I said.

Jan shook her head. "Girl, I just washed this floor." Jan put her hands on my shoulders. "Now you have to calm down. Don't make me turn you into a gel pad for my shoes."

"Say what?" I said.

Jan grinned. "When somebody does something that messes up my school, I teach them a lesson. I turn them into a gel pad and stick them in my shoes. Right now, Cindy Love is in my right shoe due to that heart she drew on the wall. That big bully, Tony Wall, is in my left shoe due to dropping papers all over the school. The kid doesn't seem to care." Jan reached down and pulled off her right shoe. There inside was a flattened little blond girl, Cindy Love.

"Jan please put your shoe back on," I asked.

Jan laughed. "Yeah, they can pack quite the kick. You're lucky you're super or you probably would have been out for the count."

"How long do you keep people in your shoes?"

"Just a couple of hours to teach them a lesson. They don't remember anything once I turn them back. They just know not to litter or clutter the school again. It's really a human service," Jan insisted.

"Ah, okay," I said. I noticed my hiccups had stopped. "Hey, I'm okay now!"

Jan smiled. "Yeah, you've calmed down."

"Do you have some magic that can keep me calm?" I asked her.

"I do. It's the best magic of all." Jan put her hand on my shoulder. She looked me in the eyes. "Just trust yourself. You're a good kid. You're smart, and you try to do the right thing. Just tell your classmates that and you'll be fine."

"Really?" I said.

Jan shrugged, "I sure hope so. If not, just hit them all with a super fart and none of them will remember a thing when they come to," Jan laughed, leading me to the door. "Now get back and give them a great speech. Knock em dead! Just figuratively of course!"

I skulked back into the auditorium as Wendi gave her speech. She must have been talking for a few minutes already but that didn't stop her from rambling on. She talked about her accomplishments, being a class home coming queen, being a straight-A student, being the star of the LAX team. How she could help lead our school into even better times. She would work on longer lunch breaks, improving the boys' LAX teams, and getting a student lounge. She concluded that she was the only person to lead our class. She did mention that I was so afraid to speak I was probably in the bathroom crying.

The class laughed. I fought back the urge to remove my shoes and clobber them all with super foot odor.

VP Macadoo took the podium and introduced me.

I stood up. I walked slowly to the podium. "Thank you VP Macadoo," I said. I saw Jason give me a thumbs up. I turned to my classmates.

"My fellow classmates. What can I say? I'm not perfect like Wendi. I don't have perfect hair or the perfect complexion. I have bad hair days. I get zits. I get nervous when I'm about to speak in front of a bunch of people. So, if you want somebody perfect, you really should vote for Wendi. But, if you want somebody who can relate to you and will be there for you, please vote for me. I may not be the best, but I do promise I will have all of your best interests at heart. Thank you."

I walked off of the podium, and the class started to clap. I smiled.

VP Macadoo took the podium. "Well, students, you've heard the candidates, and you may all vote before leaving the auditorium. Votes need to be handed to Miss Mayfield on your way out. She will be doing the counting."

I glanced towards the school administrator, Miss Mayfield, and realized that my fate was in her hands.

As I sat down, the reality of the situation hit me. I leaned into Jason. "Wait, the vote is today?"

He smiled. "Yes, and you did great."

Dear Diary: Fighting a group of super clones and drones was nearly as nerve-racking as having to speak in front of my class. I did my best. I just had to hope the class related to me.

Speech Wrapped

At the end of the day, both Jason and I were getting ready to leave school.

"Lia wait!" I heard a voice call.

I saw Steve running towards me. "Lia! You won!" he said.

"Won what?" I asked.

"Class president!" Steve said. "I'm in charge of tabulating the vote since I'm so good with numbers. You won by over 20 votes. It won't be announced until the morning, but I wanted to tell you."

"Gee thanks Steve, I really appreciate it."

Jason and I headed out of the school with Steve walking with us. "Ah, Steve, don't you live on the other side of town?" I asked.

"Yes, I do. But I like the extra walk, it's good for me. I'm in great shape you know. I run cross country. Plus, since I'm class treasurer and class secretary we'll be working together this year."

"That's nice," I said.

"So I thought it would be fun if I got to know you better."

We walked on for a while. With Steve asking me everything from my favorite color to my favorite food, to my favorite author, to my favorite show. He asked me a lot of stuff.

Jason answered most of the questions for me. I believe Jason wanted to prove that he knew me better than anybody. I'm not totally sure, but I may have detected a bit of jealousy on Jason's part. He didn't appreciate another boy butting in on his time.

Steve stopped walking with us. His eyes glazed over. "I just remembered," he said slowly. "I have to go home now and wash my underwear. After all, I've worn this underwear all week now."

Steve turned and ran off.

"Did you make him say that?" Jason asked.

"Ah, no," I said. "Though it was tempting...."

"I did!" A voice said from above.

Looking up, I saw a cute boy with curly red hair and big green eyes floating in a tree above us. He slowly lowered himself to the ground. He held out his hand. "Lia Strong, I am Zeekee Zaxxx from the planet ZZZ-333, and I need your help!"

Just when I thought my life couldn't get any more interesting, it did!

Book 5

Out of this World

The Unexpected Arrival

"Excuse me?" I said to this strange red-haired boy with the biggest green eyes I had ever seen.

"My name is Zeekee Zaxxx from the planet ZZZ-333," the boy said, as he floated from the tree to the ground. "I need your help."

I had to admit, I was intrigued. This boy looked just like a regular kid. But he seemed so different, so special. "Why do you need MY help?" I asked.

Jason walked over and stood between us. "Yeah, why?" he , curling his hands into fists. I had never seen Jason so defensive. Part of me liked that he felt the need to defend me. Although another part of me thought he was being silly. After all, I am the strongest person on Earth.

"I've escaped from my planet ZZZ-333 to seek refuge on Earth," Zeekee said, his eyes locked on mine.

"Why are you running away?" Jason asked.

"That's a very good question," I said, staring at Zeekee. Man, he had beautiful eyes. I put a hand on Jason's shoulder. "Jason, stay calm."

"I am calm!" Jason said, his gaze steadfast and locked on Zeekee.

Zeekee didn't flinch. He stood his ground. He looked directly at me and said, "I just wanted to see another planet; mingle with other types of people. After all, those of us on ZZZ-333 are mostly human. We have just developed our brains more, which gives us a few extra abilities. That's why you, Lia Strong, are so interesting to me. It appears you are the most advanced human on Earth. Yet, you seem so humble. Plus, you are willing to risk your health and your privacy to save others."

I took a step backward and lowered my eyes. That was the first time I'd heard the things I do, put into those words. My heart pounded faster.

"You should be proud of what you do and who you are!" Zeekee said.

"She is!" Jason replied adamantly, pointing an insistent finger at Zeekee.

"I am," I agreed. "I love helping people!"

Zeekee smiled. My heart fluttered a little more. "That's why I am here. I thought you could protect me from my mother's forces."

"Excuse me?" Jason frowned. "What do you mean by 'from your mother's forces'?"

"My mother, High Leader, Zela does not believe in communicating with other planets and other human types. She believes we should keep to ourselves. She, quite frankly, thinks of you as primitive hostiles. My goal is to prove her wrong."

"That's a good goal," I replied.

"Tell us again about your mother's forces," Jason was still not convinced.

"Being high leader means my mother has access to great resources. I fear she will send some of those resources after me to retrieve me and bring me back."

"We know what retrieve means!" Jason said, glaring at Zeekee. "So, basically you're saying that by coming here, you've put us in danger."

Zeekee nodded. "That was certainly not my main intention, but yes, I do believe that may be a consequence of my actions. My mother does not like being disobeyed."

"No mother does," I told him.

"True," Zeekee smiled.

"Then maybe you should just beam yourself back to whatever space ship you came in!" Jason growled.

Zeekee nodded again. "I truly understand your concern. But I believe the knowledge I gain from being here, interacting with other human types, is worth the risk. We can open up both our worlds to each other. By joining together, we can actually make the universe seem smaller!"

Wow, I really liked how Zeekee talked and thought that I could relate to his words. He just wanted to join two worlds. We could learn so much from each other. Plus, I found him way cute.

Jason stood there, arms crossed. "I'm not sure it's worth it." He took a deep breath. "Sure, I love the idea of meeting aliens from other worlds."

Zeekee held out a hand. "Well here's your chance! I'm so glad to meet you, human known as 'Jason'."

Jason looked at the extended hand, reached out, and shook it. "Nice to meet you too, Zeekee, but I don't like the idea of possibly making the leader of another world angry."

Zeekee released Jason's hand. He laughed. His laugh reminded me of a pleasant wind chime. "Oh, she is going to be so mad. But like I said, I believe it is worth the risk. Plus, I have seen Lia in action. I am sure she can protect me."

"I do like to protect people!" I said.

Jason looked at me. "He's not exactly people!"

Zeekee shook his head. "That is where you are wrong, human Jason. I am a people, just a slightly more advanced people. That's why I can do things like this." He pointed at Jason and said, "Sleep!"

Jason dropped in his tracks. He curled up on the ground and started snoring. Zeekee stepped over Jason towards me, "I'm sorry I had to do that to your aide, but I got the feeling he was being defensive when he didn't need to be."

I giggled. "Jason is not my aide...."

"But he is always by your side, assisting you."

"He's my friend," I said. "I've known him forever!"

"Oh, are you betrothed?" Zeekee asked softly. I thought I sensed a worried tone in his voice.

MAC spoke up from my watch communicator. "In case you are wondering, betrothed means engaged to be married."

I put my watch to my face. "I knew that!" I nodded. After all, I watch a lot of love stories.

"Just giving information," MAC said. "It's what I do."

Zeekee pointed to MAC. "Is that what you humans call 'Siri'?"

I giggled. "Kind of. He's my advanced version of Siri, called MAC. He likes to give me information, whether I need it or not. But, getting back to the original question; Jason and I are not engaged. We are far too young!"

Zeekee took a step back. "So you will be, once you are older?" He looked down at Jason and frowned.

I shrugged. "I'm not going there. Let's just say we're great friends. He has my back and I have his!"

Zeekee grinned. "You are truly wise, Lia Strong from Earth!"

"Just Lia, please."

"Okay, Lia please."

"No, just Lia."

"Okay, just Lia," he said.

"Alien dude, just refer to her as Lia," MAC said.

Zeekee pointed at me. "Right. You are Lia!"

"Very good," I said, patting him on the shoulder.

Zeekee's big green eyes popped open. "Oh, this is bad. Scout drones have found me…"

I turned to see about a hundred black and silver flying machines hovering over us. They looked like they had mechanical eyes. I fought back the urge to shiver. They started to spin faster and began to turn red. I figured this was a sign that they meant business.

Dear Diary: This is so amazing! I've actually met a really cool and extremely good-looking boy from another planet. Sure, he thought Jason and I might be engaged. Sure, his mom, the leader of that planet, doesn't want him to be here. And, I can't help noticing that Jason seems jealous of this guy. Not sure what to make of that. Part of me likes that Jason is so protective of me. But is this being more than protective? Man, nothing in my life is ever easy. But at least my life is interesting!

Fight and Greet

Okay, I had to deal with these spinning eye drones. They didn't look like much, but there were a LOT of them. Plus, I've been a superhero long enough to know that things aren't always what they seem. Heck, I look like a normal girl but I can flatten a herd of elephants with a fart, and not even one of my BAD farts. Dad and his team of scientists think that one of my power farts could actually drop an army! I know Dad likes to exaggerate, but I have done it in simulation. Of course, these drones were obviously machines and would probably be immune to my fart power. And truth be told, unleashing one of my farts in public would cause more harm than good.

I activated my mask and uniform.

"That is so blook," Zeekee said.

"Blook?"

"It's how we say cool…"

"Oh."

Zeekee leaned into me. "I don't think the drones care what you want. They are very stubborn."

"Man, if my neighbors see this, I'm not sure what the heck they will think…" I sighed.

"Don't worry, I'm creating an illusion so any normal humans who see this, will think the drones are flying butters," Zeekee said.

"Well, that's good," I said. "I guess. And I hope you mean butterflies. Flying butters would just be weird."

"Oh right, I knew that," Zeekee said, peeking out from behind me. "But your human language is so confusing."

"We'll talk language later. For now, I need to deal with these drones!" I looked at the drones and shouted. "Okay, you have one chance to back off!" I held up one finger.

The drones instantly bombarded me with rays of red-hot energy. I'm not sure how many beams they blasted me with, but my uniform smoked in at least a hundred different places.

I shook my head. I looked at the drones. I swear their eyes had popped opened wider. "Okay, I'm going to assume that means...*nope we're not backing off*!" I growled.

I leaned forward, squinted my eyes and thought of hot things...the sun, volcanoes, a spaceship blasting off, and Latin dancing. Okay, that last one was a little weird, but it worked. A wide cone of red-hot energy burnt from my eyes and cut through the middle section of drones. The drones I hit simply crumbled to the ground.

"Take that!" I said. The good news was, I took out at least half the drones. The bad news was, I had used up a lot of my energy firing a blast so wide and powerful. I would need a bit of time to recharge. From the way the remaining drones were swarming into formation, I knew I didn't have a lot of time.

The drones fired at both Zeekee and me again. This time I grabbed him and leaped up into the air, over the burning red beams of pain.

"Zow! You are truly splendid!" Zeekee said as I flew up into the sky.

I had to admit, I liked that he liked what I had done. It made me feel tingly. But no time for feelings now. I needed to stop these drones before they hurt Zeekee. New problem being, while I had him up in the air alongside me, I really couldn't attack the drones. I was forced to dodge attack after attack.

"Man, these drones are certainly persistent," I said, spinning in midair.

"Zeppers! And they never tire," Zeekee gulped.

We started falling back towards the ground. While I've become better at leaping and floating, I still can't hover for too long. Still, I figured I could use my falling to my advantage.

"Hold on!" I told Zeekee.

I started twirling at super speed, gaining momentum with each spin. I spun so fast, I created a whirlwind.

The whirlwind ripped through part of the drones, smashing them to the ground. I spun towards the ground, turning my body so I hit the ground first, shielding Zeekee from most of the force. I jumped back to my feet and pulled Zeekee up.

"Zow! That was mega bloop!" he said. He had turned a very sickly shade of green. He twisted away from me and bent over. "Don't look," he pleaded.

I returned my attention to the remaining drones that were now circling us. I heard barfing sounds coming from Zeekee. The drones started spinning faster and buzzing louder.

"This is so embarrassing," Zeekee groaned.

If I didn't find a way to take out the rest of these drones, barfing would be the least of Zeekee's problems.

I thrust a finger at the drones. "Okay, you crazy things have made me mad now!"

I heard a high-pitched "Hiya!" Looking up, I saw my little neighbor, half-vampire, Felipe, flying through the air at the drones. As he flew, he swatted drones left and right. His older cousin, Tomas, leaped into the air behind him. Tomas batted down the drones Felipe had missed.

Supporting the two half-vampires from the ground, was Tomas's girlfriend and my buddy, Jessica the witch. Jess used her telekinetic powers, waving her hands to smash a bunch of drones into each other.

I smiled, watching my friends clean up the remaining drones. Tomas and Felipe floated down beside me.

"That was so fun!" Felipe shouted.

"I agree," Tomas said.

Jess walked over to me, cool as ever. I don't think Jess has ever formed a bead of sweat in her life. "We thought you could use a little help," she said. "I could have banished them, but the boys wanted to have some fun."

"I appreciate the help," I told her. To be honest, I might have been able to handle the drones alone, but it would have worn me down - a lot.

Jess pointed to Zeekee, still on all fours, looking a little shaky. "What do we have here?"

Felipe looked at Jason, still asleep on the ground. "And what's wrong with Jason?"

Zeekee stood up and wiped his mouth. He looked at me. "I'm so sorry for arfing..."

"Actually, it's called barfing," Tomas corrected with a grin. Tomas looked at me. "I take it this guy isn't from around here."

Before I could say anything, Zeekee moved forward. "No, I am from a planet many light years away. I have run away from my home planet. I want to see how Earth people live."

Tomas and Felipe both sniffed him. They looked at Zeekee with squinted eyes.

"What's wrong guys?"

"Ah, nothing..." Tomas said, he just smells like alien barf.

Zeekee nodded. "Yeah, ah sorry about that. Not one of my finer moments."

I looked at Jess, looking Zeekee over. She raised an eyebrow.

Jess put her arms around Tomas and Felipe. "Okay guys, our work here is done, let's get back to the house so these two can talk."

She turned and led the half-vampires away.

"Thanks, guys!" I said again.

"So, you are not the only super being on Earth?" Zeekee commented.

"There are a few others, but we are very rare," I told him, without going into details.

"But you are the most powerful. Right? Their leader, right?" Zeekee asked.

I shrugged. I could tell this cute alien boy wanted more information but I had to be careful. Just because he happened to have big dreamy eyes didn't mean I should totally trust him. "As you can see, I'm powerful. I'm also the only super being that's open about being a hero. I guess I'm kind of the leader," I added. "Though I like to think of myself as being an inspiration, more so than a leader. I lead by example. Doing the right thing and all that kind of stuff."

I pointed to my house. "Now let's get inside where we can talk more privately. It's amazing that fight didn't draw the attention of all my neighbors!"

Zeekee smiled. "Any normal human being who was watching, simply thought you were chasing butters that fly."

I smiled back at him. "It's butterflies, but you're getting closer."

We started heading towards my house. It hit me. I stopped. I turned and pointed to Jason. "Ah, can you wake him up?"

"But he is sleeping so nicely. He's quiet. And he's calm." He paused for a moment. "Why don't you use your mind to control these simpler humans?"

"Well, I don't think of them as simpler, and I don't like to use my command voice," I said.

"But they are, and you should!" Zeekee insisted. "After all, you have power, you should use it."

He had a good point. But one I don't really like talking about.

"Can you please wake up Jason? He's going to get all dirty sleeping on the ground."

"But I don't think he likes me," Zeekee protested.

"He's just being protective of me," I said.

"I suppose that is a good trait," Zeekee said slowly. He pointed at Jason and said, "Wake up simple little human male!"

Jason started to stir. He slowly pushed himself up. He spit some dirt out of his mouth. "Yuck," he said. He looked up at us. "What did I miss?"

"Not much," I replied, innocently. I pointed to my house. "I'm going to take Zeekee into the house so he's safe. Do you want to come?"

I shot Zeekee a glance. He seemed to be concentrating on Jason.

Jason shook his head. "I'd better get home and start on my homework." He pointed at Zeekee. "I don't totally trust him, but I do totally trust you!"

I watched Jason walk into his house. I turned to Zeekee. "Okay let's get inside."

Dear Diary: Now, that was eventful! It felt great taking out a whole lot of alien drones. Sure, I had a little help from my friends, but after all, that's what friends do, they help when you need a hand. Okay, that's not all friends do, but it's a nice part of having friends. Friends have your back. Plus, sometimes they see things more clearly than you do.

I can't help but notice Jason, Tomas, Felipe, and Jess didn't seem very keen on Zeekee. Maybe they were just being over-protective. After all, Zeekee is an alien. I guess even vampires and witches can find aliens unsettling. As for Jason, sure he was also on my side, but he might have been a little jealous. He is usually the only "man" in my life. I got the idea that he didn't like sharing me. Not sure how I feel about that.

As for Zeekee…he certainly is CUTE! I love his big green eyes. He is so good-looking! But okay, that's not the main deal here. This boy is an ALIEN from ANOTHER world and he needs my help! It sounds like his mom and his people aren't very open to change. Heck, I guess they are like most humans I know. ☺
But I will make it my job to keep him safe!

Home Sweet Home

Shep, my faithful German Shepherd ran to the door to greet me, his tail wagging a mile a minute.

Shep noticed Zeekee. The tail stopped wagging. Shep took a step back. Shep started to growl.

"Bad boy, Shep!" I scolded.

Shep continued to snarl, even showing his teeth.

I turned to Zeekee, "Sorry, he's usually very friendly, but he is also quite protective towards me."

Zeekee positioned himself behind me. "Nice. A strange creature with teeth," he said.

"He's called a dog," I explained.

"Right, I knew that," Zeekee replied. "We only have cats on my planet. I never knew why. But I'm now starting to see the reason for that."

I smiled. "Ah, he must smell the cat on you. Shep and cats don't get along." I turned to Shep. "Shep, be good, Zeekee is a new friend."

Shep didn't listen. In fact, he began to snarl louder. Who would have thought I'd have a dog that didn't like aliens. I mean, I guess Shep felt like he needed to protect me from something new. But really, Shep should understand that I don't need protection. At least not from this cute alien guy. I needed to calm Shep down and fast.

I gave Shep a reassuring pat on the head. "It's okay, buddy, Zeekee is a friend."

The growling continued.

I hated to do this, but I just couldn't have my dog threatening my new alien friend. "MAC, deactivate the deodorant nanobots from my arms," I demanded quickly.

"Say what?" MAC responded from my watch communicator.

"Deactivate my deodorant," I repeated.

"Ms. Lia, do you think that's wise? You've had a stressful afternoon. Your underarms are, how can I say this politely? Less than fresh...."

"Yes, I understand," I said. It always felt weird arguing with my computer assistant. He certainly wasn't assisting me now. Though in his defense, I'm sure he thought he was. "Just do it!"

I heard MAC sigh. "Okay, let me be clearer. If I deactivate your nano deo bots and you walked into a theater and lifted your arms up, all the other patrons in the theater would fall unconscious."

"That's a really specific example," I told MAC.

"I'm a computer, specific examples are what I do."

"Look MAC, I'm not going to leave the house. In fact, I only want the nano deo bots deactivated under my left arm, and only for a moment."

A question mark appeared on my watch interface.

"I just need to calm Shep down," I argued once more.

"Okay...done," MAC said, "Proceed with caution."

"Gotcha..."

I leaned over Shep, and in my most soothing voice I softly sang, "Shep be nice and calm..." I didn't want to use my underarm scent on him if I didn't have to.

Shep kept his eyes focused on Zeekee. Yep, my loyal dog didn't trust an alien from a planet that had no dogs. I had to calm Shep down. I considered other options besides giving him a whiff of my underarm. I tried talking to him one more time. "Come on, boy, calm down..."

Shep's fur stood up on edge. If anything, he became more agitated the longer he focused on this alien boy. I positioned my underarm so it moved gently over Shep's nose. Shep, as usual, sniffed my underarm. I don't know why but he just couldn't resist.

Shep rolled over onto his back. He sighed then closed his eyes.

"Wow, your scent overpowered him!" Zeekee said.

"I like to think of it as comforting him," I told Zeekee.

Zeekee shook his head. "No way! You dropped him like a meteorite! What power!!"

"I am activating your nano deo bots again," MAC said.

"Thank you," I said.

I pointed at Shep, "He'll be resting for a while. Let me show you my house."

"Zeto!" Zeekee said. "I've never seen a house from another world before."

I led Zeekee into the living room. His mouth fell open. "I have never seen such rounded and fluffy objects before…what are they?"

"Ah, we call them a couch and chairs," I said.

He leaped into the air, onto our couch. He bounced up a bit. He settled down. He sank back into the couch. "OMS this is so soft! It's like sitting on a cloud!"

"OMS?" I asked.

He grinned, "It is short for Oh My Stars."

"Ah," I said.

He jumped off the couch and spun towards a yellow easy chair. He plopped down on the chair. "This has such comfort and warmth. It's much nicer than our metal chairs."

I pointed to the handle on the chair. "It also goes back and rocks."

"You mean it plays music?" Zeekee asked.

I smiled. "No, but some people have chairs that do that. Pull the handle and lay back."

Zeekee put his hand on the handle and pulled it back. His eyes shot open as the recliner foot section popped out. "OMS cubed!" he shouted. "This chair is awesome."

"Now move your body," I told him.

He glanced at me. "I thought you said this chair doesn't play music."

"Just trust me, Zeekee," I grinned.

Zeekee slowly rocked the chair back and then forward. His grin spread wide across his face. "This is surprisingly pleasant. For primitive beings, you Earth folk do have some good ideas!"

"Ah, thanks," I said. Though being called primitive didn't make me happy.

Zeekee pointed at the TV on the wall. "Is that big black box what I think it is?"

"If you think it's a television, yes, it is," I said.

"Oh no, I thought it was a TV," he sighed. "I so wanted to view one of those."

"A television is a TV," I replied with a smirk.

"Ah," his face lit up. "You Earth people make things so complicated sometimes!" He clapped his hands. "Television on! Entertain me!" he shouted at the TV.

"Ah, our TV doesn't respond like that," I said.

"Do I need to call it by name?" Zeekee asked.

I smiled. I reached down to the coffee table and grabbed the remote control. "No, our TV is not advanced."

Zeekee's eyes dropped. "Oh, my bad. I just assumed since Earth people spent so much time watching these boxes, they would respond to voice."

"Some do. It's just that my mom is old fashioned," I explained, handing Zeekee the remote. "Use this."

He took the remote from me and wiggled it with his hand. "It has a nice feel to it. Do I talk to this?"

I smiled. "No, you press the buttons."

"With my fingers?"

"No, with your tongue, Zeekee."

"Okay, but that doesn't seem very sanitary," he said, his tongue dropping out of his mouth.

I waved my hands in front of him. "No, no! That was a joke. Of course, you use your fingers!" I grinned.

Zeekee looked at me. He had a slight smirk on his lips. "Ha, good one Lia Strong!" He laughed. "You are so freezing!"

"I think you meant cool."

"Isn't freezing colder than cool?" he asked.

"Yes, it is."

"Therefore, isn't it better than cool?" he asked.

"You might think that, but it's not," I told him.

Zeekee started scrolling through the channels on the TV. "You Earth people sure are a bit weird, but you must be doing something right to invent something as fun and cool as TV."

"Ah, thanks," I said.

I sat and watched Zeekee. His eyes were glued to the screen as he scrolled through the channels. After about fifteen minutes of that, I said, "You know, we earthlings have other rooms too."

Zeekee's eyes remained locked on the screen. "Do you have TVs in those rooms too?"

I nodded. "In some yes, but not all. At least not in this house. Like I said, my mom is a bit old-fashioned. "Are you hungry?" I asked him.

He looked at me. "No, I told you my name is Zeekee, hungry would be a strange name."

"No, I mean do you have hunger?" I asked.

"Ever?" he asked.

"Like right now?" I laughed.

He stopped watching the TV. He patted his stomach. "Actually, I do have hunger right now. Can you have your robots bring me something?"

"Ah, not a lot of robots around, not yet anyway."

"Then how do you get food?"

I pulled him up from the chair. I dragged him into the kitchen. Once again his mouth dropped open. "I have read of these in history books. This is what we called a food preparation area."

"We call it kitchen," I said.

I pointed to the refrigerator. "That's a refrigerator, it keeps food cold." I pointed to the oven. "That's an oven, it cooks the food." I pointed to the microwave. "That's a microwave, it cooks food fast, good for warming things up. It's great for popcorn."

"What is popcorn?"

"It's tasty. Trust me."

Zeekee walked over to the sink. "I know what this metal contraption does. It's a water dispenser and water remover."

"Yep, we call it a faucet and sink," I said.

He grinned. "You Earth people, with your colorful words." He pointed at the table and chairs. "Do you consume food sitting down in groups?"

"Mom and I try to, whenever we can," I told him.

"How quaint," he told me. "Where is your female parental unit?" he asked.

I looked at the clock. "She's still at work. But she should be home anytime now. I think she has a date tonight."

"So you people still work?"

"Yes. My mom's a medical doctor."

"Wait, doesn't everybody on Earth have a date tonight? After all, you all share the same planet."

"We call it a date when two people who like each other, more than just as a friend, go out together."

Zeekee nodded. "Oh, I see." He paused. "Do you have a date tonight?" he asked.

"Nope," I grinned and shook my head. "Right now, all the boys I know are just friends."

"Even that Jake fellow?"

"His name is Jason."

"Are you sure?"

"Yes, Zeekee I am sure."

"Do you have a romantic interest in Jason, formerly known as Jake?" he prodded.

"I've known Jason all my life."

"Wait! You were born together? Do you have clone facilities here?"

I shook my head. "No, Zeekee, let me be more specific..."

"I would appreciate that, Lia Strong."

"I've known Jason for as long as I can remember."

"That does not mean you cannot have romantic feelings towards him. I think that would increase the chances. But, I could be wrong. On my planet, our dates are picked for us by computers."

"Interesting," I said. "And no, at this current moment in time, I don't have a romantic interest in Jason. He is my best friend."

"So Earth folk cannot be romantically involved with friends?"

"They can be, but Jason and I choose not to be at this present moment. We are young. Plus, he's kind of like a brother to me."

Zeekee grinned. "Ah, I understand that."

"Do you really?" I asked.

He shook his head. "Actually no, but I figure it's not that important. The important thing is, you are without romantic interest."

Something about the way Zeekee worded that statement didn't feel quite right. But sadly, he had figured out the truth. The romance in my life was zero. I just didn't need to be told that. But hey, I'm only 13. I have a lot of time. Plus, did Zeekee's interest mean he had an interest in me? Or was he just curious? I'd have to see how this played out.

I walked over and popped open the fridge. I looked over my shoulder and asked Zeekee, "What do you feel like?"

He felt his cheek. "I think I feel kind of soft and squishy, but it depends on which part of me you feel."

"Ah, I mean what do you feel like eating?"

"Do you have protein mush?" he asked.

I looked into the fridge. "Well, we do have bacon, lettuce, and tomato. I can make you a sandwich."

"It sounds fascinating! What is this sandwich you speak of?"

"In this case it's meat," I showed him the bacon. "With lettuce," I showed him a head of lettuce. "And tomato!" I showed him a nice big red juicy tomato. "Between two slices of bread!" I pointed to the bread on the counter.

Zeekee licked his lips. He stopped. "My, what a primitive reaction I just had." He grinned, showing me the dimples on his cheeks. "I liked it!"

I moved to the counter and prepared a sandwich with super speed. Not that I had to, but I wanted to impress him. I wasn't sure if I wanted him to see that Earth folk could do some amazing things, or that I, myself, could be a pretty amazing person.

Regardless, I slapped together a tasty BLT in like, under a second. Grabbing a plate from a cupboard above the counter, I darted over to Zeekee. Yep, something about this guy made me want to impress him. I placed the sandwich and plate down. I super sped over to the counter and made myself a sandwich. Then shot back to the table next to Zeekee.

"Do you want some milk?" I asked.

He raised a finger. "I know what that is…it's a liquid produced by mammals to nourish their young. Do you have a milk-producing mammal in the house?"

I got up and walked to the fridge. This time I moved at regular speed. I pulled out a bottle of milk. "Nah we just put it in bottles," I told him.

I grabbed two glasses and super sped back to the table. I poured the milk in the blink of an eye.

Zeekee had already bitten into his sandwich. "Quite impressive," he said.

"Thank you," I said with a bow.

"Actually, Lia Strong, I was talking about this bacon. It's amazing!"

"Oh right, I knew that," I said, feeling my face turn red.

Zeekee pointed at my face. "Oh, I enjoy the added color of your cheeks!" he noted. "Is that a side effect from moving so fast?"

"Yeah, sure," I told him.

I guessed it was a good thing he didn't realize he'd embarrassed me. That might have made him feel uncomfortable. It must have been a weird and strange enough experience just being on another planet. The poor guy was all alone. All because he wanted to learn and experience new things. I didn't need to make him any more uncomfortable. After all, I couldn't imagine what he was going through.

He really gobbled down that bacon, lettuce and tomato sandwich. He finished his sandwich before I had even taken a second bite out of mine. And I can really eat. One of the better things about being super is that I actually burn through a LOT of calories each day. When you have the strength of hundreds of people, you need to eat a lot.

"So, what it's like on your planet?" I asked.

He drank a glass of milk. "More please!" he said, showing me the glass.

I super sped to the fridge, grabbed the bottle of milk and put it on the table.

"My planet is very sterile and cold. All the plants and trees we have are planned. We have no wild growth left. It's a very efficient planet. Our food source is protein mush or bars, and also multi-plant."

"What's that?"

"Multi-plant is an edible plant that has the benefits of what you would call fruits, vegetables, and grains. It is quite amazing."

"Is it tasty?" I asked him.

"Well, not nearly as tasty as bacon!" he grinned.

Before we could get much deeper into the conversation, we heard the front door open.

"Hello?" Mom called as she entered the house. "Okay, Lia! Why'd you knock out the dog AGAIN?"

She walked into the kitchen. An eyebrow popped up. "So, who do we have here?"

Zeekee jumped up on the table and put his hand to his chest. "Greetings, mother of Lia Strong!" he pounded his chest three times. "It is an honor to meet you." He bowed. He dropped back down to his chair. He lowered his gaze, "I am Zeekee Zaxxx!"

"Let me guess. You aren't from around here," Mom laughed.

I could see that she found my new friend very amusing.

"I am from the same galaxy!" he beamed.

"Oh good," Mom said. "I was afraid this might be a little weird."

I gave her a grin. "You know me, Mom, these days, the new normal is…anything goes."

Mom sat down at the table next to me and across from Zeekee. She looked right into his big green eyes. "So Zeekee Zaxxx, what brings you to Earth?"

"I have a cloaked space shuttle in orbit."

Mom smiled.

"He's a bit literal. Earth languages are different for him," I said.

"So, why did you come here?"

"I wanted to see new planets and interact with special people like Lia," Zeekee said slowly like he had to think before each word.

"Okay, do your parents know you are here?" Mom asked.

Zeekee nodded. "Yes, yes they do."

Mom looked at Zeekee. She looked back at me. I could tell she fought back a sigh. She knew she wasn't getting the entire story, but decided to let it go for now. She looked at Zeekee again, then glanced at me. "Well, I trust my daughter. She is a great person, so I'm sure she will do the right thing."

"I think so too!" Zeekee said.

Mom looked at her watch. "I have a date tonight, but I can cancel it if you kids want, and I'll show you around. Or, you can come out with Oscar and me."

I answered before Zeekee. "That's fine Mom. I want to take Zeekee to Mr. T's to meet the gang and all."

Mom stood up. "Okay, I'd better go get ready. You two have fun. And Zeekee, welcome to Earth."

"Zow! Your mom is so zoopoo!" Zeekee said as Mom walked out of the room.

"I assume that's good," I said.

Zeekee grinned. "Oh, it's the best!"

Dear Diary: Okay, this Zeekee is the most unique and interesting guy I've ever met. I guess I shouldn't be surprised since he is from another world and all. I find him pretty cool. I certainly want to get to know him better. Should I be worried that he didn't tell my mom the entire truth?????

NAH! I'm sure he was just being considerate and didn't want to worry her. He knows I'm Super Teen and can handle pretty much whatever the universe throws at me. So why bother Mom with silly little details like...an alien army might be coming after him?

Pizza Hangout

I took out my phone and texted Jason.

LIA> Pizza at Mr. T's with the gang?
JASON>Is the alien dude still here?
LIA>Yes, of course.
There was a pause.
JASON>Sure.....
LIA>Good! I want him 2 meet the gang.
JASON>Probably a smart idea...if there are aliens after him it will be good to have backup.
LIA> I can handle myself.
JASON>Agreed, but it's nice to have powerful friends 2.
Now I paused.
LIA>Ur right. ☺
JASON>Meet u outside in 5.

Before I knew it, Jason, Zeekee and I were walking to Mr. Ts. I was glad that Jason had agreed to come. I wanted him to like Zeekee.

"You'll love the pizza, wings, and milkshakes at Mr. Ts," I told my alien friend.

"Yeah, they're the best," Jason agreed.

"So you humans eat wings? How do the birds fly without them? Don't you get feathers in your mouth?" Zeekee asked.

"Okay, first of all, you have to stop referring to us as...you humans," Jason said. "And the wings have had the feathers removed."

"Watching milk shake will be fun!" Zeekee said.

Jason looked at me. "How are you going to explain Zeekee to regular people?"

"Regular people?" Zeekee asked.

"People who aren't super and don't know I am Super Teen," I said to Zeekee.

I turned to Jason. "I'm going to say he's my cousin, visiting from another country. I figure I'll say Ireland. I don't think many people here in Starlight City know much about Ireland."

"Sounds like a plan," Jason nodded.

"So, there are other super people, besides you and those three that helped us earlier?" Zeekee asked. "I was unaware."

"Remember, that's because I'm the only one who is out in the open," I explained. "Two girls have been given superpowers by having bio-implants. Two others gained powers after a nuclear accident. So they are more behind the scenes."

"Oh, I understand," Zeekee said. "They want to keep their secrets."

"Yes," I said.

"And we really should keep their secrets, too!" Jason lectured, looking at me.

"Just like we have to keep your secret that you are an alien," I told Zeekee.

"Why is that?"

"It's the same reason I wear a disguise when I use my superpowers in public. When people find out you can do special things, some might want you to do favors for them, some might be scared of you, some might want to study you, and some may want to hurt your friends to get to you."

"Zow, I never thought of that," Zeekee said, hand on his chest. "I will keep your secrets from other humans. I promise."

"Thank you, Zeekee," I said, patting him on the shoulder.

We walked into Mr. T's. Zeekee's eyes popped open and so did his mouth. I found it cute. Mr. T's was packed with people. It looked like one of those nights when everybody in town had decided to eat there. The aroma of pizza and fries seemed to dance through the dining room, and music from the jukebox could be heard above all the loud chatter.

We spotted Krista and Tim at a table with three spare seats and headed towards them. Of course, to get there, we had to pass by the cool kids' table where Wendi Long and her side kicks, Patti Queen and Maggie Carr sat. And of course, Wendi's boyfriend, Brandon Gold sat alongside her. Despite being Wendi's boyfriend, Brandon happened to be a decent caring guy. Regardless of that, it definitely helped that he was so good looking and had a smile brighter than the sun.

Wendi stood up and looked at me like she was a queen lording over her servant. "So, Lia, who's your friend?"

Patti and Maggie stood up as well.

"He's my cousin, Zeekee," I said.

Wendi tilted her head back, getting a good view of Zeekee. "You share DNA with HIM? Or is he adopted?"

"Haha!" I said.

Wendi held out her hand to Zeekee. "I'm Wendi, I'm captain of the LAX team that Lia plays on."

"Oh, how nice," Zeekee told her.

Wendi shot me a glance. "Lori and Marie are putting in extra practice tonight. If you were dedicated, you would be too."

I knew Lori and Marie weren't really practicing. They were at my dad's lab, working on their powers. I could tell Wendi was trying to stir me into a fight, as well as making me look bad. But it wasn't going to happen. "Sorry, Wendi, I didn't have time after winning that election and all. I had to really get familiar with all the school laws and regulations. Plus, I wanted to show my cousin around." It felt so good letting Wendi know that I had won the election and beaten her in the process.

"Wait, say what?" Wendi gulped, her mouth dropping open.

"Steve told me. They will announce the winner tomorrow morning. But I won!" I said.

"That's impossible!" Wendi said, aghast.

"You'll see in the morning," I replied, unable to help the smug grin that had appeared on my face.

"I know one thing for sure, your cousin is dreamy," Maggie smiled.

"I assure you, ladies I am wide awake," Zeekee said.

The three girls giggled. I caught Jason and Brandon exchanging glances. They didn't see the humor in Zeekee's words at all.

Patti touched Zeekee gently on the shoulder. "Plus, you have a sense of humor," she told him.

Zeekee puffed out his chest. "Plus, I have a sense of smell, sight, and touch!" he said proudly.

Wendi, Maggie, and Patti giggled even more. "You are so CUTE!" Wendi said.

I ignored her comment and led Zeekee past the table towards my real friends.

Krista's eyes perked up the moment she saw Zeekee. "Who's this new cutie?" she asked, being much more forward than usual.

"He's my cousin, Zeekee," I said.

"Yes, I am her cousin from the land of Ireland," Zeekee said, playing along.

"Let's all just sit," Jason sighed.

Christy smiled. I could tell she was pleased to hear that Zeekee was my cousin, rather than my "friend" and she could not take her eyes from him.

Christy slid over to make room for Zeekee. "So, if you like milkshakes, let me tell you...the milkshakes here are to die for!"

Zeekee turned whiter than usual. "Well, I am interested in seeing milk shake, but I do wish to live." His voice trembled slightly.

Christy laughed. "Oh Zeekee, you have the most wonderful sense of humor."

"To die for, is an expression we use, meaning really, really good," Tim said.

"Oh, I will have one of those then! What else is good?" he asked.

"Dude, you can't go wrong with the hamburger and onion rings," Tim grinned.

"Agreed," Jason said.

Zeekee looked at me.

"These guys know their foods!" I assured him.

I don't need to go into much detail here, let's just say, Zeekee really loved Earth food.

He gobbled it down faster than I'd ever seen anybody eat. His manners were "less than stellar" but somehow he made it work. In fact, the eyes of every girl in the place appeared to be locked on him. After we ate and took in the sights and scents of Mr. T's, I suggested I show Zeekee our lake. Zeekee leaped at the idea.

A bunch of the other girls wanted to come as well, but I actually used my command voice to make them stay. Yeah, I felt kind of bad using my powers like that. But I needed to protect Zeekee's privacy. That's what I told myself, anyway.

I loved walking along Starlight City lake shore. The sparkling blue water and fresh air always seemed to revive my senses. And today, the walk along the lake felt extra special. I was able to show off our amazing lake to my amazing new friend, Zeekee. Jason walked with us too. He was such a good buddy, he always had my back.

As we walked along the pathway by the water's edge, Zeekee's eyes were wide with surprise. "I've never seen such blue water!" he said. "This is such a wonderful place. Why aren't there more people here?"

"Yeah, that's a really good question," Jason replied, looking curiously at me.

I shrugged. "I may be sending out thoughts keeping people away," I admitted. "But my thought control is a very new power, so sometimes it activates without me wanting it to."

"Yeah, well that would explain it...." Jason said.

"I like being alone with you, Lia!" Zeekee beamed.

"Why thank you!" I smiled.

"Ahem, not quite alone, standing right here," Jason said.

Zeekee smiled. He nudged me. "Maybe we should send Jason home?"

I had to confess, I had thought about it. But no, Jason was my closest buddy. And I had only known Zeekee for a few hours. "Nah, let's keep him around."

"Gee thanks," Jason replied.

Suddenly, Jason turned white. He pointed behind us and said, "This doesn't look good..."

Zeekee and I turned to see about a hundred winged monkeys flying over the lake. Each of the monkeys carried a long metal rod.

"OMS, I think my mom sent them," Zeekee said.

"How bad is this?" I asked Zeekee.

The monkey's aimed their rods, blasting us with energy beams. I moved at super speed using my body to shield both Zeekee and Jason. Still, the force of the beams sent Zeekee and Jason flying backward. I held my ground.

"I think that answers your question," Jason called to me from the ground.

"Look, flying monkey things, I'm not going to monkey around with you!" I shouted.

The monkeys opened fire on me again. Hundreds of beams of energy streamed at me. I braced for impact. The beams froze.

"Man, you get yourself into all sorts of trouble," I heard the familiar voice of Tanya from behind me.

"How'd you know I was in trouble?" I asked, now having all the time in the world.

"Jason texted me," she smiled.

"How'd you get here so fast?"

Tanya pointed to the frozen monkeys and frozen beams of energy. "Ah, time control. Remember?"

"Oh right..."

"I hate to do such a big freeze, but this called for it," Tanya said. She pointed to the frozen Zeekee and Jason. "So, what's the story with the red-haired kid?"

"He's Zeekee and he's from another planet, and I find him kind of cute," I said.

Tanya shrugged. "If you say so." Tanya turned her attention back to the frozen monkeys. "Now, what do we do about these rejects from Oz?"

"Not really sure," I said. "I could blast them with heat vision but that seems mean…"

"Mind if I try something?" Tanya asked me.

"No, of course not. What do you have in mind?"

"Well," she smiled. "I just ate garlic pizza with extra garlic."

"You're kidding," I said.

She exhaled lightly on me. I staggered backward. My head spun for a moment. If I wasn't super, I might have been knocked out cold. "Whoa, you're not kidding!"

"Yeah, what can I say…I love garlic! But here's the plan, I breathe out. You use your arms to push the breath at the flying monkeys. I'll keep them frozen but make it like they've been breathing in my garlic breath all day. Kind of like I did to you with my shoe odor that time!"

"You do have a bit of an evil side," I grinned.

She smiled at me then turned towards the monkeys and exhaled. I used my arms to push the garlic breath towards the suspended monkeys. Tanya locked her light blue eyes on the monkeys. She raised her arm. She snapped her fingers. The monkeys started to move. They all grabbed their throats and dropped out of the sky. They hit the water and then disappeared in a sudden burst of electric energy.

"Now that was different," Tanya said.

Jason and Zeekee also unfroze and moved toward us. "Who is this tall Earth girl?" Zeekee asked.

"I'm Tanya," Tanya said, seeming far less impressed than most of the other girls.

"A pleasure to meet you, Miss Tanya," Zeekee said with a bow.

"Sure," Tanya said.

"What happened to all the flying monkeys?" Jason asked.

"We blew them out of the sky and they hit the water and vanished," Tanya replied.

Zeekee nodded. "That's my mother's work. She recalled them after they failed. But she will try again."

"In that case, I suggest we get back home, pronto," I said. "Tanya, you want to come?"

"Nah, I told my mom I'd watch my little sister, Kayla tonight. But if you need me....call. I can be there in under a second."

"So she has powers too?" Zeekee asked as we headed back to my house.

"She does..." I replied.

"Yeah, but Lia's are more well-rounded," Jason said, cutting me off from saying more.

Dear Diary: It's amazing how the other girls react to Zeekee. They all agree with me that he's really cute. Well, all of them except Tanya and Jess. I guess nobody appeals to everybody. I can't help thinking that Jason might be a little jealous. I suppose I should be slightly concerned that Zeekee's mom sent a small army of flying monkeys after us. But I'm not. I can handle whatever she throws at me!

Home Front

We arrived home to be greeted by Mom, Grandma, Dad and Hana, all sitting at the dining room table. I knew this wasn't a simple meet and greet.

"Ah what's going on?" I asked though I didn't really want to know.

Dad stood up. "Is this the alien boy?" he said, pointing to Zeekee.

Zeekee nodded. "Yes sir, I am." He turned to me. "Who are these people?"

"My dad, my grandma, and Hana, my dad's assistant," I said.

"Why are they here?" Zeekee asked.

"Jason told us about the attack at the lake," Dad replied.

"We're concerned...." Mom said.

"We think Zeekee should stay at BMS Labs with us," Hana added, matter of factly.

"Wait, why?" I frowned.

"I feel we can protect him there," Dad said.

I walked to the table. I slammed my hand down smashing the table in half. "I can protect him!"

"Lia, calm down," Mom said.

"Oops, sorry," I said, looking at the cracked oak table. "But I'm a superhero. I can protect him."

"Honey, we're not saying you can't protect him, but he would be safer at your dad's lab, and so would everybody around you. After all, most of your friends are just normal kids. By having Zeekee around, you are putting them in danger," Grandma explained.

I heard Grandma's words. I knew they made sense, yet they still made me angry.

"But…"

"You can still visit with him after school and on weekends," Mom said.

"Lia, it's only logical he stay at a guarded facility where everybody around is a professional," Hana said. "Plus, we have the best defensive system on the planet."

"Honey, I told you a while ago that aliens were coming. We've been preparing for this. Your friend will be treated like a respected guest. I promise!" Dad said.

"What if he doesn't want to go," I glanced at Zeekee, who was standing quietly beside me.

"As an advanced being, I am sure he will see the logic in our thought process," Hana said. "We are better equipped to suit your needs, Zeekee." She stared towards him.

"What does that mean?" I asked.

"For instance, we have a full wardrobe of clothes for him. Can you provide that?"

I took a step back. "I guess not…"

All eyes turned to Zeekee. He lowered his head. "I do not wish to cause Lia Strong any trouble. After all, I consider her very special." He looked up. "I will go with you!"

"Good," Dad said, getting to his feet. "I've ordered a stealth hover vehicle. It will land in the backyard in three minutes."

Zeekee bent over and gave me a hug. "You will visit me?" he asked.

"Every day after school. And I will come on the weekends…I go there for training, anyhow."

Zeekee smiled and my heart fluttered. "Excellent!" he said.

He turned away and headed out the back door with Hana and Dad. I knew this was probably for the best, but that didn't mean I had to be happy about it. Sometimes doing the right thing is the hardest thing.

"Well, it's getting late," Jason said. He had been standing quietly aside, taking in the conversation around him. "I'd better be getting home. Lia, I'll see you tomorrow when we walk to school."

"Actually, Jason," I replied, "I think I'm going to leave early tomorrow. I want to prepare for being class president, and also make sure nothing slows me down during the day. This way I can get to BMS labs to see Zeekee straight after school."

Jason looked at me and paused. A worried expression crossed his face.

"Well, okay, see you in school…" He turned and walked away, his head bent down towards the floor.

Once the front door had closed behind him, Mom turned to me and spoke. "Lia, weren't you a little cold to Jason just then?

"I think I felt the temperature in the room drop," Grandma added.

I didn't answer right away. Finally, I said, "I'm going to my room. It's been a LONG day!"

Dear Diary: I'm so mad at Jason and my dad. First of all, it wasn't Jason's place to tell my family about the attack and warn them about Zeekee. And then Dad decided he should take over. How dare they both assume they know what's best for me. Men! I'm not surprised about my dad, though. That man only seems to come into my life when he needs something from me. But Jason? That was a surprise. He has always had my back. I just can't believe he's so jealous of Zeekee.
Poor innocent Zeekee. ☹

Getting Schooled

I admit, it felt weird walking to school alone. In a way, though it felt kind of peaceful. But the second I got through the door of the main building, Marie and Lori rushed at me. They each patted me on the back. "You won!" Lori exclaimed with a hint of surprise in her voice.

"I never doubted you," Marie said, smiling.

"Oh, I had plenty of doubts," Lori said.

I nodded. "Me too, actually."

"Hey, where's your faithful sidekick," Lori asked.

"Ah, who?" I asked.

"Jason!" Marie stated the obvious.

"I just needed a little space from him," I replied slowly.

"Is this about that cute guy you were hanging out with at Mr. T's?" Lori asked.

"Maybe," I said.

"That's a yes," Marie nodded. She leaned into me. "We heard he was *really* good-looking!"

"*REALLY* good looking!" Lori added.

"He's an alien," I whispered quietly. "He wanted me to protect him."

"From who?" they both asked at the same time.

"His mom," I whispered back. "Apparently she's leader of his planet, and she didn't like him reaching out to strange new worlds."

"So cool!" Marie sighed.

Lori's eyes popped open, her smile grew. "Ah, so our boy scout, Jason got jealous!"

"No!" I said. My shoulders drooped. "Yes. Maybe. I don't know. He's always been so protective of me."

"He's a good friend," Marie said.

Before I could say anymore about my feelings towards Jason, and his towards me, Wendi, Maggie, and Patti headed towards us. But instead of strutting in their usual confident manner, they seemed to hesitate before approaching us.

"So, you actually won," Wendi conceded, her eyebrows raised as she looked at me. "I guess the little people wanted one of their own. So they got what they deserved. I really don't have time anyhow, with being LAX captain and my busy social life and all…."

"Ah…ok," I said, staring back at her.

They turned and walked away. Leave it to Wendi to make my victory seem like a defeat. Before I had a chance to react, or even breathe for that matter, Steve rushed over.

"I'm so, so happy you won!" he said, taking my hand.

"Ah, thanks," I said, slowly removing my hand from his.

"I've got more great news!"

"Ah, okay…" I said.

"You know that my dad is a very successful plastic surgeon?" Without waiting for me to respond, he rushed on, "Well, he realizes the school needs to celebrate the new school year. So…." He paused for suspense. "He's funding the dance for next week!" Steve was so excited, he was almost leaping out of his skin.

"Oh, that's nice," I replied.

"He's funding all the music and food and decorations! Do you want to go with me?" Steve asked.

I sighed. My sigh actually made Steve stagger back a few steps. Oops!

But I didn't want to go with Steve. Not that he wasn't an okay guy. Right now, I didn't want to go with anybody. So of course I said, "Let me think about it!"

Steve dropped his head. "Yeah, I understand… why would a hot girl like you want to go with a guy like me?" He processed my words a little more. "Wait, you didn't say no…"

"She also didn't say yes," Lori said.

"Still, I'll take it!" He turned and ran back to his gang, which consisted of Henry Singer and Gary Nestor. Jumping with excitement, he exclaimed, "She didn't say no!" They all gave him high fives.

Marie leaned into me and whispered. "You don't really want to go with STEVE, do you? I mean, he's nice enough, but he's well…."

"Way blah," Lori said.

"I wasn't going to use those words," Marie said.

"Blander than broth," Lori said.

"Worse," Marie smiled.

"About as exciting as watching white paint dry?" Lori said.

Marie giggled.

"Look you two! One more word and I'll deactivate my super deodorant and drop you both!" I gave them a little grin so they knew I was mostly kidding.

They pretended to zip their mouths shut. The bell rang. We headed to class.

I walked into Mr. Bell's class to see Jason sitting in his customary seat, next to where I normally sat. For a moment I considered going to another seat. But I walked over to him and sat down.

"Hey," Jason said.

"Hey," I answered back.

"Look, I didn't mean to hurt your feelings yesterday," Jason whispered a little too loudly.

Mr. Bell looked at us. The class snickered.

I stood up. Using my command voice, I spoke, "EVERYBODY IN THIS ROOM WHO IS NOT JASON, FREEZE!"

Everybody in the room except for me, Jason and Jason Grant froze in place. Jason Grant looked confused.

I pointed at him and used my command voice once again, "YOU FREEZE TOO, DUDE!"

Jason Grant stopped moving.

"Wow," Jason gasped. "You've been practicing!"

I crossed my arms and glared at him. "Yeah, somehow my command voice works best when I'm angry," I said.

Jason stood up. "Look, Lia, I know you might not want to hear this, but I don't completely trust this alien kid."

"His name is Zeekee," I said. "And why don't you trust him?"

Jason shrugged. "I don't really know. Part of it is my gut feeling. Part of it is that he just seems too suspicious. I'm just trying to protect you."

I pointed to all the frozen people in the room. "I'm pretty good at protecting myself...you know, being a superhero and all. Remember, I'm the one who dropped a herd of charging rhinos with a whiff of my armpit!"

Jason nodded. "Yeah I know, you have awesome power, Lia. But even you can make a mistake, let your guard down. You may be almost invulnerable, but you still have weak spots. I think this alien could be playing on one of those."

"Are you jealous?" I asked.

Jason turned a bit red. "What me? Jealous?" He thought about his words. "Yeah, I guess I am. Maybe" he sighed. "Look, Lia, it's always been you and me. But I get the feeling this guy is trying to come between us." He dropped his head. "I just know I hate you being angry with me. Heck, I can't remember you ever being angry with me before."

I leaned into him. "Well, I am angry with you now!" I said. "I'll most likely get over it. But I need space!"

"Got it," Jason said. He pointed to the frozen class. "Now you'd better let them all move again before somebody sees this."

I sat down in my chair. I unfroze the class. The rest of the school day dragged by, but luckily it went by uneventfully.

Dear Diary: I actually hate being mad at Jason. The two constants in my life have been Mom and Jason. And right now, Mom has her dating thing going on with Oscar Oranga (Yuck). So I haven't been seeing as much of her. I can't blame her. Mom may be super like me, but she's also human and needs companionship. Dad certainly was not the best companion. I want my mom to find happiness, even if it is with the reporter who's trying to uncover my secret identity. Plus, on some level, I know Jason really mostly has my interests at heart. He has always been there for me. It's always been me and him. I guess I can't blame him for being jealous. I'm sure he'll eventually get over it. He'll realize Zeekee is just a kid from another world who needs help.

Mom's Date

That night, Mom invited Oscar over for dinner. This would be the first time Mom cooked for him, and the first time I would actually get to sit down and talk with Oscar. As much as I wanted to see Zeekee, I knew Mom needed me at home. I also knew I could spend the weekend at BM Science, training with Zeekee. And besides, MAC, Hana and Dad had all sent messages telling me that Zeekee was sleeping, and it was necessary for him to get some rest. I guess traveling from another world can be quite draining.

Mom actually took the afternoon off, which I had never seen her do before. But she really wanted to cook for Oscar, and she wanted it to be extra special. If Mom truly wanted it to be extra tasty, she would have ordered out. I love my mom, but she's not a great cook. Still, I understood she needed to make something special for Oscar Oranga. I helped her in the kitchen as best I could. By helping, I mean I gave her verbal support by saying things like...

"Pasta works. You make great pasta, Mom"...while thinking, all you have to do is boil water and drop the pasta in the pot.

"Yes, Mom, that tastes fantastic!"...while thinking, it could use less salt.

"Go easy on the amount of garlic you put on the bread, you don't want him to pass out if you kiss him." Saying stuff like that was where I lent a hand. Although, I did set the table and make the ice cubes. Yeah, not really a great help, but I made the ice cubes in under a second by using my frost breath on them. I also lit the candles on the table with my heat vision. So that was fun.

But Mom wanted me to get the use of my powers out of the way before Oscar showed up.

Once the food was prepared, I did the most important job of all. I sniffed Mom to make sure her deodorant still held. And it did. I also picked out her outfit. I decided on her short red dress. I figured Mom's food might only be average, but if she looked stunning enough, no way Oscar would care.

As Mom finished getting ready upstairs, I heard the doorbell ring. I took a deep breath. I walked to the door. I opened the door.

BAM!

A concussion blast knocked me across the house and into the rear wall. I shot to my feet. There, standing in the doorway, stood a tall girl with long black hair. She was dressed all in black, including her mask.

"Glare girl! What are you doing here?" I yelled.

Glare girl gulped. She pointed at me. "Wait, I thought Oscar Oranga was going to be here?"

"I guess he's running late. I repeat though, why are you here?"

Glare Girl shrugged. "I wanted to scare him a bit, get on the news. You know how I like my fame. Hey, how did you take that blast? That should have put you to sleep for a week!" I saw her eyes light up from behind her mask. "OMG, you have to be Super Teen, and that means Oscar Oranga is dating Super Teen's mom!" She doubled over with laughter and then looked up at me. "Does he know?"

I walked towards her slowly. "No, of course, he doesn't know." I looked at the dent in the wall from Glare Girl blasting me. "Of course, that will be hard to explain, but I'll figure something out." I glanced around. It occurred to me that my faithful dog, Shep hadn't come to my rescue. I stormed towards Glare Girl and lifted her up with my little finger. "What did you do to my dog?"

Glare Girl held up her arms. "Look I didn't do anything to your dog. I love dogs and cats! They sense my power, so they run away from me!"

I nodded. "Yeah, been there done that."

Glare Girl looked down at me. "You know, I like to think of you as a rival, but this isn't what I had in mind for today at all. I'd much prefer to taunt you out in public when you're in costume as well. I think it's better for our reputations."

I rolled my eyes. I knew Glare Girl was big on reputation, and getting famous and noticed. Whereas, I just wanted to help people. Well, mostly. I sighed. "So, if I put you down, you will go quietly?"

She held up her arms. "Yes. "

Mom glided down the stairs. "Is that Os-" she sang.

Her words stopped in mid-sentence, and then her tone changed completely when she saw Glare Girl. Mom's hands curled into fists. "What is SHE doing here?"

I dropped Glare Girl to the ground. I snickered and told her, "Man, am I glad I'm not you right now!"

Mom shook the house as she stomped towards Glare Girl. "Why are you in my house?"

"OMG! Your mother's a super too!" Glare Girl gasped.

"Yep," I told her. "She sure is!"

Mom lifted Glare Girl off the ground with her pinky. "Are you here to fight my daughter?"

"Actually, Ma'am, I just want to scare your boyfriend...." Glare Girl admitted.

'That's not much better," Mom told her.

Glare Girl held open her arms. "Look, I wasn't planning on hurting him or anything, just putting a little fright into him so I get mentioned on the news." She grinned. "It will make your girl look better...with her always using her powers for good and all."

"Look," Mom told her. "You're very lucky because I'm in a really good mood right now. Plus, I really don't want to sweat in my dress."

"You do look, lovely Ma'am," Glare Girl told her.

Mom dropped Glare Girl to the floor. She pointed to the door. "Go! Run! If I see you in my house again, I won't be so kind!"

Glare Girl gave Mom a salute. She turned and ran out of the house calling, "Bye, Super Teen!"

Mom turned and examined the wall that had a 'me' sized dent in it. "Now this might pose a problem." She thought for a moment. "I guess we could cover it?"

"Or just use command voice on Oscar so he doesn't notice it," I suggested.

"Honey, I'm not using command voice on my man friend. At least, not this early in our relationship," Mom said.

"I have an idea!" I shot out of the room at super speed. I raced up to the attic and grabbed an old rainbow tapestry that Mom and I had stored up there for a special occasion. I sped into the garage and grabbed a few nails. I sped back inside the house. I held the tapestry over the crack in the wall. I smiled at Mom. "This will work."

Mom nodded and grinned. "Yep, you're a genius!"

I floated upwards and pounded two nails into each of the top corners of the tapestry. I dropped to the ground and pounded a couple of nails into the bottom of the tapestry. I stood back with Mom. We smiled at each other.

Mom put her arm around me. "You are one smart girl!"

"I learned from the best," I replied, getting a whiff of Mom's underarm. I coughed.

"Uh oh..." Mom groaned. "Did my anger burn through my deodorant?"

"Is the room spinning?" I asked.

"I'll take that as a yes," Mom said. Now it was her turn to speed upstairs.

I heard a knock on the door. I concentrated on the door and tried to look through it. Sure enough, I saw Oscar nervously fidgeting on the other side. He had a dozen roses in his hand. Wow, I had a new superpower: x-ray vision! I kept looking. I saw Oscar's bones through his body. I shook my head. All I could see was a skeleton.

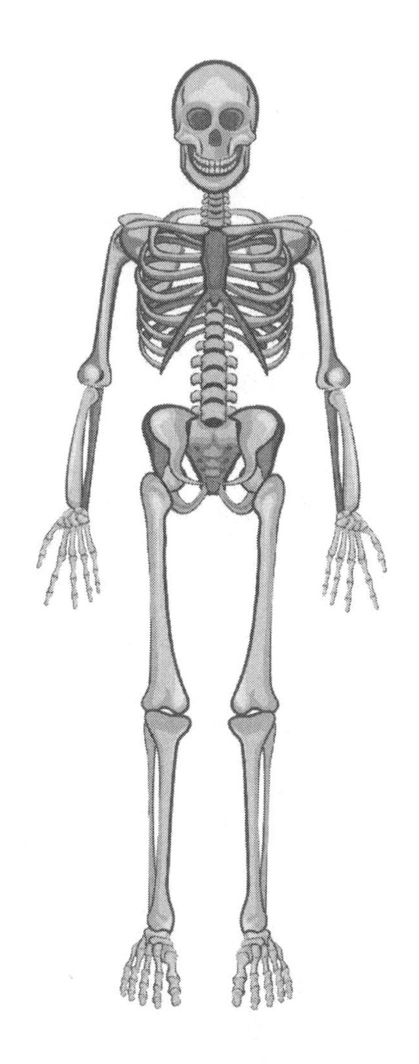

Okay, that power will need work. I walked over and opened the door.

"You must be Lia," Oscar said.

"Ah, yes," I said, opening the door wide. "Come in. My mom should be down in a second or two."

Oscar handed me the roses. "Do you have a vase for these?"

I took them from him. "Yes, I think I can find one!"

"They are for your mom," Oscar said, walking into the living room.

I headed to the kitchen to get a vase. I called over my shoulder. "Yep, I kind of figured that!"

I put the flowers in a vase and filled it water. I joined Oscar in the living room. He sat on the couch, so I sat across from him on a recliner. After a minute or two of awkward silence, Oscar sniffed the air. "Smells good!"

I gave him a polite smile. "Mom likes to cook," I said.

"So your mom tells me you are in middle school," Oscar commented.

"Yep."

"Do you like it?"

I shrugged. "I like the kids. I like some of the classes. It's okay." I paused for a second. I figured I'd give him an easy question. "Do you like being on TV?"

Oscar sat up straight. A grin expanded across his face. "I love it! I get to entertain the people as well as inform them!"

I bit my tongue. My initial thoughts were...*What a huge ego! Seriously, it's only the local news*! But I didn't say that. Instead, I asked, "Why are you so concerned with Super Teen?"

"I think she's super interesting," Oscar responded. "I mean, come on, we here in Starlight City have what might possibly be the most powerful person in the history of history."

I took a deep breath to prevent myself from blushing. "There are other powerful people popping up!" I said. "What about that Glare Girl?"

Oscar nodded. "Sure, there are some, but none seem to have the raw power that Super Teen has! I mean, she can pop off her shoe and knockout a mall filled with people."

I smiled. "Yeah, that is a pretty awesome power..." I hesitated then added, "In other words, you think Super Teen is a good story?"

Oscar nodded. "Yes, Super Teen makes an excellent story."

I leaned towards him. "Then why are you so interested in uncovering her identity."

"It's news," he said, almost without thinking.

"Her saving people is news?" I countered.

"Yes," Oscar agreed.

"Then why is her identity news?" I asked.

"People want to know!" Oscar insisted.

"Maybe. But I'm sure people also want to know your ATM password and your computer passwords. Do you tell them those things?"

Oscar grinned and shook his head. "No, of course not. Those are private."

"But you don't think a super hero's identity is private?"

He sat there in silence.

"You don't think you endanger her privacy, and maybe even her safety and the safety of her friends if you tell the world who she is?"

Oscar sat back on the couch. "I guess I didn't think that through…"

"I know you didn't," I said. "At least, I hope you didn't think it through. After all, I would hate to think you're putting a heroic young girl in danger just for your own fame."

Oscar lowered his head and shook it. "You know young lady, you're a lot like your mom. You're smart and you have spirit."

"Thanks," I said.

He gave me a crooked smile. "I guess I should give Super Teen her privacy. I should report the news and not try to make news myself."

Now I smiled. I couldn't be sure if Oscar meant this, or was just telling me what I wanted to hear. Actually, I could have used my command voice on him. But that would be unfair. I chose to believe my gut that he was telling the truth. "Well Oscar, now I see what my mom sees in you."

Oscar's eyes twinkled. "She is a wonderful lady. Sometimes I think she's a superhero!"

I laughed a bit nervously.

Mom came down the stairs. She was now wearing a pretty yellow sundress. I approved. "Are you two talking about me?" Mom asked.

"Only good things," I said.

"Isabelle, your daughter is almost as amazing and straightforward as you are!" Oscar said, standing to greet my mom.

Mom nodded. "Oh I am aware." She pointed to the dining room table. "Come, let's sit down and start dinner! All this cooking has made me hungry!"

The rest of the evening passed without a hitch. I had a surprisingly pleasant time.

Dear Diary: It's NOW official. My mom has a better love life than I do. Well, I guess any love life would be better than mine. But then again, Zeekee and I do seem to get along quite nicely.☺ Still too early to tell if anything will happen there, though. Plus, he is from another planet. Plus, his mom may be a terror. Okay, certainly not the perfect building blocks for a relationship. But hey, you never know! This could be very romantic.

I'm looking forward to seeing him this weekend. It will be a good chance for us to get to know each other. Hey, maybe my love life will become almost as good as my mom's!

Spaced Out...

I got up early the next day, anxious to get to BMS labs. My phone beeped with a text.

JASON>Hey!

LIA>Hey

JASON>U going 2 the lab right?

LIA>Yep

JASON>Want to bike there together? I'm so excited. Hana says she has something 4 me.

LIA>Nah I'm just going 2 jump there.

JASON>K

LIA>I wanna c if I can do it w 1 leap.

JASON>I know you can! ☺

JASON>C U there.

LIA>K

I knew I could have been friendlier to Jason in my texts. But I couldn't help think he was butting in where he didn't need to. Yeah, I understood he thought he was helping; doing this for my own good. But come on! I'm Super Teen. If I wanted to, I could turn a forest into a desert by just farting. (Not that I would want to do that. That is pretty disgusting. But it's cool knowing I have that kind of power.) I just didn't need Jason protecting me.

Since Mom had an early shift at the hospital, I ate a quick breakfast then took a nice shower before leaping to BMS labs. I did it in one jump, landing right in the middle of the quad area. Man...that felt good! The second I landed, Hana strolled over to me.

"Nice leap," she said.

"How did you know I was coming?" I asked.

Hana pointed to MAC on my wrist. "Remember, he has a GPS built-in. We tracked your course."

"Ah, that's right," I said. "How's Zeekee?" I asked.

Hana put a hand on my shoulder. "He is fine."

"Can I see him now?"

Hana smiled. "He's with our medical staff right now. They are making sure he is safe to be around."

"Of course he's safe to be around!" I said, stomping my foot on the ground. The ground shook. A couple of nearby workers stopped. They turned toward me.

"Sorry," I said.

Hana held her ground. "You base your…'of course' on what data?"

"My senses!" I said, sharply. "Remember, I have super smelling, hearing and other cool senses. I can tell if something is off."

Hana bobbed her head slowly. "Yes, under most circumstances you can. But this boy is an alien being. This is our first contact with an alien race. There may be factors in play that you don't know about." She put her hand on my shoulder. "Lia, you may be super, but you are still a teen."

"Hence the name, Super Teen!" I told her.

"Yes, true. But as a teen and a non-scientist, you lead with your heart instead of your head. Often that is a good thing. But in this case, a little extra caution is in order. This is a first contact. It makes sense that an alien race would want to contact you since you are so different to most humans. But we want to make sure Zeekee is safe for you and for others."

"So when I can see him?" I asked.

Hana shrugged. "In time."

I grabbed Hana and lifted her off the ground. "Can you be more specific?"

Hana didn't blink. "Of course I can, I am a machine. I am specific when called for. But I am sorry, Lia, I do not feel the need to be specific with you right now."

I curled my hand into a fist.

Hana sighed. "Resorting to violence will not help your cause. I have informed your father that you are acting a bit immature here. Punching me will only help to prove my point."

"She is right," MAC told me.

"Of course you'd side with her. Machines always stick together!" I said.

"Only when they are right," I heard my father say.

I looked over my shoulder to see Dad standing behind me, arms crossed, leg tapping away. "Young lady, please put Hana down. She is only doing what's best for all."

I sighed. Man, I didn't like my dad scolding me. I mean, come on! He's out of my life for over a decade, then he pops up again when my powers appear. And it turns out he runs this super high tech company. Now, not only is he way interested in me, he wants to be my dad again. Who does he think he is, giving me orders? I sighed. He's my dad. My flesh and blood. Sure, he went missing for most of my life, but he is here now. He is trying. Kind of. I released Hana, letting her drop to the ground.

"I'm glad you finally saw the logic," Hana said.

"Yeah, you are my dad's girlfriend, so I'd hate to break you," I told her.

Hana smirked. "Thank you."

"I'll take over from here, Hana," Dad said.

Hana turned and walked away. I swear my super hearing heard the words, "But I don't break all that easily."

Dad put his arm around me. "Honey, I know you want to see Zeekee. He should be available in an hour or so."

We started walking towards the workout and testing building.

"Why couldn't Hana have just told me that? She meets me here just to tell me nothing!" I said.

Dad grinned. "I think she wanted to test your reaction. You almost failed, by the way."

I gave him a weak grin. "Yeah, sorry about that. I know Hana is your girlfriend now, but she gets under my skin." (Plus, I also couldn't help being freaked out that my dad had made his own super powered girlfriend. But that was another issue.)

"Yeah, my Hana, she is something special, but she also takes some getting used to. I thought you two had bonded on our trip to Africa?"

"I learned to accept her a little more," I said. "But she's not quite human. The fact that she has no scent still bugs me."

Dad laughed. "That's only because you have a super sense of smell. Most normal humans don't even notice her lack of scent."

"Are the rest of the team here?" I asked, changing the subject.

"Yes!" Dad said enthusiastically. "Jess is in a meditation room, learning to control her temper. Marie is also in a meditation room, learning to control her power. Tanya is doing self-defense work with a couple of trainers. She wants to be able to protect herself without using her time powers. They are awesome but they scare her, and rightly so."

"Heck, she can knock most people out with a whiff of her shoes!" I said.

Dad laughed. "Looks who's talking."

We walked into the training building. I loved the dome shape. It made the place feel like it went on forever. "Where's Lori?" I asked.

"She's in the sparring area with Jason."

"Say what? Jason? With her enhanced legs and arms, she'll kill him if she's not careful."

"We will see," Dad grinned.

We walked through a few brightly lit corridors until we came to a large open room with a padded floor and walls; a room built to handle super collisions.

Lori stood on one side of the room in a ready stance. Jason stood on the opposite side. A robotic instructor that looked like a crash-test dummy stood between them.

I saw Hana sitting in the observing area above the room.

"Begin!" the robot said.

My mouth popped open as Jason leaped across the entire room and landed right in front of Lori.

"Holy Cow!" I said. "What the heck did you do to Jason, Dad?"

"Nothing. He is wearing our new bionic under-armor. It's an exoskeleton that communicates with his brain."

"This will be so fun!" Lori said.

She flicked a lightning-fast jab at Jason. Jason stepped to the side, letting the jab pass by him harmlessly. Jason took Lori's arms and flipped her over his shoulder to the floor. Lori kicked up back to her feet. She took another fighting pose.

"Let's see what you've got, Jason!"

"Gladly!" Jason said. He fired off seven snap kicks almost too fast for the human eye to see. Lori blocked each one, but just barely. "This is GREAT!" Jason shouted. He threw a powerful punch at Lori. Lori saw it coming and ducked under it. She sprang up and hit Jason with an uppercut to the jaw. Jason's head rocked back. Jason staggered back a step or two. He smiled.

"How did Jason stay standing?" I asked Dad.

"The suit has a magnetic current that can be used to block or soften blows. And since it's connected to his brain, it can reduce pain."

Okay, I had to admit this suit was impressive. I also had to admit it was a little scary. If a suit like this got into the wrong hands, it could do a lot of damage. This suit could make anybody super, at least while they had the suit on.

"Dad, how many of these suits do you have?" I asked.

"Just one for now. They are incredibly expensive and they have to be collaborated for each person."

"How are they powered?"

"They have solar cells. They can go at full strength for about an hour then they need to recharge. We're working on that."

I almost said, don't work too hard on that, but I stopped myself.

Jason and Lori exchanged a couple of jabs. While the body under- armor did make Jason stronger, he still didn't quite have Lori's fighting spirit. After all, Jason has never been a fighter, even in LAX. Lori, on the other hand, led our team in penalties.

Lori leaped over Jason, landing behind him. Jason turned to face her. Lori kicked him right in the gut. Jason went flying across the room. He hit the floor with a thud. Lori leaped after him, landing right next to him.

Jason held up a hand. "You got me. You win!"

Lori grabbed his hand and helped him up. She patted him on the back. "Not bad for your first time, J-man!"

I watched Lori and Jason congratulating each other. They seemed to be getting along so well. I caught Dad staring at me. "What are you looking at?" I asked.

"Nothing," Dad said. He touched his earpiece. "Zeekee is out of medical. He has been cleared to see you. If you'd like to see him now, you can."

I looked at Lori and Jason standing there laughing and talking. "Yep, I'm so ready."

Dad led me to Zeekee's quarters. The room had a bed, a desk, and a computer, but no windows. "Dad, is the best you can do?" I asked.

Dad grinned. "For now, yes. Once Zeekee is totally cleared, we will move him to nicer quarters. But I assure you, this room is very comfy."

Zeekee saw me and jumped up from the bed. "Lia, you are here!"

I loved the way he said my name. It sounded like music to my brain. He took my hand. "Have you come to take me away?"

I glanced at Dad, he shook his head. "Not yet," Dad said. "We still have to run a few tests."

Zeekee looked me in the eyes. "I had been hoping for a friendlier reception."

Dad went into full scientist mode. "Zeekee, you must understand that it is critical for us to be careful with you. We want to make sure you are both physically and mentally ready for Earth's people and culture. It is best for all if you do not stand out."

"I thought humans loved individualists who do their own thing?" Zeekee countered.

"True," Dad said. "But, we don't want you standing out too much. It could attract attention you don't want or need. I'll leave you kids alone now." He turned and walked out.

Zeekee looked at me, trying to read my reaction.

"You have to trust my dad," I said.

"Do you trust your dad?" Zeekee asked.

I thought for a moment or two. Of course, I did. After all, this was my dad we were talking about. Sure, he wasn't the greatest dad during the first dozen years of my life. Sure, he had left me and Mom alone. But he knew Mom was a strong powerful woman who could handle anything she was faced with. But he was back in my life now, helping both Mom and me when we really needed it. He and his team were aiding me in developing my powers. Plus, he had even helped Jason by letting him trial that super cool, body under-armor. Sure, Dad and his company also benefited from all of this. But that still didn't mean that I couldn't trust him. Right? I mean, he was my dad first, scientist second. He had my back, sometimes when I didn't even want him to. Right? I mean, come on!

"How well do you know your dad?" Zeekee asked.

"He's my dad!" I said.

"Well, my mom is trying to hunt me down because she doesn't like the idea that I want to communicate with other planets!" Zeekee said.

I shook my head. "My dad's not like that. He's a man of science. He loves exploring and helping people. It's what he does."

Zeekee looked down at his feet. "If, you say so…"

"Of course I say so!" I told him. "He's my DAD!"

"Your words say one thing, but your feelings say something else," Zeekee said.

Yeah, Zeekee read me well. He sensed I still didn't totally, 100 percent, trust my dad. He hadn't been there for my first lost tooth, my first skinned knee, or for that matter, even my first steps. He had also let Mom down. She'd had to carry a pretty heavy load, acting as both my mom and dad. That's tough, even for a super mom.

Zeekee took my hand. "See, you have doubts!"

"A few really small ones," I admitted.

"You see, I will be safer with you!" Zeekee insisted.

I liked the sound of those words. After all, I did protect people. That's part of what a superhero does.

I noticed a round sparkling ball of energy in the corner of the room. It started crackling. It split into many other sparkling, crackling balls of energy. Each of the balls moved like they were alive.

"What the…" I said, mouth open.

Zeekee turned to the ball of energy. "Energy Wisps!" he gasped.

Before I had a chance to even say, "What the heck are those?" the wisps sent bolts of electricity into Zeekee. Zeekee fell to the ground, sizzling and convulsing. The wisps kept shocking him. I jumped in front of the bolts. I felt the energy rip through my body. It kind of tickled but not in a good way.

"I've called for medical team and security," MAC told me.

"Good," I said, energy still pulsating through my body, "but security won't be needed!" I focused my eyes on the glowing wisps. They danced and darted back and forth. I blasted them with a wide beam of heat vision. The wisps sizzled out and turned to dust.

I faced Zeekee still shaking on the ground.

A couple of wide-eyed emergency medical people arrived in the room. "Don't touch him!" they ordered. "We will look after him," they tried to reassure me.

I ignored them. I had taken on the full power of the wisps. There was no way that touching Zeekee would hurt me. I felt his pulse beating. I breathed a sigh of relief.

Dad, Hana, Tanya and a group of heavily armed men and women came into the room. Dad rushed up to me. "Honey, are you okay?"

I looked up at him. "Yes, it takes more than a couple of energy wisps from space to hurt me."

Dad glared at Hana, "How did those things get in here? Aren't we scanning and shielding the building?"

Hana nodded. "We are. And we're now recording the energy readings from these things so we can adapt our defenses."

Tanya put her arm around me. We watched the medical people work on Zeekee.

"His vitals are good. I think once he becomes conscious again, he will be fine in a day or two," the person said.

I nodded with relief.

Jason and Lori arrived on the scene. Jason ran up to me just as the medics started to carry Zeekee away. "Are you okay?"

"I'm fine," I said.

"From what I hear, Zeekee will be fine too," Jason said.

I shook my head. "No thanks to you!"

Jason took a step back. Tanya put her hand on my shoulder. Everything around me froze into place. Tanya stepped in front of me. "Be careful with your words here, Lia!"

"If Jason hadn't reported Zeekee to Dad in the first place, none of this would have happened!" I insisted.

Tanya waved a finger in my face. I figured she was probably the only person in the world besides Mom or Grandma, who could get away with that. "Lia, those electric thingies would have found Zeekee if he was at your house. But you wouldn't have had an entire staff of medical and security personnel to deal with them. By telling your dad about Zeekee, Jason may very well have saved Zeekee's life. Now, I'm going to start time again. I want you to think about your words." She grinned, "Don't make me revert you into a baby!"

I felt pretty confident I could stop Tanya before she actually turned me into a baby, but her words still made sense. Maybe I had been a bit, just a bit hard on Jason. "Can you turn time back a little so I didn't say what I said to Jason?" I asked.

"I could, but I'm not going to," Tanya said. She walked behind me and time started up again.

Before Jason could respond I said, "Jason, I'm sorry. I should never have said that. I know you were only doing what you thought was best for me and Zeekee."

"Mostly for you," Jason replied.

I gave him a little grin. "I appreciate it." I started walking out of the room to check on Zeekee. "I'll talk to you later, Jason."

"Later," Jason said.

Dear Diary: Man, I was scared those things might have really hurt Zeekee. I don't think I've ever been so worried in my life! Not sure what that means. But Zeekee gets me. At least I think he does. I hope his does. Funny how he knew I still don't 100% trust my dad. Yeah, he's my dad but he still left both Mom and I. I like to believe he means well, I do…I just hope I'm not being naïve. Being super doesn't make me totally aware of things. Too bad I can't read minds. I guess I could use my command voice to make Dad tell me if I can trust him, but then he might not ever trust **me** *again if I did that. He's my dad, I want to give him the benefit of that and believe that I can trust him.*

As for Jason, I'm still so mad at him. Not because I think he was jealous of Zeekee (which he still might be), but because he didn't trust me to protect Zeekee. Of course, he might have shown good sense there, since Zeekee did get attacked while I was in the room with him. One thing I know is that Jason always means well. Man, I am confused.

Friends

I received a text from Jason early on Monday morning, right before school.

JASON>Hey…

LIA>Hey

JASON>How's Zeekee?

LIA>MAC tells me he's still sleeping but they expect him 2 b fine.

JASON>That's great!

LIA>Yep

JASON>Walk to school together?

LIA>Not today…

JASON>OK C U there.

LIA>Sure

I felt kind of bad giving Jason the cold shoulder again. But I still couldn't shake the feeling that Zeekee would have been fine if he'd stayed at home with me to look after him.

When I got downstairs, I found Mom sitting at the kitchen table. She had made me a plate filled with bacon, eggs, French toast and fresh fruit. Mom knew that being super meant I needed a lot of calories to power me.

"Heard you had a crazy day yesterday," Mom said, sipping on a cup of steaming coffee.

I sat and started gobbling down the bacon. "Yeah, nothing I couldn't handle."

"I hear your alien friend got hurt. Your dad said he took a lot of volts. He was lucky you were there to step in."

"Just being a hero, Mom."

"How are *you* doing?" Mom asked. "MAC sent me a read out from your suit. You took enough of a jolt to stop a school of whales…."

"I'm fine," I told her. "I'm like way strong," I grinned.

"I looked at your friend's medical records, he's going to be fine. Everything seems stable. His alien body just needs time to recover."

I smiled and cut into the French toast. "I can't wait until I can talk to him again."

"So, why are you mad at Jason?" Mom asked.

"I'm not mad," I insisted. "I'm disappointed. He didn't trust me."

Mom reached across the table and grabbed a red juicy raspberry off my plate. "Honey, I don't know a lot of things. But I do know that Jason trusts you."

I ate a couple more raspberries before Mom could nab them from me. I sighed. I knocked Mom off her chair and also blew her plate to the floor.

Shep jumped in on the opportunity to clean the floor for us.

"Sorry!" I said, standing up to help her to her feet. "Sometimes I forget my own strength!"

Mom laughed. "Part of the deal when you are a mom to a superhero. Just glad you had fresh breath. But it's nice to see your power is still growing."

"Plus, Shep, really scored some tasty human food," I added.

"Just glad I was pretty much finished eating," Mom said with a grin. "Do me a favor kiddo, give Jason a break. The boy is your best friend."

I sat down and got back to eating. "I will," I said. "Just not today."

Once again, I headed to school alone. I admit I did kind of miss Jason's company. But I looked at this as a time to think; a time to collect my thoughts about the coming day. After school would be my first student council meeting.

Now that I was class president, I needed to decide what would be the best way to help my class and the school, and maybe even our community. Sometimes older people don't give kids enough credit, I wanted to do something to show them we care about what's going on around us.

We had the dance coming up, thanks to Steve's dad who was sponsoring it. I thought we could maybe suggest that everybody who comes to the dance, donates a dollar or two to the city beautification fund. Yeah, I liked that idea. Maybe I could even get them to donate their time.

I bumped into something. The weird thing was, I couldn't see anything. I reached out to feel for whatever was blocking my path. I felt a jolt of energy pass through my arm. I staggered backward but didn't fall.

"What the heck?"

A voice, neither male nor female said, "Lia of Earth, I am Gaadaa, personal robotic bodyguard of High Leader, Zela. Your people are hiding Zeekee Zaxxx from his mother, our leader. You will surrender him to us, or else!"

"Or else what?" I asked.

"I am so glad you asked!" Gaadaa said.

I heard a high-pitched tone ringing in my ears. I slapped my hands over my ears. The sound still echoed through my body.

"Your primitive efforts to stop me from harming you will not work! This tone has been designed by our best scientific minds specifically to harm you."

I staggered backward. With the sound clanging in my head, seemingly bouncing from ear to ear, I found it hard to stand.

"Hey, Lia, are you okay?" I heard a familiar voice that I couldn't quite recognize. The words seemed to be in the background of my mind. "Lia, what's going on?"

I wanted to answer, but I couldn't. I needed to focus all my attention on just standing.

"Stop!" I shouted.

For a second, the sound stopped bombarding my brain. I leaped forward, swinging wildly.

"You are powerful, indeed," Gaadaa told me. "But even you cannot hit what you cannot see. Wait! What is happening to me?" Gaadaa screamed.

A large square cheese humanoid appeared in front of me.

"What the? I got attacked by a robot made of cheese?"

Marie smiled and popped out from behind the now cheesed Gaadaa. "It wasn't originally made of cheese," Marie told me. "I just thought cheese would be more fitting."

I hit the cheesed robot with heat vision, turning it into a pile of melted cheese for the birds.

Jason came up and put his hand my shoulder. "You okay?"

I nodded. "Yeah, weird experience, but I'm fine."

"I saw you were in trouble and sent out a mass text to the team," Jason said. "Marie was the closest. Good thing her powers were best suited to handle something like this."

Marie grinned. "I'm just glad I only turned that nasty robot to cheese and not everything else around it. The training with your dad's people at the lab has really helped me."

Lori and Jess ran up to us. "Is it over? Did I miss the action?" she asked.

Jess pointed to the pile of cheese. "I'm guessing, yes."

Lori smiled at Marie, "Did you do that?"

"Yes!" she admitted proudly.

Lori held up her hand to give Marie a high five. Marie slapped Lori's hand. Lori turned to cheese.

"Oops," Marie said. "I guess when I get excited, my power still sneaks out!" She took a deep breath. She touched Lori on the shoulder. Lori turned back to the original Lori.

Lori looked at us all looking at her. "What, why are you all staring at me like that?"

"No reason," I said.

"Nothing to see here," Marie smiled.

"Everything is normal," Jess grinned.

"Let's get to school," Jason suggested.

"Did you turn me into cheese again?" Lori asked Marie.

The rest of us just giggled.

"You did! Didn't you?" Lori persisted.

"Not on purpose!" Marie told her.

We laughed and continued on our way to school.

Jason and I walked silently for a few minutes. "It's nice to be walking with you again," Jason told me.

"I have missed you a little," I admitted. "And thanks for the save."

"I do always have your back!" Jason told me. "You know that, right?"

I gave him a nod.

"I need to hear it from you," Jason insisted.

"Yes, I know you have my back. You always have and you always will," I groaned.

Jason smirked. "Now, that wasn't so hard!"

"Why don't you trust Zeekee?" I asked Jason.

Jason looked me in the eyes. "I don't know him well enough yet to trust. He's a guy who literally just fell from the sky. He might be the most trustable guy in the universe. But he hasn't done anything to earn my trust."

"Fair enough," I nodded.

Jason grinned. "But Lia, I do trust you. And if you trust Zeekee, I will trust your trust."

"Thanks, buddy," I said, smiling at Jason for the first time in days.

Jason's grin widened.

"Wow, I needed that," he said. "I really don't like it when you're mad at me. It's an experience I don't think I've ever had and one I don't want to go through ever again."

"Agreed! You definitely want to stay on my good side," I told Jason with a little wink.

"You ready for your first student council meeting?" Jason asked.

I shrugged. "We'll see. Truthfully, I'd rather be fighting robots from outer space."

"Did you really turn me into cheese again?" Lori asked Marie.

We all laughed as we walked into the school.

Dear Diary: I must admit, my world didn't seem quite right when I was mad at Jason. I'm glad we're getting along again. I hate to say this, but Jason MAY have been right. Being at my dad's lab MAY be the safest place for Zeekee. After all, that robot thing had me in trouble. Yeah, I have been in trouble before and always fought my way out of it, but this time it certainly helped that Jason and Marie were there. These aliens sure are alien to me. They seem to know a lot more about me than I do about them. That's not good. When Zeekee wakes up, I'll have to talk to him. I need to be better prepared in the future. I want to keep Zeekee safe of course, but I want to keep my world safe too! It's a good thing I have my team.

School Governing

The school day went by as smoothly as a school day could. Truthfully though, the day actually dragged by a bit as I anxiously awaited my first school council meeting. Of course, I did have this conversation with Steve on my way into lunch…

"Oh hi, Lia. Imagine meeting you here!"

"Yeah, imagine meeting you in the lunch room, the same room as all the other students in the school."

"So Lia, have you thought about the dance?"

"Being the new class president, I have."

"So Lia, what are your thoughts on the dance?

"I'm glad you asked, Steve!"

"You are?" his face started to beam.

"Yes, I think we can use the dance to build a little community awareness. I'm going to have a volunteer table where we'll get kids to donate money or their time to help make Starlight City even nicer."

"Oh," Steve said. He thought about what I had said. "That's actually a good idea."

"Thank you, Steve."

Steve looked down at his shoes. "Have you given any thought about who you might go with to the dance?"

"Yes, yes I have," I said.

Before I could say anything else, Steve's face lit up again. "Oh who? Is it somebody I know?"

I nodded. "Yes, I'm going with some of my teammates. They can help me at the volunteer table."

"Oh," Steve said, seemingly trying to sink into the floor. "Do you think you'll have time to maybe have one dance with me?"

"I'll do my best to fit you in for one dance," I said.

"A slow dance?" Steve asked.

"Let's not push it, Steve!" I pointed to the cafeteria. "Now, if you don't mind, I'd like to eat while I still have time."

"Right, right," Steve said. "See you later at the council meeting. I'm my homeroom rep!"

"That's nice, Steve!" I told him.

While our school did house middle school kids and high school kids in the same building, the two student councils were separate. Therefore, being the oldest grade in the middle school meant that I was not only my class president, I was also the leader of the student council. Which meant (much to my surprise) that not only did I have to come up with ideas for my class, but I also needed to run the meetings and come up with ideas that were good for the entire school. I thought, no problem. If I can fight alien wisps and robots, then I can handle a room filled with middle school student politicians.

I could sense though, that my nano deodorant had to work overtime to keep me fresh smelling. I told myself that it was a great thing my dad was back in my life to help me with cool technology like that.

When I arrived at the classroom that would hold the meeting, I noticed I was the last one there. The student council sat at a big round table in the middle of the room, and there was just one spare seat. I headed towards that seat. Of course, it would be situated between Wendi and Patti.

"Well, look who has decided to turn up, the queen of the student council," Wendi scoffed.

"Do you want us all to bow?" Patti smirked, standing up as if I was royalty.

"Yes, Patti. Bow to me!" I said in my command voice. Yeah, it was a bit petty, but I wasn't in the mood for any mean girl games. Time to show them I meant business.

Patti raised her arms over her head and bowed down on the table. "As you wish!" Patti said.

I sat down next to her. "Rise!" I ordered.

Patti sat up. Wendi shot her a *why the heck did you do that* look. Patti only shrugged. I fought down the urge to smile. Yeah, I know I should have felt bad about using my power like that, but really, Patti had it coming. She's actually lucky I didn't make her cluck like a chicken. In a way, I had restrained myself.

"Okay, we all know each other," I said. "So I don't think there's any need for introductions. Is there?"

I looked around the table. Everybody shook their heads. I got the feeling that most of the kids thought the less they talked, the better. But not Wendi, of course.

"Well, since I have the most experience at student council, I can lead if you wish," Wendi told me.

"That's okay, Wendi. I can handle this."

"But…"

"Wendi, sit there and don't talk unless called on," I said in my command voice.

Wendi sat there and zipped her mouth shut.

I noticed Jason (who was school secretary), giving me a look. I knew I'd get a lecture about this later. But really, by using my powers like this I helped everybody.

"Okay, student council here's what I want to do. We have this dance coming up on Friday. Right?"

All the kids nodded their heads.

"And thanks to Steve's dad's generosity, the dance is free. Correct?"

All the kids nodded their heads again. Steve sat across from me beaming.

"Well, here's what I propose. We have a volunteer table at the dance. The table will have a sign-up sheet and a jar and a box. Kids can either volunteer their time to help beautify the town, or donate money and put it in the jar or donate canned food for the box. What do you think?"

Jason spoke up, "I like the idea."

Steve spoke up, "I love the idea!"

Brandon, who was there as masters of arms (which was pretty much a token position) said, "That's a great idea!"

Krista spoke up. "Sounds good. I'll man the table if you like."

"We'll all take turns," I told her.

"Any objections?" I asked.

A sixth grader named Henry Singer raised his hand.

"Yes, Henry?"

"Can my A cappella group, the Starlight City Sound Machine, sing at the dance?" Henry asked.

"Don't you have a concert for that?"

"Yes," Henry said.

"Then let's wait until the concert," I said.

Jason spoke up. "Lia, I know you're new to all this, but student council is a democracy."

"Jason has a point," Brandon said. "For these types of decisions, we usually take a vote."

I nodded. "Fair enough." I took a deep breath. "Please raise your hands if you think the Starlight City Sound Machine should sing at our dance?"

Interestingly enough, six kids raised their hands. Another six kids didn't raise their hands. "Looks like it's a tie," I said.

"Ah, Madam President, you get to vote too, Henry told me."

I grinned. "Yes, good point" I looked at Henry. "So, how many songs will you guys sing?"

"Just one," Henry said.

"Will you donate time to charity?" I asked.

"We can sing at the senior center." Henri grinned at me hopefully.

I raised my hand. "Okay, you guys have a deal."

Walking home from the meeting, Jason turned to me. "I noticed you used your command voice on Patti and Wendi."

I turned away from him. "Yep."

"I mean, Lia, I can't blame you. It must be so tempting to use those powers. But until this afternoon, you've only used them in an emergency."

"I just wanted the meeting to go smoothly. It was my first one. I wasn't in the mood for any of their mean girl stuff. I let them know who the boss was," I avoided eye contact with Jason as I spoke.

Jason looked at me. He started to open his mouth. He raised a finger. He considered his words. He patted me on the shoulder. "Great job. I think it went well."

"Thanks, Jason."

"It's a great idea about the dance."

"Thanks again, buddy."

"Do you need help at the volunteer table?" he asked.

"Of course," I said.

"Well, I'll gladly work your shift with you."

"Okay," I told him.

"So we're best friends still, right?" he asked.

I stopped walking. "Jason, we've always been best friends and we always will be. No matter what. But that doesn't mean I can't be mad at you from time to time. I'm sure you've been mad at me before."

Jason shook his head. "Never! Lia, you were an amazing person even before you had your powers! I could never be mad at you."

"How about when I use my command voice to make people do what I want?"

"Just a little disappointed, but I can't blame you...."

"How about when I take my shoes off and knockout the mall?"

Jason laughed. "That, I know you can't help. That's just you being you. Besides, it's relaxing."

We both laughed.

Dear Diary: Okay, Zeekee still hasn't woken up. But the docs at BMS Labs assure me he will, which is great. I can't wait to talk to him again. My first student council meeting went well. Sure, I used my powers, but I truly believe I used them for good. After all, nobody wants to hear Wendi and Patti carry on and on and moan and complain. I think even Jason got that. I'm glad Jason and I are talking again. I know he's a little jealous of Zeekee, but really, he doesn't need to be. Jason will always be my BFF. Not sure what Zeekee is yet.

The dance is on Friday. I just hope it will go smoothly. Of course, it will go smoothly! I'll be there to make sure it does.

Dancing Machine

Friday came really quickly. Zeekee still hadn't woken up, but his brain activity and vitals were getting stronger. The docs assured me he would become conscious again anytime now.

I gotta' admit, most of the school seemed excited about the dance. I liked the idea of helping the city, plus getting a chance to listen to music and hangout with my friends and the other kids. The student council members stayed after school and worked on decorating the gym. The theme of the dance was '*Giving*'. A nice theme, but a bit hard to find decorations that would fit. So we went with the standard balloons and streamers and glitter.

Of course, Patti and Wendi had opinions on everything we did. I thought it would be nice to go with bright primary colors like red, blue and yellow. Wendi thought we should go with green and orange because as she put it, they looked better. For a brief moment, I thought about using my command voice on her, but Jason shot me a look. So I decided to ride out the storm.

I hung some streamers, while Wendi and Patti stood next to me, telling me to move this way or that way. I fought back the temptation to deactivate my nano deodorant and drop them both. But I didn't dare. If I hit the room with too much power, the dance would be canceled due to half the student body being knocked out cold.

All and all, it took twice as long as it should have to get the gym ready, but we had it acceptable by five. That gave me time to leap home, hit the showers, grab a bite to each and get ready.

Preparing for the dance, I tossed open my closet door. "Man, I have nothing to wear," I moaned.

"Excuse me, Ms. Lia," MAC said. "But I detect that your closet is filled with clothing. Most of it clean."

"I meant I have nothing special to wear!" I sighed.

"Ah, Ms. Lia, the suit you are wearing is composed of nano-technology that will change to your liking. I call that pretty special. Plus, we can simulate any look. I call that mega special. In addition to that, the nanobots keep you fresh and clean, unless you are under lots of stress. And I call that uber special!" MAC said.

I watched as the outfit I was wearing began changing. My faded jeans and t-shirt transformed into a sparkly sky-blue dress that shimmered and shone as I swished from left to right. My feet had been fitted with a pair of shiny black heels that buckled around the ankle. Although this was my chance to wear heels, something I had never done before, I knew Mom definitely wouldn't approve. As I stared at myself in the full-length mirror, the dress was abruptly replaced with a pair of black skinny jeans that were teamed with a pretty white top, patterned in silver sequins. Threaded around my waist was a studded belt with a cool silver buckle, and on my feet, a pair of black high-top sneakers... "Okay, I get the point, MAC," I said. "Yes, I have options, but I really don't know what I should wear."

I heard a knock on the door.

"Come in, Mom," I said.

My mom and Grandma Betsy entered the room. "We detect a disturbance is the force," Grandma Betsy said.

"Really?" I asked.

They laughed. "No, you're just a 13-year-old girl getting ready for a dance, so we figured you'd be nervous."

I lifted up my arms and sniffed. "You can't smell my fear. Right?"

"Nope," Grandma said, coughing.

Mom put an arm on my shoulder. "Why are you so nervous, honey?"

"Well, this is my first dance as a teen, and as a superhero, and as a student council leader. Plus, I'm a girl…I want to look my best…" I said. "This Steve guy drives me crazy, yet a part of me kind of likes the attention. Plus, I will be sitting at the volunteer table to get kids to volunteer to help the city, so looking my best will help!"

Grandma grinned. "Plus, Jason will be there!"

"Grandma! Jason and I are just friends, buddies, BFFs!"

"But granddaughter…friends often make the best boyfriends! They've seen you at your worst and stayed by your side."

I shook my head. "I do NOT want to go there. NOT now." I couldn't believe my grandmother was talking about boyfriends!

"Let's just help you get ready for tonight." Mom said, cutting Grandma off. "What sort of style are you thinking of?"

"I'm not sure, something pretty, I guess. It is the school dance, after all," I said.

"Well, you have a computer controlled suit that can accommodate any look," Mom noted.

"Yeah, MAC's told me that, and that is cool, but still I'd love to wear something normal too…" I replied.

After about 10 minutes, we settled on a spotted pink dress from my closet and a pair of flat heeled shoes, topped with little bows. I slipped a matching headband onto my head. Finally, I felt satisfied with how I looked.

It was nice to wear my own clothing instead of my nano suit. Yeah, the nano suit was cool, but sometimes you can't beat your own clothes. (Of course, I still carried the nano suit in my bag. And I wore the holo-earing for a fast mask if needed.)

Mom and Oscar were heading out on a dinner date and dropped Jason and me off at the dance on their way.

Mom tried to reassure me, but I told her that really, this dance was no big deal. I was there as a student council member and as a friend. I probably wouldn't even dance. Well, at least I wouldn't do more than one or two dances, and definitely no slow dances. In fact, I felt pretty certain that Vice Principal Macadoo had informed the DJ to play no slow music.

When I entered the gym, my heart jumped a beat. Sure, it was the same old gym I had been in like a billion times, but the loud music and flashing lights made it seem way cooler than I had ever expected. It was still early, but a lot of kids had already arrived.

Janitor Jan walked over to me. At first, I didn't recognize her because she was wearing a really pretty blue dress and had her hair down over her shoulders. "Jan, you look great!" I said.

"Well, I figured if I am going to chaperone this dance, I should look half decent!" she laughed.

"That's great. Glad you could come," I told her.

"I do like to get out!" she said. "Plus, this way, if anybody messes up my gym, I can turn them into a nice clean turnip." She winked at me before turning and gliding into the middle of the dance floor.

"She was kidding. Right?" Jason asked.

"I doubt it," I shook my head. "But wow, good crowd here!"

Jason grinned. "Free food and good music, makes for a fun night." He looked at me. "I see Krista and Marie are manning the volunteer table. Think maybe we could have a dance?" He paused for a moment. "As friends...."

I smiled. "I want to see how the girls are doing with getting people to donate and sign up," I told him.

"After that," Jason said. "As friends," he added again, this time with a smaller smile.

I stopped and turned to him. "Sure, I'll have a dance with you later. As a friend..."

Jason's smile grew. "Awesome." He pointed to the food table. "I think I'll check out the eats. I hear Steve's dad went all out!"

"Go for it!" I said.

As I headed across the dance floor, I caught Wendi staring at me. Of course, she and Brandon were holding hands and dancing slowly, even though the music playing was upbeat. As I passed them I said, "Careful guys. VP Macadoo is watching."

"Jealous?" Wendi smirked.

I actually was a bit. "No," I said. "Just trying to be helpful!"

"Thanks, Lia!" Brandon said. "We appreciate you looking out for us!"

"No, we don't!" Wendi told me. "Now go sit at your table where you belong, while those of us with boyfriends dance."

I wanted to say something back to her. But nothing appropriate came into my head. I also wanted to level Wendi with a fart. But that would have ended the dance for everybody. I took a deep breath and silently walked to the volunteer table.

"So, how's it going?" I asked.

Because this table had been placed alongside the DJ, as well as a massive set of speakers, Marie and Krista couldn't hear me. They held their hands up to their ears.

"SO HOW'S THE VOLUNTEER TABLE GOING?" I shouted, just at the exact moment the music stopped. Half the room began cracking up. Man, the urge to fart grew, but I fought it back. I shot the DJ a look. He shrugged.

I focused my attention on Krista and Marie. "We've had some canned food donated, and two people have signed up to volunteer at the senior home. Plus we've raised $25 dollars."

"Well that's a start," I said.

I turned to the crowd. "Remember people, we're here to have fun and…."

The music blasted loudly once again. Kids started jumping around and dancing. I sighed.

Marie tapped me on the shoulder. "Don't worry, Lia everything will work out fine."

The moment she said those words, I saw Steve strutting across the floor towards me. He seemed to be empowered by the success of the dance his dad had funded. "Hey, Lia!" he said, standing alongside me and grinning widely as he spoke.

"Hey," I replied.

I pointed to the list of volunteers. "I don't see your name yet," I coaxed.

Steve leaned over the table and signed the list. "I love helping! I think I'll do clean up duty in the park, and sign up for visiting the senior home."

"That's nice," I said.

"So, what are you signing up for Lia?" Steve asked.

He had a point. My name was still missing from the list. "I'll sign up for visiting the senior home as well." I picked up the pen and wrote my name under Steve's.

Steve pulled his wallet from his pocket. He dropped a fifty-dollar bill into the money collection. I knew he did it to impress me.

"Nice job!" I said.

Steve leaned closer to me. "Do you want to dance?" he asked.

I was saved from answering Steve, because a few guys from our class, Aaron Ross, Dan Jenson and Mitch Eagle appeared at the table.

"Hi Lia!" they all said at once.

"Ah, hi guys…" I pointed to the table. "So, you guys are here to donate and volunteer. Right?"

The three of them nodded. They took out their wallets and dropped money into the collection box.

"You wanna dance?" the three of them asked in unison.

I sat on the table and crossed my legs. I kind of enjoyed this attention. "Tell you what guys, if we make a thousand dollars tonight for charity I will dance with each of you!"

All three smiled.

"We're onto it!" Aaron said.

The three boys turned and began talking to people in the crowd.

Marie tapped me on the shoulder. "What's going on with you? I mean yeah, you're pretty and all, but it's like you have these guys under your power."

I felt my phone vibrate.

I picked it up. I saw a message from MAC.

MAC: Lia, since you are not wearing your suit, you are sweating more than normal and your scent is attracting the boys.

LIA: Good to know. I'll be careful.

"What's going on?" Marie repeated.

"According to MAC, it's my scent," I explained.

Marie leaned over and sniffed me.

"Careful, on a bad day that will drop you!" I warned.

Marie smiled. "Actually you smell great!" she said.

I forced my arms down to my sides.

"*Lia! Lia! I'm here*!" I heard the words inside my head.

Looking around, I spotted Zeekee strolling in through the entrance. He stood in the doorway and glanced around the gym.

I leaped off the table and rushed through the crowd. I reached Zeekee and threw my arms around him. I hugged him.

"Zeekee! It's so great to see you!" I released him from my grip but kept hold of his hand as I looked into his huge green eyes. "I was so worried about you!"

"I missed you, Lia! But I needed to regain my strength."

He gazed around the room. He shuddered. "I feel all their eyes on me. The females like me but the males do not!"

"They might be a little jealous," I whispered to him.

He whispered back, "Can we please get out of here?"

"Excuse me?" I asked.

"All these humans worry me. I need to get away from them. So many thoughts in my brain. I can hear them all."

"But these are my friends," I said. Then added, "And then there's Patti and Wendi!"

He locked eyes with me. My mind flooded with the thoughts Zeekee was hearing…

"Why is that freak guy here?
"He's so good-looking!"
"I hate the way the girls look at him."
"Wow, he's like a dream."
"I don't like that kid!"
"I so like that kid!"
"These kids better not scuff my floor! Or else!"

Pretty sure that last thought was from Janitor Jan. Outside of that, I understood how Zeekee felt.

I took his hand. "Let's get out here!"

We started running. "I know a place outside the city where we can go! It's where my ship dropped me off!" Zeekee told me.

When we reached the gym doors, I paused. "Wait, I left my bag on the table inside. My special suit is in there!" I said.

Zeekee pulled me forward. "Doesn't matter, you don't need it."

I shrugged and followed. At least I still had my holographic earring so I could have a mask if I really needed it.

Dear Diary: Yes, I left the dance and ran off into the country with an alien boy I barely knew. A small part of my brain (as well as MAC), said this wasn't bright. A much bigger part of me (my heart), said…'go for it girl!'

Spacey

I told Zeekee, "Just give me the general direction you want to go in. I

can leap there!"

"Ah, my ship is exactly 2.8 miles due east of here. Near the big body of water."

"You must mean, Star Pond," I said. Yes, our town is near a lake and a pond. I pointed to my back. "Grab on!"

He took hold of me. He pointed over my right shoulder.

I bent down to leap in the direction he pointed.

We glided through the air.

"This is so sub zero!" Zeekee shouted.

We dropped down right next to the bright blue pond. The setting sun reflected off the water.

I knelt down and ran my hand through the rippling surface. "I've forgotten how pretty it is here!" I said.

Zeekee smiled. "You are prettier than any body of water!"

"Thanks," I said. I felt my cheeks blush. I turned away from him so he couldn't see.

Zeekee took my hand. I let him. "You know Lia, I like you. You are special to me."

I giggled. Yeah, not the most mature response, but this guy was getting to me. I turned to look him in the eyes. "I like you too. But we're just getting to know each other."

"Yes, but I can sense we will have a great relationship," Zeekee said. "Do you feel it too?"

I nodded. "I think so. But it's like I said…we only just met."

Zeekee smiled. "We will have plenty of time to get to know each other."

Okay, a part of my brain started yelling…*Alert, Alert! Something is not right here.* But a bigger, dumber part of my brain said…*Be quiet, this is fun. OMG, a very cute alien boy likes me!*

"So you like it here on Earth?" I asked, my gaze still locked on his.

He shook his head. "Oh no. Not at all."

My body started to tingle. Like each separate cell had come to life and wanted to leap up. My body became engulfed in a blue orb. I felt an even bigger tingle. Everything blurred.

The next thing I knew, I found myself in the middle of a spaceship. I was standing on a round platform and trapped in by bars of yellow energy. I knew I was in space because looking out through the ship's transparent walls, I saw Earth below me.

Oh, this was bad. There were five pale skinned people around me. Four of them were short and stocky bald men wearing green uniforms. They growled at me. The four men stood in front of a tall, commanding woman with bright green hair. She wore an elegant purple dress.

Zeekee ran over to the tall woman. "I have done it, Mother. I have brought you Lia of Earth."

The woman smiled and placed her hand on his shoulder. "Very good, my son!"

"I've learned there are others like her on Earth," Zeekee said. "But she is the most special, their leader."

"Yes, we will start with her." the tall woman stated firmly. "We can always come back for the others, in time. Once we learn what we need to learn."

"Zeekee, how could you do this to me?" I gasped.

Zeekee stared back at me. "Lia, I do like you and I find you interesting. But I love my planet and will do whatever it takes to protect it."

"Huh?" was all I could say.

The tall woman walked past Zeekee and the other men. She stood between us. "I will explain it, son." Looking directly at me, she spoke.

"I am High Leader, Zela." She pointed to the stocky bald guys, "These are my personal guards, Alpha, Beta, Omega, and Harold. You, Lia Strong, have been deemed an enemy of our planet ZZZ-333."

"Ah, lady, I didn't even know about your planet until your son here came to me."

"Ignorance is no excuse!" she shouted. "Your powers threaten us! That is why we had to prepare for you, make you let your defenses down!"

Wow, it had worked! Man, I had let them sucker me in. I still couldn't believe that Zeekee would do this to me.

Zeekee walked up to the enclosed space that had become my prison. "Don't worry, you will like our planet. You will have plenty of time to get to know me and appreciate me."

I curled my hands into a fist. "So, I get no say in this?"

"Of course not," Zela laughed. "You may be super, but your brain is unable to handle such power. That is why we will drain you of your power. At least most of it. Once I have your power in me, if you act civilized, we will return you to your planet."

I pleaded with Zeekee. "Zeekee, how could you take me away from my family and friends?"

He shrugged. "Well, your mom works a lot, she will get used to life without you. Your father left you for many Earth years, I doubt he will miss you much. Your friends, Jason, Lori, Marie, and Steve will miss you a bit, but they will find others to replace the time they spent with you. Human teens leave for college all the time. Think of this as a way to get your education."

Ouch! That stung a bit. Some of it hit home, especially the part about Dad. But I knew they wanted to play mind games with me.

"College is a choice. This is not my choice," I stated slowly.

Zeekee nodded. "I guess, but the stuff you will learn on our planet is far greater than anything you will learn in college. Believe me, you will thank me later."

I thought about what he had said for a second. Could this be a good thing? I'd get to experience something no other person on Earth could. I took a deep breath to clear my head.

Nope, this was not a good thing. Time for me to end this now! I reached out at the yellow beams that acted as bars. They pushed my hand back, sending a shock that jolted through my body. It didn't really hurt but my hand could not pass through the bars.

"Our prisons adapt to the strength of the being they are holding," Zela told me with a laugh. "There is no way you can escape."

Okay, time to evaluate my options. I had my holographic earring and MAC communicator, but no uniform. I didn't dare look at my watch to see if MAC had alerted my friends, but I felt pretty sure he had. Of course, I had no idea how they'd get to outer space. That meant, even if my friends knew what had happened to me, I'd still be on my own. But wait, no uniform meant no nano deodorant bots. These aliens needed to breathe oxygen just like regular people.

I lifted my arms up over my head to yawn. I placed my hands on my forehead, keeping my underarms exposed and pointing out at the aliens. Zeekee staggered back, holding his throat. He fell forward.

"Serves you right!" I said.

"Ah, that stench..." one of the bald men frowned with disgust.

His face turned green to match the color of his uniform. He dropped to the ground. In fact, all the guards around him fell over.

I pointed my armpit at Zela, giving her a good blast. She staggered then fell over.

"You are lucky the ship is on autopilot," MAC told me. "This has kept the ship in Earth's orbit."

"Yeah, crashing a spaceship to Earth would be bad," I admitted.

I noticed Zela starting to move. She pushed herself up from the ground. "Impressive, girl!" she said. "But my system is stronger than my people! I am their leader, after all." She pointed at my wrist. "I see my silly son forgot that you have a computer on your wrist. It can't help you while you are trapped in my cage! You cannot break the energy beams! They have no physical form!"

I drew a deep breath. Some situations call for jumping into action. Some call for thinking, then jumping. Jumping! That was the key. Sure, the bars were made of energy, but the pad at the bottom of the cell seemed to be made of some sort of metal. Being metal, I bet I could smash it.

I jumped up and slammed my feet down on the pad, leaving a dent in it. The energy bars started to fizzle and fade.

"Stop that!" Zela ordered. "That's a really expensive piece of equipment!"

"Not for long!" I told her.

I slammed my right foot down.

BAM! The crack grew.

I slammed my left foot down.

POW! The pad split into two.

The energy bars fizzled out. I leaped out of the cage at Zela.

"Okay, Zela, it's you and me now!" I told her.

Zela faded away.

"Silly, Earthling fool. That was a hologram!" I heard from behind me.

I turned. Zela punched me in the jaw. She pulled her fist back. I could see it throbbing red.

"Now who's silly?" I asked.

I lifted her off the ground with a finger. "If I were you, I'd give up!" I told her.

"I'm a leader! I do not give up!" She said, her green eyes almost turning red. "You will surrender to me!"

"Ah, lady, I have the upper hand here. I've knocked out all your people. I'm about to clobber you. There's not much you can do to hurt me!"

"Not you, but the people you love!" she said. "SHIP! I ORDER YOU TO CRASH INTO STARLIGHT CITY!" she shouted.

"Order acknowledged!" The ship said.

I felt the ship start to move.

"Surrender to me, Lia Strong of Earth or all your loved ones are doomed!"

Dear Diary: Yikes! Yikes!! Yikes!!! I let my guard down because of a handsome face. Man, my mistake big time. That got me captured aboard a spaceship. Okay, nobody can say I don't have an exciting life! But this was too much excitement. Now, the crazy alien lady wants me to surrender to her or she will crash her ship into Earth. You know, right now I could certainly use a little boring

End this Mess

I had to do something and fast. The problem was, I had no idea how to stop a spaceship (that I was in), from colliding with Earth. My only hope was to reason with the crazy alien lady who wanted to crash that spaceship.

"Ah, Zela, crashing your ship and killing yourself isn't the best way to get me to work with you!"

Zela thrust a finger in my face. "I have no interest in working WITH you. I want you to do as I order." She started tapping her foot. "Ship, how long until you crash into Earth?"

"Two earth minutes," the ship replied.

Zela laughed. "You don't have much time to cooperate. You can't win. You either come with me or I destroy all you love!"

"Including yourself and your people," I pointed out.

Zela laughed louder. "Just a small price to pay for stopping the threat you pose to us."

"I repeat! This crash won't stop me!"

Zela stopped laughing, she leaned into me, her breath smelled like sour lemons. "You are a hero. You know you can't let your friends and your city be destroyed. You will give in to me. I will win!"

At least a million thoughts raced through my brain. And I didn't like any of them. I couldn't let this mad lady destroy my town. I WAS a hero, and heroes have to be willing to make sacrifices.

I took a deep breath. "Stop, your ship." I put my hand over my heart. "I will go back to your planet with you so you can drain my powers."

Zela sneered. "I so love...."

She froze in place.

"Not so fast, strange, nasty, alien lady!" I heard from behind me.

Tanya, Jason, Jessie and little Ellie Mae Opal appeared on the ship. Ellie Mae wore a ruby red costume and mask.

She smiled. "Wow, I've never teleported into space before."

"And I've never frozen an alien space ship in time before," Tanya said.

"How'd you find me?" I asked.

Jason pointed to MAC on my wrist. "GPS locator, of course. It works in space. As long as you are close enough to Earth." Jason looked at Zeekee laying there out cold on the floor. "I see his intentions were less than honorable." That was as close as Jason ever came to saying, 'I told you so.'

I sighed. "Yes." I took a deep breath. "His planet fears my power, so they want to drain me of that power. Zeekee's mom, Zela, wants me to surrender to them or she will crash her ship into Earth. So we need to figure out how to turn this space ship around!"

Jason nodded. "That is so uncool! But yeah, we tracked the ship and figured out that they want to crash it." He turned to Jessie. "That's why Jessie is here."

Jessie grinned. "I can banish this space ship into another dimension!"

"No, you can't!" I exclaimed.

Jessie nodded. "Pretty sure I can!"

I shook my head. "I mean, let's try to find another way first. I want to show them they have nothing to fear from me. Or from any other super teens!" I glanced at the still sleeping Zeekee. Sure, he had used me. Sure, he had hurt me. But it couldn't have been all fake! Could it? I pointed to Zeekee. "Let's see if we can get him to turn this around."

Tanya shrugged. "The creepy alien kid?"

"Yes," I said, walking over to him. "And he's cute in a different way, not creepy."

"I vote creepy and sort of cute," Jessie said.

"He's different looking," Ellie added.

I bent down and gave Zeekee a shake. "Wake up, dude," I ordered.

He laid there like a log.

I shook him. "Hey, Zeekee! Rise and shine!" I shouted.

His eyelids squeaked open. "Ah, did you get the ID number of the space bus that crashed on me?"

"That's not important," I said. "What's important is that your mom wants to crash your ship into my planet, which will destroy my city and all of you."

Zeekee's eyes crept open a little more. "Oh, that is not good." He sat up. "My mom really likes to get her way...." His eyes popped open. "Why aren't we moving?" he asked.

"Trade secret," Tanya told him. "But we can't keep this up for long. Manipulating time and space for too long can be more dangerous than crashing a spaceship into Earth."

I helped Zeekee to his feet. "Can you override the computer?" I asked.

He patted himself on the chest. "I am a computer genius!" he said.

I sighed. Suddenly I found it hard to believe that I had actually liked this guy. And not just because he space nabbed me and wanted to drain me of my powers. Okay, that was a big reason.

"Computer, show me the controls!" Zeekee ordered.

"Passcode," the computer asked.

"One, two, three," Zeekee said.

"Confirmed!" the computer beamed.

A holographic control panel appeared next to Zeekee.

"Wait...one two three?" Jason asked, frowning and shaking his head, "That's a terrible passcode."

"Big picture here, Jason," I said.

Zeekee shrugged. "My mom has a really bad memory." Zeekee ran his hands up and down the control panel. "I've programmed the ship to return to ZZZ-333."

"Great!" I said.

Jason stepped forward. "Yeah, but what prevents you from coming back to Earth and trying this all over again?" Jason always had my back.

Zeekee looked Jason in the eyes. "My word."

Jason shook his head. "Dude, your word doesn't mean a whole lot to us anymore."

Zeekee lowered his head. "Yes, I understand. I lied to you all. I misled Lia." His eyes found mine, even though his head was still lowered. "But I do truly care about you, Lia. I would not let my mom harm you, by harming people you love."

"But you'd let her drain my powers?" I asked.

"Draining would allow you to live your life as a normal person. I thought you might find that to be acceptable…"

Jason made a fist and walked up to Zeekee. "That wasn't your decision to make!" he frowned angrily.

He lifted Zeekee off the ground with one hand. A pleased grin appeared on his face. "Okay, this exoskeleton is so cool!"

Zeekee nodded. "You are correct on both terms." He pointed to the floor. "Please put me down. I am cooperating. I will open up a wormhole to our planet. And we will leave and never come back to bother you."

"I still don't think we can trust you!" Jason glared at Zeekee and lifted him higher in the air.

"You have my word. When my mother, our leader, Zela sees how easily you defeated us, yet you let us go, she will understand you are no longer a threat."

"I trust him," I said.

"If Lia trusts him, I do too," Ellie said.

Tanya shrugged. "Whatever. If they attack Earth again, I'll just reverse them through time until they don't exist."

"Or I can turn them all into toilet paper," Jessie said. "Now that would be fun."

Jess may be cool but she certainly had "issues".

Zeekee gulped. "I understand!"

I nodded to Jason. He let Zeekee drop to the ground. "Finish your calculations," Jason ordered. He turned to Ellie, "We need you to port us out."

Ellie nodded. "Got it!"

Jason eyed Zeekee carefully.

Two of Zela's guards started to stir awake. I cracked my arm up, aiming my underarm at them. They both dropped back down to the ground, face first. I lowered my arm and sniffed myself. Whoa, that packed quite the wallop.

"Zokay," Zeekee said. "The course is laid in. I can get us back to our planet now." He gazed at me. "I promise that if we ever return, it will be in peace."

"Yeah, yeah," I said. "Not falling for that twice!"

Zeekee nodded. "I understand."

Jason pointed to Ellie. She brought her hands together, then opened them wide. A large glowing sphere appeared. It was quickly increasing in size. Looking into the sphere we could see Star Pond.

"Okay, everybody in!" Ellie said.

Tanya snapped her fingers. Zela started to move.

"What's going on...."

She never got to finish as I waved my foot under her nose. Even with my shoes on, the odor still dropped her. "Now that's power!" I told her unconscious body.

Tanya and Jessie disappeared into the sphere.

Jason took my hand. "Come on, let's get out of here."

I walked into the sphere without even looking back at Zeekee.

We arrived at Star Pond, Ellie by our side. "Phew, that took a lot out of me," she said. "I am just a kid, after all."

"Are they leaving?" I asked.

Jason pointed up to the sky. We saw a bright ball of energy. The energy whisked off. "Yep."

"So, do we have to take them at their word that they will never come back?" Ellie asked. "I know I'm just a kid, but gee, I don't trust 'em."

I put my hand on her shoulder. "Sometimes Ellie, we have to trust the other side."

Jessie snickered. "Trust is all fine and good and all that jazz, but I zapped their minds."

"You did what?" I asked.

"I magically removed all thoughts of our planet from their alien minds. You might not have wanted me to banish them, but I banished the thoughts from them. I hope that's okay," Jessie said.

"It is," I said.

Jason looked at me. "I know this might sound kind of silly, but you do owe me a dance.... if we hurry we can still make it."

I took his hand. "Hold on tight!" I told him.

We leaped into the air towards the school.

"Ah, that's sweet," I heard Tanya say.

"True, as long as she doesn't lift her arms up or kick off her shoes and knockout the school!" Jessie said.

"Yeah, I had to remember that!"

Dear Diary: Wow! Wow! Wow! I was taken in and fooled big time. Yep, I let a cute face and amazing eyes convince me. I almost got pulled off the planet because of that. Heck, I almost got my city destroyed because of that. The good news is, I learned from my mistake. The better news is, my team came through for me. The best news is, I learned (which I should have already known), Jason always has my back; even when I don't make it easy for him. Regardless of whether I'm making sensible choices or not, Jason will find a way to be there for me. I am one lucky girl! Oh, we also made over a thousand dollars. So I had to dance with three different boys (apart from Jason), but it was worth it!

Epilogue

That night after the dance, I joined Mom at home to watch her boyfriend, Oscar on the evening news. We were both feeling worn out. I kicked my shoes off and dropped Shep from two rooms away. Poor guy!

When Oscar appeared on the screen, he made a special announcement. "Tonight's special guest is lawyer, Callie Hanson. Callie, like me, believes Super Teen should not be allowed to run unchecked! Her goal is to stop her."

Mom turned to me. "Sorry about this honey."

I looked at Mom and sighed. "I'm too tired to worry about this right now. That's a problem for another day.... for now, let's just be happy." I knew that whatever the world or the universe threw at me, I would be ready!

Book 6

Saving the World!

Crime Doesn't Pay

Jason and I sat in his living room playing one of the Mario racing games. Jason had a huge smile on his face. "Man, I am so winning!" he said. He nudged me.

"You should be proud of yourself. You're really good at pressing buttons on a console!" I told him.

We steered our cars around a bend. Jason increased his lead. "I would think having super reflexes would give you an advantage!" He laughed.

"See Jason, you're not so smart after all! Cause super reflexes don't do that!" Truthfully, my powers would probably have an impact, but whenever I played a game with someone who doesn't have superpowers I tried to curb my strength. After all, I truly believed my powers should be reserved for emergency use, and of course the occasional fun use. I was still a teen and teens need to have fun. But, I was always careful not to abuse those powers. Like my mom says, "With great power comes great caution". I'm pretty sure she got that from a movie or a comic book and just changed it a bit. Still, it makes sense. I know my powers are a gift and not to be abused. Though man, sometimes it was tempting to crush Jason at this Mario game. Maybe if he used the body under-armor my dad designed for him it would be a fair battle? But no, that would be a waste of the body under-armor's charge. Dad would not be happy.

Sure, Dad did disappear from my life until my superpowers showed up. Sure, Dad can be kind of awkward and a little weird. But he does help with cool tech stuff. So, it's good to keep him happy. Plus, I really didn't want to get on my mom's bad side. So I figured it was best for everybody's sake if I just let Jason win.

After all, he's been my BFF since I could first walk and talk. He and Mom are the two people who have always been there for me, no matter what. And Jason always had my back. Even during the times I didn't think he needed to have my back. BTW, most of those times he was right. Yep! No matter what, Jason always had my best interests and safety at heart. I was glad he was a part of my life, regardless of the fact that he couldn't help boasting about his skills with computer games.

"Man, Lia! For a superhero, you're really bad at this game." He paused for a moment, "Wait? Do you always let me win?"

"No…no of course not," I said in a slightly cynical tone just to make him think a bit.

"Hey, are you ready for that comet in a couple of days?" he asked, in an effort to change the subject.

"Ah, what comet?" I frowned.

"It's called K-9 the Dog Comet. It's going to pass really close to Earth. Within just 10,000 miles."

"That doesn't sound very close!" I said.

"In comet terms, it's like…way close. We'll be able to see it in a couple of days through my telescope!"

"Oh so cool," I said with mock excitement. Though truthfully, I did think it was pretty cool. "You science geek!" I laughed.

Before Jason could respond, we heard the police scanner in the room go off. "Alert, all squads report to the Starlight City Museum. There is an armed robbery in progress."

I shot up from the sofa.

"What the heck? Why would anybody rob the museum? I've been there on school trips. It's kind of nice, but boring…"

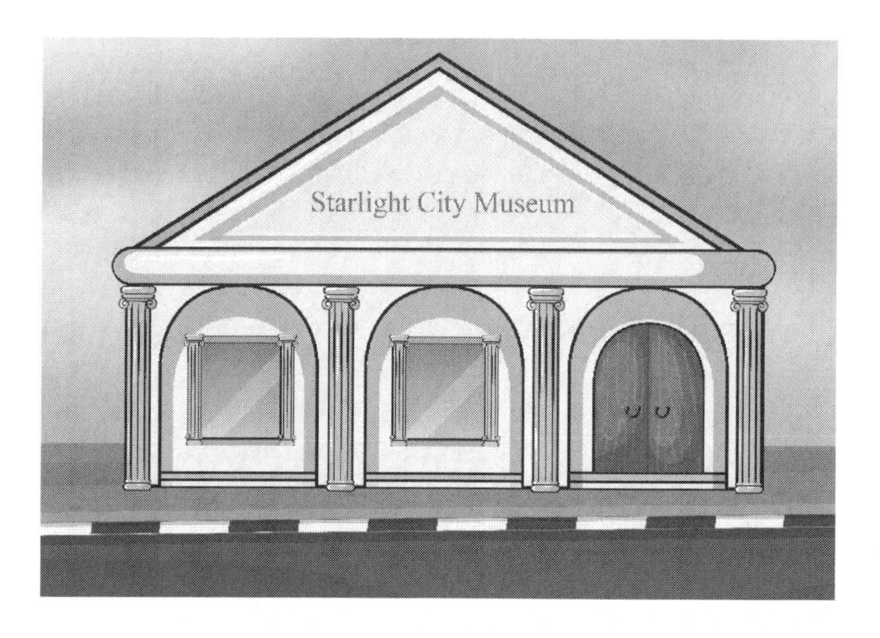

Jason looked at me. "First, the museum is amazing. Second, this week there is an exhibit on display from the renowned artist, Patrick David. His pieces are worth millions. Dad has extra security on the grounds."

"Okay, I guess that answered the 'why' question. Now for the 'how.' How do they think they are going to get away with this in my town?"

I turned to MAC, my wrist communicator. "MAC, activate suit and give me a nice pink holo-mask!"

"Check!" MAC said.

Jason looked at me. "You're lucky my mom's not around at the moment. You should be more cautious when turning on your Super Teen uniform. Someone could see you."

"I used my super hearing, so I knew she wasn't at home yet," I told him.

I opened up a window. "I should be able to get to the museum in one leap!" I said boldly. It was the way I thought a superhero should talk.

Jason pointed behind me. "Ah, the museum is that way."

I turned and walked towards the window on the other wall. "Right. I knew that!"

I opened up the window. I leaped up into the air. Extending my body into the glide position, I flew (well, glided) towards the museum. A part of me thought about flapping my arms. But a bigger, more logical part, figured that would just make me look silly.

Closing in on the old museum, I used my see-through vision to see through the ceiling. I saw five armed men with gas masks on. They were prowling along the main floor. All the other people and guards laid unconscious on the ground.

"I see they gassed the people!" I said, landing on the roof.

"Very good, Ms. Lia," MAC told me. "These crafty, cunning bad guys may not be super but they understand you need to breathe. I am sure they think the gas will stop you, hence the reason they can rob the museum in your town."

"I don't like bad guys on my turf!" I said, curling my hand into a fist. I paused. "Will this gas hurt me?"

A question mark appeared on Mac's interface. "I literally have no idea. I cannot analyze the gas until we are in the gas. By then it's possible that it will be too late for you."

I took a deep breath. "Looks like it is…hold my breath and force out the gas time."

"So it would appear."

I held my breath and started spinning really fast. As I spun, I pushed myself downward bursting through the top floor of the museum. I hit the floor. I kept holding my breath and spun again, pushing through to the main floor. I crashed down between the bad dudes.

One of them pointed at me. "It's Super Teen!" He looked at another bad dude. "I thought you said the gas would overpower her, too!"

The other bad dude shrugged. "She must be holding her breath. Fire at her and force her to breathe."

Extending my arms, I twirled them in circles super-fast, creating powerful mini-whirlwinds. The whirlwinds blew through the room, knocking down the bad guys. I hoped they would also blow all the sleeping gas out.

Only one way to tell. I ran forward at super speed and pulled the gas mask off one of the thugs. Moving from thug to thug, I pulled each of their masks off.

They all looked at each other. They smiled. "Looks like the gas is gone!" one of them said. "Which means we can breathe."

"Also means I can breathe!" I said, pointing at the thugs.

They all aimed their guns at me.

"You know those bullets won't hurt me!" I boasted.

"True," one of the thugs said. "But if we fire at you, the bullets bouncing off you will do a lot of damage to the art here as well as all the innocent people!" he laughed. "So you let us go and nobody gets hurt!"

Tapping my foot slowly I told them. "That could work."

I could see them all smiling under their commando hoods.

I continued. "But now that your gas masks are off I prefer a different approach."

"And what would that be?" One of the armed baddies spat.

I turned my back, and more importantly my butt, to the five thugs. I released a silent but near-deadly fart. I aimed my butt upwards making sure the standing bad guys would take the worse of it.

Before I could even turn around I heard...*Gasp. Plop. Plop. Plop. Plop. Plop.*

I turned to see the five thieves laying flat on their faces on the ground, each holding their throats. Sure, maybe not the most lady-like of attacks, but it certainly was efficient and got the job done fast.

I heard somebody clearing their throat behind me. I turned to see a tall, slim, dark haired lady. She looked vaguely familiar.

"And you are?" I asked.

"My name is Kalie Hanson," she said slowly. "I'm a lawyer."

"Oh right," I smiled. "I've seen you on TV with Oscar Oranga. Now, you can see that I am no threat to society!"

Kalie walked forward. She handed me a letter in a white envelope.

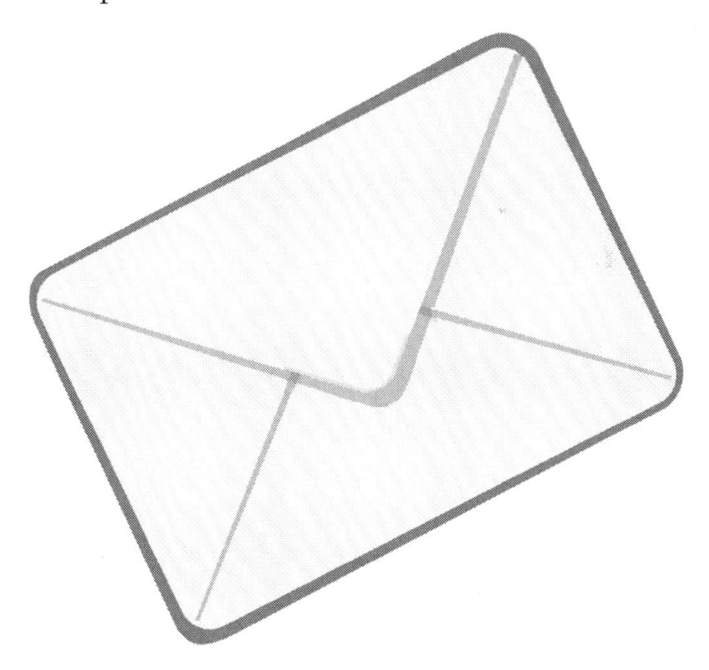

"I don't want a reward. I know it might sound corny, but good work and knocking bad guys out is its own reward."

Kalie pointed to the letter. "Please open it, Miss."

I used my see through vision to make sure this wasn't a weird trap. I only saw a piece of paper in the envelope. I opened it up.

"It's a letter," I said.

"Very good," Kalie said. "A legal letter. Please read it."

I started reading out loud, "Super Teen, you are hereby forbidden to take the law into your own hands. Doing so again will be taken as interference with justice and you will be arrested."

I looked up at Kalie. "This is a joke. Right?"

"I'm a lawyer. I never joke about the law. The law is what separates us from animals. "

"But... but...I saved the day...."

"Perhaps, but you are not a sworn officer of the court. Not only that, you also damaged the museum. In addition, you used gross force...the silent but near-deadly fart."

"Hey, it's fast and efficient!" I protested.

Kalie looked down at me. "It's not lady-like."

"Who made you in charge of what's lady-like?" I countered.

"Good point. As a legal professional though, I can say your silent but near-deadly farts endanger innocent people."

"I aimed high..." I said.

Kalie shook her head. "Not good enough."

Jason's dad, Chief of Police Michaels, arrived on the scene. He was an olive-skinned, tall stocky man. Not a person to be messed with. "What's going on here?" he barked, at Kalie.

Kalie turned and adjusted her glasses. She held out a hand. "Police Chief Michaels, I am Attorney at Law, Kalie Hanson. I am representing the people of Starlight City and the world. I have issued a cease and desist order for Super Teen. She cannot be fighting crime. She is not an officer of the court or the land." She scoffed. "She's just a kid."

"A very powerful kid!" I said.

Kalie turned back to me. "All the more reason to cease and desist. There is a reason why we don't let young kids drive tanks."

I tried to think of some witty and strong retort but nothing popped into my head. Instead, I said, "Well, ah...."

"I rest my case," Kalie said. She handed Chief Michaels a copy of the order she had given me. "If Super Teen arrives at another crime I expect you to arrest her!"

The chief took the paper. He eyed it. He sighed. He looked at me. "Sorry, Super Teen, the law is the law."

This couldn't be happening. Could it? All I wanted to do was to help people. Now, this lawyer lady wanted to stop me because I was a kid. "But, but..." I said. "Ms. Hanson..." I muttered.

Hanson grinned. Before she could say anything cold and cutting, chief Michaels chimed in, "Wait, Hanson! Are you related to those bozos who tried to terrify our town a while back? The ones Super Teen stopped."

Kalie adjusted the glasses on her nose. "Yes, I am sad to report that they are my cousins. But this has nothing to do with them. I wouldn't even defend them in court. They wanted me to do it for free!" She snorted. "I wouldn't even defend those guys for a billion dollars. I am ashamed to share DNA with them!"

"So you admit I did good work stopping them?" I asked Kalie.

Kalie shook her head. "I admit you were lucky that nobody got hurt. I feel your luck will run out. Hence my court order." Kalie had to see the frustration on my face. She walked forward and put a hand on my shoulder. "Look, I get it. You want to help the world. And you can. Graduate high school, go to college and then go to law school or the police academy. Then you can fight crime the legal way."

"But... I want to help now!"

Kalie laughed. "I wanted to marry Tom Cruise, we don't always get what we want." She turned to the chief. "Chief Michaels, I expect you to enforce this order."

Chief Michaels lowered his head. He walked over to me. "Sorry, Super Teen. Next time I see you fighting crime I will have to order my team to arrest you."

"I don't understand, but I do understand," I told him.

I leaped up into the air. I fought off the image to drop Kalie with a fart.

Dear Diary: OMG!! Here I am only trying to do good in the world and now this Kalie woman pops up and she's trying to stop me. She calls me a menace. I'm not a menace, I'm just really powerful and I want to help the world. Sure, my farts can drop an army. Sure, I'm strong enough to cause the earth to rumble when I slam my foot down. Sure, my breath can freeze a lake. Okay, yeah, I can see where some people might be scared of me. But really, I am just trying to help. I need to convince her and others of that. The world is better with Super Teen in it.

School is in Session

The next day, during my walk to school with Jason, I vented. "I can't believe that Kalie Hanson lady! How can she want to stop me? Doesn't she see all the good work that I do? How I help people!"

"Well, you did knockout the mall once, trying on a pair of shoes. You have dropped a herd of hippos by lifting your arms. You can fart and be the only one left standing for miles…."

"First, it was a herd of rhinos. Second, it's not like I do these things on purpose. Third, you're not helping here, Jason!"

"I'm just trying to get you to see her point. The fact that you can casually or by accidentally knock out the entire state might scare some people," Jason said.

I sighed. My sigh knocked him down. I helped him up. "Sorry!" I said. "OMG, I *am* dangerous."

"You're not dangerous, well not deadly at least. You just need to work on controlling your power."

"I'm doing that!" I insisted. I pounded my foot on the ground, making the ground shake. I pulled my foot back and dropped my arms to my side. "Sorry…" I said, "Still working on it."

Jason put a hand on my shoulder. "I know that. A lot of people know that. But you can't blame some people for being scared. You do pack a lot of power."

I took in Jason's words. I knew they made sense. I don't feel like a powerful dangerous weapon. I feel like me, Lia Strong. I'm not Super Teen, I'm just a teen who happens to be super. I use my powers for good. To help people. To help the world.

But yes, I guess I could sort of see how some insecure or cynical people could be worried about me. I stopped walking. I looked Jason square in the eyes. "So then, what do I do?"

He grinned. He patted my shoulder. "Just keep being you. You'll win people over."

I dropped my school bag on the ground in frustration and shrugged. "Don't see how."

"Listen, Lia, you were the most special person I knew before you became super. Now you are super special. It's only a matter of time until everybody sees that." He collected his thoughts. "Well not everybody. Some people are always going to complain or be scared. But you will get the vast majority on your side. Heck, many people already see how special you are!"

"You mean special in a good way. Right?" I grinned.

"In the best way!"

I picked up my bag and started walking towards school again. I didn't want to be late and get on Vice Principal Macadoo's bad side. He had a pretty big bad side.

"So, how can I keep showing them how special I am if I can't help by fighting crime and saving the day and all that stuff?"

Jason laughed. "Who says you can't?"

"That court order...."

"That just says you will be arrested if they catch you," Jason said.

"Correct..."

"Catching you and arresting you is a lot easier said than done. Especially since I happen to know the chief of police is on your side. At least unofficially. No way can they stop you!"

Walking up the school steps I said, "You want me to break the law?"

Jason opened the door for me. "I just want you to keep being you."

Before I had a chance to say thanks, Wendi and Patti shot over to me. From the frowns on their faces I knew they had a complaint or an insult; or a complaint-insult. They had a talent for putting everybody down.

"About time you got here, Lia!" Wendi scolded.

"Yeah!" Patti agreed.

I pointed to the clock above the lockers. "I still have five minutes to homeroom bell. I am not late!"

"Not for school," Wendi admitted. "But we have a problem. A problem that you, as leader of the student council, needs to fix."

I headed towards my locker. Krista and Tim Dobbs were putting their bags in their lockers. They wore much friendlier faces. "You know I don't have a lot of real power. Right?" I told them.

"Well, of course, that position is just a token position, hence the reason I let you win," Wendi told me. "But you do speak for the kids in this school. Well, at least the middle-school part of this school."

"Yeah!" Patti said.

I looked at Patti. "Can you say anything but yeah?" I asked.

"Yep," Patti said. She seemed proud of herself for that.

I sighed, making an effort not to knock her and Wendi over. "Okay, what do you want me to try to do?"

"Fix the school lunches," Wendi said.

"I don't even think Super Teen herself could do that," I said. Truthfully, our lunches that weren't that bad. Most of the time we could recognize what we were eating. At times, the food even tasted pretty good. But I wanted to get on Wendi (and Patti's) good sides.

"Of course, Super Teen couldn't fix them! She is so overblown and over-rated. Just because she can fart down a herd of elephants, she thinks she's ridiculously amazing."

"It was a herd of rhinos," I corrected. "And she used her underarm odor. But that's all beside the point."

"Oh, I forgot you were her number one fan," Wendi said snidely.

"How can I try to help, Wendi?" I groaned.

"The lunches. We want more options. Like, it would be nice if they had a veggie option. You know, some of us don't like to eat meat." She touched her own cheeks. "That's how we get this great skin."

"You know, more options would actually be nice," Todd said.

"I hate to put pressure on you, Lia, but man, I would love a salad bar!" Krista said. "I mean how hard can that be?"

Okay, the masses have spoken. I hated to admit it but more food options did make sense. "Who do I talk with to see what I can do?" I asked Wendi.

"VP Macadoo," Wendi said.

"Yep!" Patti agreed.

"I'll make an appointment to talk to him ASAP!" I assured them.

"Good," Wendi said.

"Yeah," Patti agreed.

They turned and walked away. Suddenly everything froze. There was only one person who I knew could do that. Sure enough, I saw a smiling Tanya walking towards me looking as cool and confident as always.

"What's up?" I asked her. Yep, this is my life now, talking with a girl who can stop time is just the everyday normal.

"Your dad wants to study my sister, Kayla," Tanya said. Never being one for small talk she added, "Do you think I can trust him?"

"He is my dad," I said.

"He also runs a super big company that we didn't even know existed until your powers showed up. He is kind of a mad scientist."

"But a nice one who means well," I insisted.

"So Mom and I should let him?" Tanya asked, her eyebrows raised.

I nodded. "Yes, but let's keep an eye on him and the people around him. I don't think they're bad but sometimes they can be scientists first and humans second."

"Gotcha," Tanya said. Okay, I'm keeping everybody frozen until I get to homeroom. Stay cool!" she gave me a nod.

I watched Tanya walk away thinking, *Man, I wish I had control of my power like she does.*

Dear Diary: Sure, I have a crazy lawyer who has convinced the police and some other people that I am dangerous. But I somehow get the feeling that asking for a variety of new lunch options for Wendi and Patti is going to be even more challenging. Still, I hate to admit it but that's actually a good idea. This school could use some more green food. Well, at least food that is supposed to be green.

Training

After the day I'd had dealing with normal kid problems (and lawyers), it felt good to be at BMS labs to let loose a little. But I needed to remember to make an appointment with VP Macadoo about the lunch program changes. That idea made me more nervous than fighting deadly robots. With the robots, I could smash em to pieces. I couldn't do that with the VP. Man, that would definitely be a blemish on my record!

Speaking of robots, well androids, Hana was practically giddy as she stood with Marie, Jessie, Tanya and I in the huge practice gym. I haven't known Hana very long but I did know that anything which made her so excited involved a challenge for us.

Hana stood before us in a white jumpsuit. "You super gals all know that I always stress you should work as a team, right? Together you are more powerful than you are alone!"

"That does make sense," Marie agreed.

"Yes, together your sum is greater than your parts. Therefore, we've come up with what we think is a suitable challenge for the four of you.

"I think we can handle whatever you throw at us!" I said.

"Yeah," Jess said.

"We are pretty darn powerful," Tanya agreed. She looked around. "Hey, where are Jason and Lori?"

Hana smiled. That smile sent a shiver down my spine. "They are part of your test. They are actually your opponents."

Jessie licked her lips. "This will be fun. Truthfully, I don't see how it will be much of a challenge for us. After all, Lori's bionics are neat. And that suit Jason wears lets him do cool stuff." She pointed to the four of us. "But we are the power four in this group. Any of us can take the two of them down." She stared at Hana as if stating an obvious fact.

Hana grinned. She pointed across the huge gym to two very large doors on the far wall. Each door had to be at least five stories high. Like I said, this battle gym was way big. The doors slowly rolled open to reveal two massive robots. I mean they were as thick as they were tall. Each robot had a colored dome on top. Using super-vision, I saw Lori sitting in the dome of the green robot, Jason was in the other purple robot. "Tada!" Hana said. "These robots have human operators and are also the latest in artificial intelligence. They have many defensive capabilities. Plus, your friends are up in the control domes and you need to defeat the robots without hurting your friends."

"Still Easy!" Jessie boasted. She ran out into the middle of the gym. She motioned for the robots to come at her. "Come on, let's see what this mix of human and robot has to offer!"

Jess pointed at the robots and wiggled her fingers. "Going to use my magic to shrink these things down to size!" she boasted.

The robots clanked forward. They each crackled with energy. They kept coming forward. In fact, the energy ricocheted off the bots back towards Jess, frying the ground at her feet.

"What the?" Jess said.

"We built in an anti-magic generator," Hana told her. "After all, magic is just another form of energy."

Jess looked at us. Her dark hair popped straight up. "Ah guys, a little help here!"

Marie stepped forward. "I might be able to turn those robots into tinfoil!" She moved towards them quickly.

I tossed a glance at Hana. She shook her head.

I lifted my wrist computer aid to my face. "MAC, buddy what do you think we should do?"

"I am not allowed to give hints," MAC said in a robotic voice. "But if I could, I would say work together," he whispered in a quieter voice.

The giant humongous bot operated by Lori reached a long mechanical hand down towards Marie. Marie grinned. "That was a mistake, friend!" Marie touched the hand with her finger. "YIKES!" she screamed. We heard a loud zapping sound. An electrical charge sent Marie flying backward. She crashed to the ground yards away.

She raised her head. "I can't touch those things!" She dropped her head back to the ground. "Now if you don't mind I'll just lay here until my ears stop ringing and ringing and ringing." She smiled, "It sounds kind of soothing."

"I gotta admit, this is way fun!" Lori announced from her robot.

"Glad I am not scared of heights!" Jason added.

"Do you last two want to give up now?" Lori asked.

Tanya looked at the slowly approaching robots. "I got this!" She held her hands up, framing Lori and Jason's bots in between them. "Stop!" she ordered.

The two humungous bots froze in place.

Tanya smiled and turned to Hana, "Game over. We win!"

Man, sometimes I was so envious of Tanya. She had her act together. Always calm and cool. She knew the score. Plus, OMG, she had the power to control time. Maybe even time and space! Like, holy cow, what a cool power! I know, I know...Jason will always tell me that Tanya may have great powers but she can't bend steel with her hands, bullets don't bounce off her, she can't freeze a lake with her breath, she can't drop an army troop with a fart. Yeah, that last one might not seem too useful but it is kind of fun to do.

Getting back to my original thought, Tanya just knew what to do and when to do it. I think she sweated confidence.

Hana crossed her arms. She sighed. "Yes, you have frozen your friends in time forever. Bravo, you must be so proud," she gave a little mock clap.

Tanya seemed unaffected. She pointed at the time-stopped robots. She looked at me. "Go take those two overgrown legos apart. Be careful not to hurt our friends though."

Yep, that Tanya…she really did have it figured out. I shot forward using super speed. I didn't need to but I wanted to show off some. I spun up the length of Lori's robot smashing it over and over as I rose. Knowing that the robot was frozen in time, I was aware that I could smash it without having to worry about it falling over and hurting Lori. Reaching the top, I popped off the dome and dropped gently to the ground. I placed the dome down carefully.

With Jason's robot, I took a different approach. I leaped up to the top and removed the dome that was holding Jason. I gently lowered it to the ground. I leaped back to the top of the now dome-less big bad bot.

I crossed my arms to my body and started spinning down. Spiraling down through the middle of the bot's body, I was pretty sure I had split it in half. I smashed through its metal legs and jumped to Tanya.

Tanya smiled and snapped her fingers. "Time to move again!"

The two bots crumpled to the ground.

Jason ran over to Tanya. "Man! That was so way cool being frozen in time like that. Great way to use teamwork."

Hana groaned. "I guess that was…not quite what I had envisioned. But I can't argue with the results. Nice work Tanya. I'm impressed that your control of your power has improved. I am so glad we have your little sister to work with now. Teaching one so young will be very beneficial for us and for her."

"I hope so," Tanya said. "Mom and I are hoping that some training will help her learn to control her power."

"I'm sure it will!" Jason said. "The people here are great." He pulled back his sleeves showing Tanya his advanced under-armor. "See!"

Tanya touched the armor gently. I wasn't sure why but I didn't like that much. No, not much at all.

"Nice," Tanya said politely.

Jason couldn't stop gushing. "I think you and your sister have such great potential with your powers. Time is something the entire universe shares."

I leaned forward. "Yeah, but can she lift her arms and let her BO clobber a city?" I regretted saying that for a number of reasons. I flushed a bright shade of red.

Jason and Tanya both turned to me. "You do have awesome raw power," Jason said.

"Agreed," Tanya said. "Of course, it's not a contest. We are a team."

I gulped. "Great point…"

Jason took Tanya by her hand. "Come on, let's go greet your sister!"

Tanya looked at me.

"Go!" I said. "Make her feel at home, she is a kid."

"See you later, Lia!" Jason said.

I watched as Tanya and Jason walked out of the training area.

Lori came up and patted me on the back. "Are you okay?" she asked.

I nodded and forced a grin. "Yes, of course. Jason and I are BFFs. We are great BFFs. He is allowed to have a life without me."

"Should we keep training?" Marie asked. "My head isn't spinning as fast now."

"I'll give it a shot," Jess said. "I'm not used to my magic being fizzled out."

Hana looked at us. "Well, I have to go and supervise Kayla's training. But I approve of you three working alone."

"Actually, I'm going to check in on Kayla's training, too," I told the others.

Dear Diary: Okay, what the heck just happened to me? I've never really been jealous before in my life. I've been angry, sad, mad and not glad, but never ever jealous. I am pretty certain I felt a little spark between Jason and Tanya. Maybe nothing will come of it? Maybe I'm imagining it? But even if something does happen between them, I need to find a way to be happy for them. They are my friends. Jason and I will always be BFFs. Right? Of course, we will! Right? Right?

Mixed Feelings

I followed Tanya and Jason to the training area where Kayla was to begin work with Dad's people. Dad was talking with Kayla and Tanya's mom, Mara. Kayla had four, white coated training experts around her. Using my super hearing, I heard Dad reassure Mara that Kayla would flourish here and that she would learn to control her powers. He also mentioned that spending the weekend here would be great for Kayla. Mara seemed to reluctantly agree.

She kissed Kayla goodbye and then slowly made her way out of the room.

"I'm not sure this is such a good idea," Tanya said. "Kayla is so young. I mean, she's just a kid...."

"All the better reason to teach her to control and use her powers now," Jason lectured politely. "The people here are pros and they have everyone's best interest at heart."

That's one of the traits I loved about Jason. He always saw the best in people. He believed that everybody was like him and wanted the best for everybody else. I really admired that. And I may be the only person who sees that in Jason.

But then I listened to Tanya speak and I realized I wasn't the only one to see that quality in Jason at all.

She put her hand on his back, she looked him in the eyes. He smiled. I fought back the urge to frown. "Jason, I love the way you see the world. You see everybody as pure as you are!"

Jason looked away from Tanya and began to blush. "Ah, gosh," he mumbled. "Thanks, Tanya. That's so nice of you to say that!" He glanced over at me, "I think Lia thinks the same thing."

"I do!" I said. "I do!"

Tanya rolled her eyes. She looked into Jason's eyes as Jason continued to talk. "I do believe that if you treat people properly they will treat you properly!"

"I hope you're right," Tanya said.

"I know you're right!" I said.

Tanya snapped her fingers. Jason and the rest of the people in the room, except for Kayla, froze in time. Man, she had control of her power.

"What gives, big sis?" Kayla asked, walking over.

Tanya eyed me. "Am I fishing in your waters here?"

"Huh," Kayla said, "there's no fish or water here. I guess I could make some if I wanted."

Tanya turned to her little sis. She bent down to her. "That was just an expression."

"Oh… bummer, making water here might be fun…."

Tanya waved a finger in front of Kayla's face. "No, we don't use our powers like that. It's too dangerous! That is why you are here!"

"But you're using your powers now," Kayla protested.

"True, but only a little local time stop. Nothing big!" Tanya insisted.

"Okay," Kayla said taking a step back. "What do you want to talk to Lia about? How to do super farts?"

"Ah, no!"

Kayla licked her lips. Her eyes popped open, she stood on her tip toes. "Do you want to talk to her about how you and Jason look at each other?" she asked.

"Maybe," Tanya said.

"That means yes!" Kayla said, jumping up and down.

Tanya frowned and pointed at Kayla. Kayla froze in mid jump. Tanya turned to me. "Now, we can talk in private."

"Unless Hana or somebody comes in," I joked.

"Nope, the entire world is frozen except for the area around us now," Tanya said.

OMG! She could freeze the world easier than most people take out the trash. And she was so calm about it.

"Really?" I gasped.

"Trust me, we can talk…about everything."

"Everything?" I said.

Tanya lifted a finger. "First, can I trust your father and his people? I know you aren't as naïve and sweet as Jason."

"Nobody is," I said.

"Great point, but it doesn't answer my question."

I sighed. My sigh sent Tanya staggering back. I stopped myself from grinning. "You ask a good question. I love my dad. After all, he is my dad, and in many ways, he wants to help the world just like Jason does. Sure, he's more secretive.

Sure, he disappeared from my life. But he's been a big help since he's been back. And I truly think that he wants what is best for everyone.

"Okay, good," Tanya told me.

"That said, I can't say all his people agree with him. I have no idea about his backers. But we have to admit they have really helped Marie and the others get a good grip on their powers."

Tanya nodded. "Okay, I'll trust him, for now. If it doesn't work out I can always reverse time."

"Can you do that?" I gasped.

Tanya simply smirked. She looked at me. "Now back to the BIG question. Do you have an interest in Jason?"

Wow, she really was forward. I think I liked that. The problem was I didn't know what I thought about me and Jason as more than BFFs.

Tanya tapping her foot said, "Well, while we have all the time in the world, I don't want to keep them all frozen like this for too much longer."

I grinned meekly. I shook my head. "I love Jason, but as a great, amazing friend."

"You sure?"

My mind said, *NO OF COURSE I'M NOT SURE.* But my mouth quietly said, "Yes, I am sure."

"Then you don't mind us getting closer?" Tanya asked.

I took a deep breath. "I just want what's best for Jason."

Tanya smiled. "Good. He's one lucky guy. We may be the two most powerful people in the world and we both like him a lot!" Tanya pointed at Kayla and she rewound backward to the point she was before Tanya had stopped time. Tanya snapped her fingers. The world started up again.

"Shall we get working on your powers?" One of the trainers asked Kayla.

Kayla jumped up and shouted. "Sure!"

The trainer showed Kayla a big clock. "Now, concentrate on turning this back a minute…"

Tanya took Jason by his hand. "Hey, let's go for a walk."

"Sure!" Jason said.

I stood there and watched them leave. I fought back the temptation to stop them with a fart.

Dear Diary: OMG!! I really, truly, really have no idea what to think about Tanya and Jason. I mean, I've known Jason FOREVER. I think of him as a BFF a BRO. Somebody who is always there for me when I need a friend to laugh or cry with. I should be happy for him. Tanya is an older cool girl. Any guy would be lucky to be with her. I should be so, so happy for Jason. I mean, he's my best friend. I guess I'm just worried that if he spends more time with Tanya, he might not be there for me when I need him. Yeah, I know that's selfish. But I can't help it. I might be super but I'm still human.

The Rescue

I walked home from my training session alone. I needed a little me time to get my head on straight. Obviously, I could have leaped home in a single bound. But instead, I walked slowly, just breathing in the air and soaking up the sun. I couldn't blame Jason for liking Tanya. After all, Tanya was cool, collected and seemed to have total control of her awesome power. Jason would be lucky to be with her. As Jason's BFF, I should be happy for him. And I kind of was. I guess I just felt sad for me.

I walked along, wallowing in self-pity when MAC broke my train of thought.

"Ah, Lia, there is a problem!" MAC said.

"Of course, there's a problem! My BFF is hanging out with another girl!" I moaned.

"Well, ah, yeah, I guess that is a problem," MAC said. "But this problem is much more life threatening and dangerous."

"Say what?"

MAC spoke fast. "I've picked up a mayday from a commercial airplane above Starlight City. They have lost power and they are crashing!"

I tuned in my super hearing. I could hear the jet plummeting towards the ground and the voices of the scared passengers. Then I heard the pilots' desperate calls to the control tower in Capital City. I jumped up into the air towards the sound of the falling plane.

"MAC, activate my costume!' I cried.

"Already done!" MAC said.

I leaped up with so much power, I soon reached the plane and found both of its propellers gushing smoke.

Luckily, I'd been practicing controlling my air leaps. By shifting my weight in one direction, I could cause myself to float in that direction. I "flew" towards the plane. I realized that even if I caught the plane at this speed it wouldn't be much different than the plane hitting the ground. Either the plane's momentum would carry me forward and I'd crash into the plane, or the plane would smash into me. The plane would lose in both cases.

That meant I had to slow the plane down slowly then catch it and then lower it gently to the ground.

I inhaled then exhaled super-breath and sent just a touch of freezing air onto the plane. My frosted breath hit the plane and slowed it down while blowing out the flames in the burning engines.

I dropped down under the plane and pushed upwards with my hands as well as more cooling breath. I wasn't sure how, but the plane stopped nose diving, and with my guidance, it turned horizontal to the ground. Of course, the plane was still falling, but it was a controlled (by me - mostly) fall.

I needed to find a safe spot to guide this plane down. The schoolyard was big and at this time of day, pretty empty.

It made the perfect landing spot for an out of control plane.

Looking down, I scanned the landscape and searched for the school. I saw it fairly close to where the plane's momentum was taking us. I only needed to nudge the plane a little to the left. When the plane rocked to the left, the passengers screamed.

"Sorry!" I told them. "But don't worry, I have this under control!" I said this as much for my own confidence as theirs.

I remember once when Mom and I went on vacation and I tried hang gliding. It occurred to me that this was pretty much the same thing. Only now, instead of a big kite, I had a huge aircraft to guide down. I bore my hands into the bottom of the plane, giving me a really strong grip. Now I could guide the plane down just like that hang glider.

I took a deep breath. I watched as the ground grew closer and closer. This would be tricky but I could do it. The ground came clearly into view without me needing to use Super Teen vision. We passed over the school's fence, barely clearing it. I tilted my body just a bit to steer the plane towards the big field. We were falling fast, but it was nothing I couldn't control. My feet touched the ground first, in fact, they dug into the ground. The force of the plane pulled me forward, digging two ditches with my legs. I held onto the plane. We slid across the field. I felt our momentum slowing down. The plane and I dragged a few hundred feet then came to a stop.

I had done it. I had landed a plane on my back. I stepped to the side and guided the plane off my hands onto the ground. It hit with a thud. All the passengers cheered.

I heard police car sirens coming towards us. In minutes, police, fire, and ambulance would be surrounding the plane. Of course, Oscar Oranga was already there with his news crew. He'd arrived even before the emergency personnel.

Oscar thrust a microphone into my face, "Super Teen, how does it feel to have saved a plane?"

"Pretty darn good!" I said.

"Does it worry you that the police consider you to be a criminal?" Oscar asked.

"I'm not a criminal!" I insisted.

"Well then…a vigilante who works outside of the system and the law," Oscar said.

"Oscar, I just saved a plane full of people from crashing!"

"True, you did, and I am sure they are grateful," Oscar said. He pointed to my skid marks on the school field. "Of course, you did totally dig up this field, causing damage to the school grounds which are public property."

"But way less damage than an airplane crash would cause!" I insisted strongly.

"Good point. But that still doesn't stop you from being wanted by the police," Oscar said.

I saw Chief Michaels and a bunch of his men walking towards me. Kalie Hanson stood there right behind them, smirking.

"Super Teen, I would like to thank you for saving the airplane and its passengers. I am sure the courts will go easy on you because of..."

Everything froze in place. I saw Tanya walking towards me, flipping all the hats off the police officers as she passed by.

"Jason said you might need my help," Tanya grinned. She raised her hand for a high-five. "Man, excellent save of that plane!"

I returned her high five. I frowned. "Lot of good it did me... I'm still wanted!"

Tanya looked at the happy faces of the passengers and onlookers. "Yeah, but you scored major brownie points here. The tide will turn in your favor, just give it time. Luckily, when you have me on your side, time is also on your side." Tanya looked up to the sky. "Now get out of here. Let the events speak for themselves."

I took Tanya's advice and leaped home.

Dear Diary: Wow, it's nice to know I had it in me to save that plane. It took a combination of power and planning, but man oh man, I did it. I saved the plane!!!! That makes me feel great. Of course, saving that plane didn't stop the police from trying to detain me. That made me feel kind of lousy. The good news is, watching the news afterward and checking my social media, I could see that most people were way happy that I did what I did. In fact, most of them thought it was ridiculous for the police to try to arrest me. Of course, Wendi thought I was a nuisance and should be stopped at all costs. Sigh.

Oh, it also feels weird to be saved by Tanya. I know it shouldn't but it does. Okay, I admit it, I am a little kind of slightly jealous of her relationship with Jason. Yep, I have to share Jason, and I have to learn to deal with that, pronto. I can do it. If I can catch a falling plane out of the air and land it safely, surely I can learn to live with a nice girl getting along really well with my BFF. Man, I just used the word really a real lot. ☺

Surprises

The next morning I looked forward to going to school and dreaded it at the same time. Part of me was so anxious to learn how the rest of the school reacted to Super Teen's saving of the plane. I wasn't thrilled though with the idea of watching Tanya and Jason interact with each other.

While sitting at the breakfast table, of course, Mom had to notice the frown on my face. "What's wrong?" she asked.

"What do you mean, Mom?"

Mom pointed at my stack of pancakes. "You've hardly touched your pancakes!"

"Mom, I've eaten three stacks!"

"Yes, Lia, for you, that is just a warm up snack. You need your energy, especially if you're catching falling planes!"

I crushed my fork in my hand. "Oops! Sorry, Mom."

"Something tells me this isn't just about the lawsuit and the police trying to arrest you," Mom said.

"I'm not a criminal, Mom! I help people!"

Mom grinned. "I know. Once people understand that, this will blow over." She shrugged. "Besides honey, the police can't hold you. The only people who ***might*** be able to do that would be those at your dad's company."

"Still, I don't like being thought of as a criminal," I groaned.

"The truth will come out!" Mom insisted. She looked at me as I stared at my breakfast. "But something else is on your mind."

"Yeah," I admitted. "Jason and Tanya are talking a lot. They're getting real friendly. I overheard Jason telling Tanya how excited he is about comet K-9. The one that's going to pass just 50,000 miles from Earth. He says he can't wait to see it on his telescope with her!"

Mom grinned. "Ah, good for Jason, that Tanya is quite pretty!"

"Mom…not helping! Just a few days ago, Jason said he wanted to see that comet with me!" I slammed my hand on the table, breaking the table in half. "Oops…"

"That's coming out of your allowance, young woman!"

"Fair enough," I sighed.

Mom's eyebrow popped up. "My keen mom instincts tell me you're not happy with Jason growing closer to Tanya. Do you like Jason as more than a great friend?"

I actually thought about my response. "No, yes, maybe…" It was hard to believe I had to think before making such an indecisive response.

"What you're trying to say is, you don't know," Mom said with her hand on my shoulder.

"Exactly," I moaned.

"Well honey, I hate to say this, but you are being very selfish."

My eyes popped open. "Say what?"

"Just because you don't know how you feel about Jason doesn't mean he can't build relationships with other girls. Especially when that girl is as nice as Tanya. She's older right?"

"Not helping, Mom!"

Mom just smiled. "Not much I can do here to help. Though I can help you see when you're being selfish." Mom pointed to the front door. "Jason is here, go walk to school with your BFF."

I stood up. My first thought was to get up and walk away. Instead, I leaned into Mom and kissed her. "Thanks, Mom."

I met Jason on the porch. I had to admit I was really glad Tanya wasn't with him. Jason, of course, was all smiles. "Man, Lia, that rescue of the plane by Super Teen yesterday was awesome!" he said loudly.

I smiled and nodded. "It was," I agreed.

We headed in the direction of the school. "Plus, the way you used your head and your powers to slow the plane down, that was amazing!" Jason continued. "Your powers and knowledge of your powers is growing each day!"

"Thanks," I told him with a friendly shove.

"Plus, I loved watching you and Tanya team up like that!" Jason added.

Yeah, he just had to bring up Tanya. "So, how are we going to stop your dad from arresting me?" I asked.

Jason stopped walking for a second. "Actually, that one may be pretty easy. The lawsuit says that Super Teen isn't a deputy of the court."

"I am aware. And no, I am not," I said, dragging Jason towards the school.

Jason raised a finger and grinned. "But you could be. My dad actually has the power under the town's charter, to deputize you. Heck, Governor Tom Condor could do it for the entire state if he wished.

Now I stopped walking. "Wait, so this is possible? How can we make it happen?"

"Well, we need an online petition," Jason said. He showed me his phone. There on the screen was a web page: Let's get Super Teen Deputized. "We already have 5000 signatures," Jason told me.

I hugged him, lifting him off the ground. "Jason, you're amazing!"

"Hey, just doing my share to help make the world a better place," he smiled. "Now please put me down."

"Right!" I said dropping him to the ground.

We reached the school with me feeling better than I had since this whole Kalie thing had started. This looked as though it could work out well for me. Of course, my mood shifted when I saw Wendi and Patti rushing over to me.

"So?" Wendi said.

"Yeah, so?" Patti said.

"So what?" I asked.

"Any progress on changing the school lunches? Adding more green? Maybe getting a vegan option?" Wendi said.

"Maybe getting more dessert choices," Patti offered.

Wendi shot her a disapproving glance.

"Hey, I workout hard for this body!" Patti said pointing to her hips. "I deserve a little dessert now and then."

They both turned their venom towards me. "So?"

"I have an appointment to talk to VP Macadoo before classes," I said, lying a bit. But hey, sometimes when it comes to dealing with mean girls, it's easier to let them hear what they want to hear. Well, it would have been easiest and most fulfilling to drop them with super BO, but not very hero-like.

Patti and Wendi strutted away, a pleased look on each of their faces. At least, they appeared as pleased as Wendi and Patti can be when they aren't making somebody else feel miserable. I headed to VP Macadoo's office. I walked by Jason talking with Tanya at her locker. I gave them both a nod and a smile. Jason deserved to be happy.

VP Macadoo's office manager, Barb Bane met me outside of his office. She was a cold, unfriendly woman. I figured she lived with like a million cats.

"What can I do for you, Miss Strong?" she said in a sharp and irritable tone.

"I would like to see the VP. It's official class and school business," I told her.

She didn't even check his availability before replying. "I'm sorry, he's busy all week working on real issues, not student's concerns."

I pointed at her and said with my command voice, "He'll see me now!"

Barb Bane smiled. She waved to his office like she was showing me a prize I had won. "Of course, he will see you now. He's just playing his morning game of solitaire on his computer."

Walking into VP Macadoo's office, he noticed me and quickly activated the screen saver on his computer. "Ms. Strong, what can I do for you?" he asked.

I sat down in the chair next to his desk. "I'm here on school business."

"I would hope so, Ms. Strong."

"Many of the students want to see a change in the school lunches. They would like more options, especially more green options. And by green, I don't mean foods that aren't supposed to be green."

VP Macadoo chuckled. That relieved my stress a little. "I love that idea," he said.

"You do?" I asked. He'd caught me off guard. I didn't expect it to go so easily. Had I worked up a sweat for nothing?

"I do." He nodded.

"So it's settled?" I asked.

He frowned and shook his bald head. "I do wish it was, but for that to happen, the order has to come from the school board."

"Then let's make an appointment to see the school board," I said.

"Well, there is a meeting tomorrow," he said.

"Great!" I smiled.

He lowered his head. "But they won't see me." He sighed. "They never want to listen to me."

Wow, who would have thought that big strong Mr. Macadoo could be so easily brushed aside?

"Wait, weren't you a navy seal?" I asked him.

"Yes, I served the country proudly. But the board says I am only a vice-principal and it's my job to discipline, not to give suggestions...." He told me.

"That doesn't seem right," I said.

"I agree, but I'm still a good soldier and I listen to orders from those above me."

"What about the principal?" I asked.

Mr. Macadoo shrugged his huge shoulders, "He says it's his job to keep the school afloat. He can't sweat the little stuff. But you know what, I'll ask the board again."

"Okay, if they say no I'll just show up anyhow!" I said. "I can be very convincing!"

Mr. Macadoo held out a meaty hand. "Let's hope for the best then, Lia."

Dear Diary: Things certainly went differently than I expected. First off, sure Jason may be getting closer to Tanya but he's still my BFF. He always has my back. I feel great about that. He's trying to help me become a legit crime fighter. Man, I would never have thought of creating a petition! Second, I always thought of Mr. Macadoo as this big gruff guy who really didn't care much about the students. He wanted discipline above all else – or so I believed. Turns out he does want what's best for us, he just has very little actual power. Well, I am going to do whatever I have to do to get into that board meeting tomorrow to convince them we need better lunch choices. Sure, I am kind of doing Wendi's bidding, but when she's right, she's right.

Time and Space

Sitting up in my room that night, I wanted to do something nice and normal. I decided I would work on my history report. We had to write a 500-word report on a person in history who we thought was amazing. I tossed around a lot of names: Einstein, Joan of Arc, Gandhi, Mrs. Gandhi, Madam Curie, Michael Jackson, Babe Ruth, Mother Teresa, Lincoln, Malala…after all, she wasn't much older than me. But I settled on Leonardo da Vinci. I mean the guy was amazing.

In fact, I think da Vinci may have been the first super hero! Heck, there's even a teenage mutant ninja turtle named after him! I mean, come on, the man painted the Mona Lisa!

He was an amazing artist but it didn't stop there! He lived almost 500 years ago but he had diagrams and plans for flying machines, a mechanical knight, and parachutes. Plus, he made and played his own musical instruments. He created the first texts on human anatomy. Oh heck, it was even said he could bend horse shoes. Yep, I'd made a great choice here! The guy was amazing! The trick now was to keep from writing too many words. Believe you me that hardly ever happened.

Who would have thought I could have fun doing a paper for school?

My thoughts were interrupted by a text from Jason.

Jason>Hey
Lia>Hey. What's up?
Jason>I'm at BMS Labs
Lia>Why so late?
Jason>Kayla is having some issues…
Lia>Wait, Kayla is still there?
Jason>Yeah, she decided she feels more comfortable here
Lia>Ah…ok…

Sure, that was kind of weird that Kayla felt more comfortable in a cold sterile lab than with her mom and sister. But I guess when you are young and have powers, you might find some comfort in a controlled place like the lab.

Lia>So, y r u there?
Jason>Kayla is having some issues…she wants 2 b here but she's also homesick.
Lia>Fair enough. But y r u there?
Jason>Well, I was just talking with Tanya at her home
Lia>Okay
Jason>And the next thing we knew we were both here
Lia>Yikes!!
Jason>In fact…her entire home is now here ….
Lia> That's either cool or creepy
Jason>It's a little of both

Lia>So do you need me?
Jason>W…
Lia>Jason?
Lia>Jason???
Lia>Jason???
I turned to MAC. "MAC what's going on at the lab?"
No response.
"Mac?"
Still none.

This couldn't be good. I raced to my window, threw it open and then leaped towards BMS labs. I didn't know what was wrong but I knew something was. My gut and my brain both told me this was bad! Way bad. Flying through the air, I started thinking, *how bad can this be… Kayla is only like 8 years old. I mean how much damage can she do?*

I landed where the lab should be. There was nothing there except a house. It was a nice normal looking red roofed house with an attic window. It was an average type of house, yet it totally freaked me out.

"Hello?" I called.

My voice echoed back to me.

"Now this is creepy…." I said.

"It sure is." I heard from behind me.

I literally jumped fifty feet in the air. I landed and turned towards the voice. It was Janitor Jan. She stood there with Lorie and Marie by her side.

Patting my chest I said, "You scared the heck out of me. What the heck are you doing here?"

Jan looked at me. "I detected a disturbance in the force!"

"Say what?" I said.

Jan grinned. "I felt a ripple in time and space. It led here. I brought these two along, because well, you will need backup."

"Where's Jess?" I asked.

Jan shook her head. "She's part of that ripple. I can't find her…."

Lori looked at the lone house standing in the dark where a massive lab had been. "Please tell me I'm not the only one freaked out by this…"

"You are so not!" Marie told her. She shivered.

I looked at Jan. "So you're the most experienced of us all…"

"You mean I'm old," Jan grinned.

"Have you dealt with anything like this before?" I asked.

Jan nodded her head. "A displacement in time and space? Sure, every day. Turn somebody into a toad…that's a displacement in time and space."

"Phew," I said. Then how do we deal with this?"

Jan shrugged. No idea at all." She pointed at the house. Turning a person into a toad is a small, tiny displacement in time and space. Removing a huge complex and replacing it with a house, now that's a big freaky displacement. I have no idea, none at all, zilch."

She leaned towards the house. "Never in my almost 50 years have I seen anything like this! The power.... the pure raw power..." She collected herself. "Why are you here?"

"I am Super Teen," I said.

Jan rolled her eyes. "Yeah I know that, but how did you know to show up here?"

Oh, I was on the phone texting with Jason and he just stopped texting. I knew he was here with Tanya. They were trying to calm down Kayla...."

"Wait, Kayla is still here?" Marie asked. "Why?"

"Apparently, she likes it here," I said.

"Well she likes the spot.... but not the lab," Lori said.

Jan walked past me up to the front door.

"What are you doing?" I asked.

She looked back over her shoulder at me and said, "Knocking on the door, of course!"

Jan knocked on the door three times.

She waited.

No answer.

Jan put her ear to the door. "Hmm, I hear breathing..."

"From inside?" I asked.

"Nope, from the door, the door is breathing."

"Say what?" Marie said.

Jan pointed to the door. "This door has a person inside of it..." She put her hands on her hips. "I thought I was pretty clear." She tapped on the door. "There is a person inside this door."

"How could that be?" Lori asked.

"I'm guessing that Kayla didn't like this person so she put them in a door. Kind of makes sense in its own weird way."

"Can you get them out of there?" I asked.

Jan ran her hand up and down the door slowly. "Nice oak," she said. "And nope. They are part of the door. This isn't magic, this is manipulating time and space at a greater scale."

"Then how do we free them?" I asked.

Jan pushed the door open. "Easy, we convince whoever did this to let the person out and put everything back the way it should be."

"How do we do that?" I asked.

Jan walked into the house. "How the heck should I know?"

We followed Jan inside and entered a big living room area. There, on the fairly modern looking couch, sat Tanya and Kayla. They had their eyes locked on each other. And they were surrounded by a shimmering transparent bubble.

"Took you guys long enough to get here," Tanya said. "Not sure how much longer I can hold her. I may have more power than Kayla, but she's not afraid to use the full force of her power. I'm keeping her from ripping time apart."

I was not really sure what Tanya meant by ripping time apart, but I felt pretty confident it couldn't be good.

"How can we help?" I asked.

"Kayla, here, has let the power get to her little head. We have to stop her!" Tanya said.

"How?" I repeated.

Tanya turned towards me. "She's a kid…knock her out!"

"Right." Taking a step forward, I touched the glowing sphere. I was abruptly shot back and bounced off a wall.

"But don't touch the sphere," Tanya warned me, a second too late.

"Right, got that," I stammered, stumbling to my feet.

"I'm trying to keep her from increasing the size of the sphere… if she does, time will be changed all around us," Tanya said. "But it's way hard. Like I said before, she doesn't care about consequences. Just results."

Jan raised a finger. "We can help keep that sphere from growing. Between my magic, the energy from Lori's bio-bionics and Marie's molecular rearrangement ability, we can hold it steady!"

"You sure?" Lori asked.

Jan laughed. "No of course not, but it's all we can do."

Jan, Lori, and Marie outstretched their arms and concentrated on the sphere. The sphere condensed then expanded, condensed then expanded, kind of like a bouncing ball hitting the ground.

"We can hold her for now!" Jan said. She looked at me. "You gotta get in there and knock her out!"

"How? I can't touch that sphere." Then it hit me. "I can teleport in!" I shouted.

"Ah, you can't teleport," Lori told me.

"True, but Ellie Mae Opal can, and she's just one town over in Moon Town. Be back in a flash." I darted out of the room at super speed. I jumped into the air and headed towards Moon Town. I smiled. That name always makes me laugh. I guess it's nice to know I can still laugh in the face of little eight-year-old Kayla rewriting time.

I was standing at Ellie Mae's front door in less than three minutes. Man, I was getting fast. Okay, it wasn't the best time to be congratulating myself. I knew it was late and Ellie Mae was probably getting ready for bed, but when you are protecting time, sleep can wait.

I knocked on the door.

Ellie's mom, Jeanie opened the door. "Lia, what's wrong?" she asked.

"I need Ellie to teleport me into a temporal sphere to stop a little kid from rewriting time!" I said.

Jeanie put her hands on her hips and grinned. "Is that all?"

She turned towards the staircase. "Ellie, come downstairs. Lia is here to see you."

In a poof, Ellie Mae stood next to me. She had pink PJs on. "What's up, Lia? I was just brushing my teeth for bed."

"Ah, I need you to teleport me into a temporal sphere so I can stop Tanya's little sister from changing time!"

"Oh, that would be bad." She turned to her mom. "Can I go, Mom?"

Jan nodded. "Yes, of course!"

Taking Ellie by the hand I said, "Come on, I'll fly us there."

Ellie laughed. "Too slow. Where do we need to go?"

"BMS Labs!" I told her.

The next thing I knew we were standing outside of the red roofed house that stood where BMS once did.

"Oh, how freaky!" Ellie said.

We rushed into the house. Jan, Lori, and Marie still had their arms outstretched, they were each covered with sweat. The sphere pulsated faster and faster.

Ellie Mae pointed to the inside of the sphere. "So you want to go in there?"

"Yes."

Ellie licked her thumb and held it up. "Hmm, I have to take into account temporal drift." She took my hand. We blinked forward.

I found myself standing right on top of Kayla. "Hey!" she said.

I pinched her on the side of her neck. She dropped to the floor. The house flashed once, then twice. I noticed Jason fall out of the door. Well, that explained who was in the door. We were standing in a bedroom in BMS labs. Kayla laid on the floor. Dad, Hana and a bunch of scientists and security personnel looked on, confused.

"What happened?" Hana asked.

"My little sis made you all go bye-bye," Tanya said.

Dad scratched his head. "Amazing…"

"Hard to compute," Hana said.

"Scary," Marie said. We all nodded in agreement. Well, all of us, except for Dad.

Dad went into full mad scientist mode. "Truly amazing." He concentrated on Tanya. "She has your power without your control, and without the limitations you place on yourself. So amazing."

"You keep saying that," I said to Dad. "It's not amazing, it's scary."

Dad shook his head. "It is amazingly scary but the potential has so much potential." Dad pointed to a couple of scientists in white lab coats who were standing nearby.

"Put her on her bed and keep her under sedation," Dad instructed the scientists.

"I'm not sure I like that!" Tanya protested. "She's just a kid, a dumb, scared kid."

Dad looked Tanya in the eyes. He turned away just a little. "Would you prefer her changing time again?" he asked. "Making poor Jason a part of a door."

"No, of course not," Tanya said.

"Yeah, what was that all about?" Lori asked.

Tanya sighed. "Apparently, my little sis thought Jason might come between us. So...."

"Wow, holy symbolic time change," Jason said.

"Do you remember anything?" I asked Jason.

"Just Kayla glaring at me..."

"We'll keep her in her room, sedated. It's lucky she is here because we can teach her to control her powers. Once we control her control, we will ease up on the sedation. All will be well," Dad said.

"I believe that is a wise course of action," Hana said.

Yep, it wasn't a surprise that Hana agreed with Dad. After all, he did create her to be his personal "yes women". But I kind of agree too. I feel bad for Kayla, but uncontrolled power like hers has to be kept restrained.

Dad kept his attention locked on Tanya. "Has this incident made you inclined to accept more training for yourself and your sister?" he asked.

"That would be wise," Hana told her.

Tanya took a step back. "I'm not a kid who can't control her urges…" She took a slow breath. "I can control my power."

"You sure?" Hana asked.

Tanya locked her gaze on Hana. Hana shrunk down to the size of a toy. In fact, she became a small wind-up toy. Tanya bent over, picked Hana up and wound her up. She put Hana down on the ground. Hana mechanically walked away. Tanya grinned. Hana became Hana again.

"Yes, I am sure!" Tanya said.

"Amazing," Dad said.

"Wow," Jason gushed.

"Okay, I gotta admit that was impressive," Jan said.

"Good control of power," Marie said.

"You're so cool," Lori told her.

Jason nudged me. "Isn't she amazing?" he asked.

"She sure is…" I sighed.

Ellie Mae walked over to me and grinned. "It's past my bed time. Do you mind if I port myself back home?"

I returned her grin. I gave her hug. "No of course not, you were great. We couldn't have done it without you."

She hugged me back. "Just glad to be part of the team." She disappeared in my arms.

I looked at my phone. A text had popped in.
Ellie Mae> Home and tucked in. Goodnight.
Lia>☺

Dear Diary: Not sure what bugged me more… Jason hanging out with Tanya, Kayla's raw power, or Tanya's control of her power. Or my dad being so fascinated with their power. Or Jason being so impressed with Tanya. Okay, I gotta admit, this is a side of me I don't like. I don't enjoy being jealous. But am I being jealous or just cautious? I mean, come on, Kayla pretty much made all of BMS labs just go away. If we hadn't all teamed up to stop her, who knows what would have happened? And she's only a kid. Dad says that's part of the problem…she doesn't know how to control all that raw power. But really, does anybody know how to control all that power? Maybe Tanya being older and more in control could make her more dangerous?

I gotta shake these feelings and thoughts out of my head. Tanya is a nice girl, a friend. A friend who likes Jason and who Jason likes back. I can't let being jealous cloud my judgment. Besides, once I got to her I was able to take Kayla out with a pinch. I could do the same to Tanya if I ever had to. But I would never have to – right? Of course, I wouldn't!

Am I a bad person for even thinking like this? I know in the comics Batman had a plan to take out all the other superheroes if they went bad. He's Batman, he protects people, and it's what he does. So, I'm just being protective of my people. Right? I take my role as protector very seriously. (Even if the police and the law don't want me to.) I'm just doing what I was born to do…making sure everybody is safe. I'm covering all my bases.

Plus, Jason seems happy and I have to learn to be happy for him. Yes, as a friend I have to support him. That's what I'll do. Okay, I've got to get some sleep. Tomorrow, I deal with something just as scary as a time controlling kid – the board of education.

Questions

Arriving home from a long weird evening, I found Mom in the living room having coffee and cake with Oscar Oranga and Kalie Hanson. Great! Just when I needed to talk to Mom about my super problems, I find the two people who are trying to stop Super Teen in my house! Oscar wasn't a big surprise. After all, he and my mom are dating. I guess the universe doesn't want my life to be too easy. But Kalie…now that was somebody I wasn't expecting. That Oscar, he'll stop at nothing to get a story.

"Ah, hi," I said walking into the room.

Mom and Oscar smiled at me. Mom pointed at Kalie, "Lia honey, I assume you know the world famous lawyer, Kalie Hanson."

Kalie grinned and looked away. "Oh please, I'm far from ***World*** famous. "

I offered Kalie my hand. She took it with a firm grip. "Well, you are kind of famous," I said. "After all, you're trying to stop Super Teen from helping people."

Kalie released my hand. Looking me in the eyes, she said, "I'm keeping her from hurting people. She has no training."

I crossed my arms and glared at her, concentrating hard on not to fry her with heat vision. "She has great power!"

"All the more reason she needs training!" Kalie glared back.

"I hear she's training with BMS labs!" I said far more defensively than I would have liked.

Kalie nodded. "So they have shown us with some training videos. But I don't trust them much more than Super Teen." She looked at me. "Frankly, I'm surprised you trust them so much, given your personal history with their founder."

Well, well, Kalie certainly had done her homework.

Mom stood up. "No reason to bring my ex-husband into this!"

Oscar cleared his throat. "Yes, Kalie, no need to bring up her super rich ex-husband."

"I thought it was relevant. He hasn't been the most responsible father figure to you. Why do you think he can be a good guide to Super Teen?"

"Cause the two aren't related," I insisted.

"Sure they are!" Kalie argued. "If the man wasn't a good father to you, why do you think he can help Super Teen? And if he did help, I would think you'd be jealous."

I knew Kalie was trying to get me to lose my cool. So I did. Using my command voice, I ordered, "Oscar, you're a dog. Kalie, you're a fire hydrant!"

Kalie stood up, dropped her arms to her sides and went stiff. Oscar dropped to all fours and crawled over to Kalie. He started sniffing her.

"Lia!" Mom scolded.

"What?" I said. "It popped out of me. I did it by accident..."

Mom waved a finger at me. "Young lady, you don't accidentally make one person think they are a fire hydrant and another a dog!"

"At least I didn't make Oscar think he was a dog that had to pee," I said.

Mom crossed her arms. "He is my current boyfriend."

"Hence, the reason I took it easy on him." I looked at Mom. "But come on, Mom, he brought Kalie Hanson into the house...the woman who is trying to stop me from helping people!"

"She thinks she's doing the right thing!" Mom insisted.

"Well, she's wrong. I help people!"

Mom pointed at Oscar and Kalie. "How is ***this*** helping anyone?"

It did help *me* feel better but I knew that wouldn't help my argument. I sighed and looked at Mom. "She was bad mouthing Dad."

"Your dad is a big boy with a lot of resources. He can defend himself. Plus, I know you mumble complaints about him sometimes, too."

"He's my dad, I'm allowed to complain."

"She's a lawyer, it's her job to protect the city."

"Mine too, Mom."

"Then it looks like you need to convince Kalie that she and Super Teen are on the same side. And fast, before my boyfriend wets her."

Mom had a point. By doing what I was doing, was kind of supporting Kalie's argument that I could be dangerous. This might be considered an abuse of power.

"Sorry Mom, I just have to put up with so much of this bullying stuff at school. I don't like having to deal with it at home as well. Kalie reminds me of other mean girls."

Mom put a hand on my shoulder. "She's a woman doing a job. Not a girl trying to make herself feel better by making you feel worse!"

"Wow, Mom you know mean girls so well."

"Trust me, honey, mean girls are not a modern phenomenon. It's just that these days, social media makes it so much more anonymous and easy to be mean."

"True that," I said.

"You need to use your words not your powers," Mom told me.

"Got it." I pointed to Oscar, who had a leg raised at Kalie. "You two, go back to being people and forget about this!"

Oscar lowered his leg. He stood up and walked back to his seat. Kalie sat down. Her eyes blinked.

"Sorry, I lost my train of thought for a moment," she said.

Oscar jumped up. "Excuse me, I have to rush to the bathroom." He darted out of the room.

I sat on the chair next to Kalie. "My point is, Super Teen is just trying to help."

"My point is, she's not qualified to help. She's a kid and not a deputy," Kalie countered.

"There's the petition that's getting signatures to make her a deputy!" I said.

"I saw. Hopefully, the police chief will be wise enough to ignore it. The will of the people is prone to emotion, not logic," Kalie said.

"Super Teen has saved the town a number of times," I replied.

"True, she's also knocked out the mall, dropped herds of cattle with farts, dropped charging rhinos with BO. The list goes on...."

"But all those people and animals just took naps. There was no lasting harm done," I said.

Kalie shrugged. "She got lucky."

"Come on, fighting a giant robot isn't luck. She saved the town and more."

"I will give you that. But since Super Teen has shown up, other super beings have also appeared. Like that Glare Girl," Kalie said.

Oscar walked back into the room. "Yeah, she's nasty. I've had experience with her. She's just in it for the fame."

"See!" Kalie said.

"Just because one super being is a fool doesn't mean Super Teen is out to do harm!" I said.

Kalie looked at her watch. "It's getting late. I should be going." She stood up. "I'll call an uber."

Oscar jumped to his feet. "I brought you. I should drop you home." He looked at Mom. "If that's okay with you, honey?"

The word 'honey' almost made me barf. But Oscar somehow makes Mom happy so I fought down the barf.

"That's fine, honey, I'm on call tomorrow."

Kalie smiled. She looked at me. "Now, your mom is a real hero. She has the training and the knowledge to save people."

"She does," I agreed.

Kalie patted me on the shoulder. "Look, Lia, I get it. It's cool to see a person your age using super powers and seemingly helping people.

But if I ever see Super Teen, I will tell her…I appreciate what you are trying to do. Get some training from trained professionals. Go to the police academy and come back when you are older. Use your power wisely."

"I hope you do get to meet her and tell her that!" I said.

Kalie grinned. "Hopefully, she won't use her command voice on me and make me do something ridiculous," she smirked.

Oscar gave Mom a kiss. (That I could barely watch.) Then I watched him and Kalie leave. Once we heard Oscar's car rev up, I turned to Mom.

"Do you think she knows anything?"

"She knows a lot of stuff, she's a lawyer and a sharp lady."

"Ha. Do you think she has any idea I could be Super Teen?"

"I doubt it," Mom said. "But just be careful around her." Mom looked at me. "So where did you head off to earlier in such a hurry?"

I groaned. "To BMS labs…I was texting Jason. He was there with Tanya trying to comfort Kayla then he went silent. Plus MAC went silent too. So I flew there as fast as I could."

"And?" Mom said.

"Kayla had replaced the lab with a strange, eerie version of her own home, complete with Jason as a door."

Mom's eyes narrowed. "Alright now, that just seems freaky."

"Believe me, weird doesn't begin to cover it. Especially when you are there looking at it. If there was creepy music, I would have thought I was watching a horror movie. But this was actually real life. At least, how my real life has become."

"How did you stop her?"

"Tanya held her off with the help of Jan, Marie, and Lori. I got that cute little Ellie Mae to come and teleport me next to Kayla. I knocked her out with a neck pinch and everything went back to normal."

"Kayla's power is amazing and scary…."

"True, luckily beneath that power is a scared, average eight or nine-year-old. Doesn't take much to stop her."

Mom quivered a little. "It could have been very bad if you hadn't stopped her. How did your dad react?"

"Dad was kind of like a kid in a candy store. He loves Kayla and Tanya's potential. But he did acknowledge that Kayla will be dangerous until she learns some control. Like Tanya has."

"How are YOU handling all this?" Mom asked me.

"Which part? Jason hanging out with Tanya? Or me seeing Kayla's power? Or do you mean, realizing that Tanya has the power? Or maybe, coming home to the reporter who is trying to figure out my secret identity, as well as the lawyer who's trying to stop me from helping the world? Which one are you referring to, Mom?"

"I didn't know Oscar was bringing Kalie, but he thinks of her as his ticket to the big city media."

"Is that what ***you*** want, Mom?"

"I'm okay with whatever he decides. I like the guy, he's nice and makes me feel good. But I won't stand in the way of his career. This is about you, though. Jason has always been your BFF."

I smiled. "He still is. It's just that now I have to share him more. But he's happy and that makes me happy."

As weird as it was, that was the truth. Jason was a great guy and he deserved a great girl. I had to admit, Tanya was a great girl.

Dear Diary: Yes, I might have abused my power a little on Kalie, but she had it coming. She's trying to stop Super Teen from doing her job. She bad mouthed my dad. She's so high and mighty.

But yeah, I really shouldn't have mind-controlled her like that. That might have felt way good but it was wrong (well wrong-ish) ☺

Her last comment kind of freaked me out though. Could she have any idea that I am Super Teen? Nah, no way. Right?

Mental Links and TP

As I walked to school with Jason, we talked about the events of the day before.

"Unbelievable that you had a face to face with Kalie Hanson in your own home yesterday!" Jason said.

"Yeah, I really wasn't expecting that. I mean, come on. You don't expect to see your arch enemy sitting on your recliner."

"She's not really an arch enemy. She's a lady trying to do a job." Jason reminded me.

"I know, but arch enemy seems more fitting. Then again, I guess Wendi would be my real arch enemy. Even though, Glare Girl claims she wants it to be her."

"Wendi isn't sharp enough and Glare Girl is nicer than she lets on," Jason said.

"So, how did it feel to be a door?" I asked. Part of me wanted to snicker, a bigger part was concerned.

"Weird. I was kind of me but then at the same time, I was a door," he shivered. "Can't really explain it. It was like I had a brain but I was a door...."

"Sounds freaky," we heard the familiar voice of Jess say.

We saw Jess and cute little half-vampire Felipe walking towards us.

I grinned. "Jess, I haven't seen you at school lately. Where have you been?"

"I decided to try home-schooling. I've been finding school...how do I say this politely...way boring and filled with jerks." Jess said.

"Glad you were being polite," I told her.

Jess shook her head, her hair was now black but with red streaks, it worked on her. "Nothing to do with you two. But there are so many mean girls at school. I decided if I hang out there much longer, I'll vanish them – or worse."

"What's worse than being vanished?" Jason asked.

"I'm not sure I want to know…" I said.

"My own personal TP."

"By TP, you mean toilet paper, not an Indian home. Correct?" Jason asked.

"Smart boy!" Jess answered.

"Yeah, probably a good thing you decided to try home-schooling," I told Jess.

Turning to Felipe, I asked him, "And where have you been, Felipe?"

Felipe glided up and hugged me. "My family when on vacation!" he said bouncing up and down.

"Oh, where did you go?" Jason asked.

"Transylvania," Felipe said. "It was way cool. I had to wear a coat and everything."

"Ah, funny," Jason said.

Felipe shook his head. "No joke. That place is cold! But still fun. I'm hoping though, next year we go to Disneyland."

I nodded. "Yeah, that would be fun too…"

Felipe looked me in the eyes. "How's Kayla doing?"

"Why do you ask?" I asked, a bit taken aback.

"Ah, sometimes, once in a while, I feel her thoughts," Felipe said, shaking a bit.

Now, that may have been a little freaky, but it certainly wasn't surprising. I've pretty much figured out that in my world now, anything goes. It kind of made sense that two powered kids would be on the same mental wavelength.

"Oh?" I said, cautiously. "So what has she been thinking?"

Felipe shook his head and shrugged his shoulders. "Not sure, she seems angry, sad, confused, scared..."

"That pretty much sums her up," Jason said under his breath.

Felipe's half-vamp hearing picked that up loud and clear. "What does that mean?"

I bent down to him. I looked him in the eyes. "It means she is just learning to use her powers and her powers scare her."

Felipe thought for a minute. "I think she thinks other people are scared of her too...."

I nodded. "Yeah, she may be right there."

"I certainly am scared of her!" Jason said.

I gave Jason a glare. He took a step back. "Sorry, slipped out, but I am," Jason said.

"Why? Kayla is nice!" Felipe insisted.

Leaning into Felipe I said softly, "She's still learning to control her powers. That's going to take some time because, well, her powers involve time, and that's complicated."

Felipe smirked. "I get it. But she'll be alright?" he asked, a worried frown crossing his face.

"My dad and his best people are working with her. I am sure she will be fine," I said.

"Okay, I trust you," Felipe smiled. He gave me another hug. "Thanks, Lia!"

"No problem, kid!"

I heard Jess's voice in my mind, *"You're not lying to the kid. Are you?"*

I thought back, *"I don't lie."*

"Are you holding back any truth?" Jess thought to me.

I considered my thoughts very carefully. Jess was not a person to mess around with. There was so much going on, I needed Jess on my side. Or at the very least, not against me. *"The kid is scared, people are scared of her. Everyone is wary of her except my father who is fascinated by her…"* I thought to Jess.

Jess smirked and thought back to me, *"Your father is an odd man. But I like him, he's easy to read. If you trust him, I do too."*

Once again I considered my thoughts carefully. *"I do trust him. He is my dad and he's been a big help. Yeah, sometimes he lets the science get in the way of logic; if that makes any sense. But he means well. He truly wants to help,"* I thought to her.

"Why are you two just looking into each other's eyes?" Jason asked.

"I think they must be mind-chatting," Felipe said.

"Oh cool," Jason said. "Right, mind chatting." He stopped to think about his next words. "I guess it's best if I don't ask what you were talking about."

"Smart boy," I said.

MAC beeped from my arm. "Ms. Lia, the school bell is in ten minutes. Unless you are planning to move at super speed, you'd better get a move on."

Jess pointed at MAC. "I can't tell if that thing is cool or annoying."

"Cool!" MAC told her. "Very cool and helpful. I do not want Lia to be tardy."

"He's a little of both," I said.

"Hey, I can hear you!" MAC said. "Just because I'm a machine, doesn't mean I don't have feelings, well e-feelings."

"Mostly helpful," I said.

"I can live with that," MAC said. "You now have nine minutes until the bell."

Jason and I started walking to the school. "See you guys later," I said.

"Yeah!" Felipe said.

"Be cool," Jess said.

"You sure you don't want to come back to regular school?" I asked.

"You just want me to turn those mean girls into TP, don't you?"

I headed to school thinking she may actually be right.

Dear Diary: It's always nice to see Felipe. He brings a bit of added sunshine into my life with his upbeat spirit. Kind of interesting that he and Kayla share a little mental link. Well, I guess there aren't many young kids with power, so it makes as much sense as anything in my world does. I hope I reassured him. Heck, I hope I reassured myself. My dad may be a nearly mad scientist, but he does mean well. He does want to help the world, and teaching Kayla to control her powers will help the world. I know it will.

And yes, it was good to see Jess again. She never did fit quite in at school, but she is a friend and certainly somebody we want on our side. Maybe she'll come back to school sometime? Heck, maybe I do want Patti and Wendi to be turned into TP!

The Meeting

When we arrived at school, VP Macadoo was waiting at the door. He had a strange look on his face. I couldn't quite make out what was so unusual about it.

"Wow, I've never seen Mr. Macadoo smiling before," Jason whispered to me as we approached the VP.

That was it! The VP was actually smiling.

"Great and surprising news, Lia!" VP Macadoo beamed. "The school board will hear our augment for more diverse foods today at 3:30 pm."

"Oh good. But I'm not surprised," I said.

"I'm shocked! They've never positively acknowledged my requests before. They meet in the school conference room next to the teacher's staff room. I will meet you there."

"Sure," I said.

He pointed at Jason and me. "Now hurry to class, I wouldn't want to mark you two as tardy!"

For some reason, I started to sweat. Man, I hate nervous sweat cause it tends to burn through my deodorant. The weird thing was that I had no idea why I had this nervous sweat. I've fought androids, killer robots, alien queens, giant mad scientists and mutant apes. I could certainly handle a room full of normal people who just happened to have nothing to do, so they get put on the board of education. Yet for some reason, I nervously watched the clock all day.

In history class, I wasn't paying attention when Mr. P asked me what I thought the greatest invention of the 20th century was. I blurted out "toilet paper" because come on, it was a great invention.

I got the class to laugh, even though I still insisted it was an important invention for sure. But Mr. P pointed out that toilet paper or TP was actually invented well before the 20th century. Though he did say, modern toilet paper, the kind that rolls, was invented in the 19th century. So, I was sort of close. Mr. P had a way of making you feel good even when you messed up.

At lunch, I had to admit it felt kind of weird when Jason sat next to Tanya instead of me. But I forced myself to be happy for Jason. And for Tanya too. After all, Jason was a great guy. Any girl would be lucky to have him as a friend and more.

Tim and Krista noticed me staring a bit too long at Jason as he chatted and laughed with Tanya.

"You okay?" Tim asked.

"No thanks, I don't need the salt," I said.

Krista looked at Tim. "I think she just answered your question."

Krista nudged me. Normally I would have reacted, but I was so engrossed in Tanya and Jason, I didn't budge.

"Boy, you sure are solid!" Krista said.

"Yeah, she works out a lot," Marie said covering up for me.

"She just needs to concentrate more on the matters at hand," Lori said loudly.

I turned my attention back to my other friends. "Ah, sorry," I replied.

They all shrugged. "No problem. We understand this must be a bit weird for you," Krista said.

"That Jason is one lucky, dude," Tim said. "Man! Tanya is so pretty."

The other three girls at the table hit Tim with glares. He sank back into his chair. He nibbled on a fry.

"He's right," I said. "She's older than I am. She's prettier than I am. She has awesome power…"

Lori coughed.

"Power of persuasion," I finished.

Just as I sat there, wallowing in my woes, Patti and Wendi came marching over to me. Yep, nothing is ever so bad that Patti and Wendi can't make it worse.

They both shoved their food under my nose.

"Look at this!" Wendi said. "Do you see a lot of green in these meals?"

"I don't!" Patti answered.

I forced myself to look up at them. I contained myself from wilting them. I returned their glares. "Actually, I have an appointment to talk to the school board at 3:30 today!" I told them.

Patti dropped back. Wendi remained in my face. "Well, you might actually get something done. I'm surprised!"

"I'm not surprised you are surprised," I told her.

"Of course, we're helping you do your job," Wendi reminded me.

"How?" I asked.

Wendi turned her phone so I could see it. She had an online petition that read: *Give us More Healthy Foods at School.* "We have over 500 signatures," Wendi said.

I looked at the list. "Pretty sure that Snoopy, Elvis, Pikachu and Bart Simpson, don't go to this school," I told her. Still, it was a pretty impressive list.

"I think there might be a Bart Simpson," Patti insisted.

I glanced down the list. "Whatever. That will help, thanks."

"Hey, we're just helping you do your job!" Wendi told me.

"Thanks. I'll tweet my results after the meeting," I said.

"Hang on, I just figured out this means you won't be at LAX practice, today!" Wendi said. Yes sir, no matter what I did, Wendi could find something to complain about. I could cure the common cold and Wendi would complain that the medicine I'd invented didn't taste savory enough.

"I can be there at the start, then head off," I told her.

Wendi stood there in thought. "Nah, we don't want you getting all sweaty and smelly! You're going to have a hard enough time convincing the board even at your best. This is too important and too close to my heart as well as those of our school mates. I don't want you risking it all because of Lia body odor." She left on those words.

"I don't have Lia body odor!" I mumbled under my breath.

Marie and Lori both looked at me.

"Well, it's not ***that*** bad! And only when I get nervous."

"And you won't get nervous talking to the school board?" Tim asked.

"Okay, maybe a little."

Jason and Tanya had been listening intently to the conversation. "I can go with you if you want," Jason told me.

I smiled at him. "Actually, I would appreciate that," I answered. I looked at Tanya. "Is that okay with you?"

Tanya shrugged. "We're just dating. It's not like I own him. Of course, he can go. I know you guys are great friends."

I should have been relieved. But somehow, for some reason, hearing those words...*we're just dating*, made my heart sink. I forced a smile. "Thanks, Tanya," I told her.

The next thing I knew it was 3:30. I found myself standing outside the school conference room with my buddy, Jason, and VP Macadoo who seemed almost as nervous as I was.

"Finally," the VP grinned. "After all these years, the school board will hear my thoughts!"

"Well, actually ***my*** thoughts," I told him.

He grinned and bobbed his head. "Yeah, but when it comes to the food we serve, our thoughts are the same."

Now, that was a scary thought. But in a way, it was fun to be bonding with this big hulk of a man. Nice to see that he, like everybody else, had fears and goals. It made me smile.

"Of course, once I pitch the more green foods idea, I'll give them my other ideas," the VP said, rubbing his hands together.

"Such as?" Jason asked.

"Longer detentions, longer school days, more math, less art, just for a start," he rattled off.

"Oh..." Jason said.

Yeah, I wasn't a fan of any of those ideas. But I didn't want to mention it now. After all, VP Macadoo was my ticket into a board of education meeting. I couldn't risk that. I had to hope that after I said my piece, the board would be too busy to listen to anything else.

The door opened. An older looking woman with a beehive hairdo came out.

She looked at me. "Ms. Strong, the board will see you know."

I stood up. Jason and Mr. Macadoo both stood up also. The old lady held a hand up. "Sorry, Macadoo, the board only wants to talk to the student."

Mr. Macadoo looked at me, pleading with his eyes.

I shrugged. "Sorry!"

I followed the lady into the conference room. There, sitting at a big long table were eight older men in poorly fitting jackets, and three older women dressed like ancient grandmas. They looked like the type of people who had nothing else to do besides being on a school board. But the person at the head of the table was quite different. She was a very pretty younger woman who wore a stylish and fashionable outfit. She had the biggest blue eyes I'd ever seen. She certainly stuck out in this crowd. The others had donuts and coffee in front of them. She had a glass of water and nothing else. She smiled at me.

"Nice to meet you Ms. Strong. I'm Tina More. I'm head of the school board."

"Nice to meet you too, Ms. More," I said, sliding into my seat. "Wait, are you related to Tammy More? I know she's a great junior LAX player."

Tina smiled. "Yes, she's my daughter."

"I can tell. You have the same eyes," I told her.

"Thanks," she said. "Now, Ms. Strong do you mind if I call you, Lia?"

"No, not at all, that is my name," I told her with a smile.

"Lia, what can the school board do for you?"

I stood up. "Well, a lot of my fellow students would like more green food and more healthy lunch choices served at school. We also want healthier options for the breakfast menu, so the kids who eat breakfast at school can benefit from those as well."

Ms. More didn't blink. "That is an interesting request. We will take it into consideration."

Okay, I didn't come this far to let a bunch of older people tell me "we'll think about it." I've been around enough to know when I'm getting the brush off. This was the school board's version of "maybe". A maybe that meant most likely not.

I held my ground. "I'd like a more solid answer please."

Ms. More smirked and shook her head. "My, you are a feisty one. So, so much like your mom when she was your age."

"I'll take that as a compliment," I told her.

She nodded. "It was meant as one. Still, we can't just give in to every student request."

"This isn't every student request. This is just one that makes sense. We have an online petition with over 500 signatures."

"You kids today with your online petitions," Ms. More laughed. "As I said before, we'll take it into consideration." She shooed me away. "Now, run along please."

"No!" I said using my command voice. "You will approve of my request," I ordered.

I watched as the eyes of the eight men and three older ladies all glazed over. "We will approve it!" they repeated.

Tina More just grinned. "You are so much like your mom. Your powers won't work on me."

"Ah, what? I asked, unsure of what was going on.

In less than the blink of an eye, Tina stood behind me. "I'm super too, my cousin."

"Say what?" I repeated.

"The Mores and the Strongs are third cousins. We're super too. We just keep our powers to ourselves. After all, we're outnumbered by the non-powered. There are billions of them and maybe a hundred of us. If we come out like you do, sooner or later they will be after us and we will lose. After all, they are scared of us. Look at what that lawyer is trying to do to you."

"Look, the way to make people accept us is to show them we can help them and do good!" I insisted.

"Let's just agree to disagree," Tina told me. "You go around being a goodie in a cape. My family and I will stay behind the scenes."

"Fine," I said "But here's the thing. I really need to get this done for the school."

Tina sped back to her chair and sat down. "Okay, convince me."

I thought for a bit. What do school board members usually want? They want fame and proof that their school is better than all the other schools in the area. "We can claim to have the healthiest food in the district. You will be trendsetting. You'll become the school board who all the other school boards want to be like."

Tina grinned. "Convincing argument. I will add some green choices and more salads."

"Plus, you won't raise lunch prices. Correct?" I said.

Tina nodded. "Sure."

I walked up to her and offered my hand. She shook it. "We have a deal!"

I stood up and walked out of the room. Jason and VP Macadoo met me as soon as I opened the door.

"How'd it go?" Jason asked.

I gave him a thumbs-up. He leaped from his seat and hugged me. "You rock!" he said. The hug felt good.

VP Macadoo leaned over to me. "Did you manage to get in any of my talking points?" he asked.

"Sorry, no," I said. "Next time!"

Dear Diary: A couple things…First, I was able to get something done as school council president. That felt good, way good. Nice to know I can always do things without power. Of course, I also learned that my family isn't the only super powered family around. We have third cousins who also appear to have powers. I will have to talk to Mom about that.

I also think I was so cool when watching Jason with Tanya today. I handled it really well. I am getting this. I really am. Plus, Jason did hug me. But that was just a BFF hug. Right?

The Secret Revealed

When mom got home that night, I kind of ambushed her at the door.

"Why didn't you tell me about the Mores?" I demanded. Our faithful dog, Shep picked up on the tone of my voice and quickly ran out of the room.

Mom looked at me. "I'm fine too, honey. How was your day?"

I took a step back. I took a breath. Then another. "Sorry. I just met with the school board today. I got them to put more healthy green options on the school lunch and breakfast menus."

Mom walked over to the living room. She plopped down on a chair. She popped off her shoes. She leaned back. "That's great, Lia. But what's this about our third cousins?"

"Tina More, she's head of the school board," I said.

Mom put her arms behind her head. She sniffed herself. "Sorry. I probably should have mentioned our cousins to you sooner. But the Mores and Strongs have a long history of pretty much avoiding each other. Things got worse when I met your dad. Things got ***way*** worse when I married your dad."

"Why?"

"The Mores are very much into hiding their powers. They think we should all use them only in emergencies, for the most part. The Strongs are a bit less conservative. We like to be in the foreground with our powers and our careers. They like to do their work in the background. They are always the woman behind the man. And that's fine," Mom said.

"I kind of get that, but why did things get worse when you married Dad?" I asked.

"Ah, I thought that was obvious. Sorry, long day. The Mores think if regular folks keep seeing us, they will fear us and eventually come after us. They think your dad and his inventions will lead that charge."

"But Dad only wants to help!" I said.

Mom grinned. "Yeah, but some of them think he has alternative motives. They think he's planning to capture us all." She laughed. "The Mores didn't approve of my marriage to him at first. But then Tina told me it's a good way to keep an eye on him, keep him under control. Then when I left him, they didn't approve of that either. They actually thought I should wipe his mind. Which I would never do. That made a bigger rift. The Mores are good people, mostly. They are just worried and scared."

I took in Mom's words. Yeah, I could kind of see how some supers might be worried about Dad and his team of robots, scientists and all their inventions. They do appear to be helping us but they could also be studying us and looking for weaknesses; building weapons to stop us if they needed to. "But Dad has been a great help to me and the others," I argued.

"True, but Marie and Lori wouldn't be supers if it wasn't for scientists like your dad. Same with Ellie Mae and Glare Girl, they were made super by science. In fact, even Tanya and her sister were made by science. Sure, it was an accident, but science nevertheless. So, that's the More's other worry. That your dad and others like him are trying to make everybody super."

"Is that such a bad thing, Mom?" I asked. "Think of it as the world where everybody has powers...." To tell the truth, I wasn't sure if that would be good or bad. Then one of Mom's earlier statements got to me.

"Wait, you said most of the Mores like to stay in the background. That kind of tells me that one or two don't. How come I haven't bumped into them?"

Mom frowned. There is Kara More, she has the strange power of being able to duplicate another super's powers if she touches them. She can absorb a lot of powers making her difficult to deal with. Along with each power, she also takes on a little of their personality."

I shivered a little. "That's weird. Why haven't I seen her anywhere then?"

Mom laughed. "You have…on TV. She goes by the stage name, Kara Star."

"You mean the movie star, Kara Star?" I gasped. "I love her movies. The one where she was a vampire in love with a zombie was so good. She played the vampire part perfectly. Do you remember how amazing she was in that movie?" An image of Kara Star as a vampire came to mind. That movie was one of my all-time favorites.

Mom rolled her eyes. "Yeah, I remember."

"So much for the Mores being in the background," I said.

"Kara believes in hiding in plain sight," Mom told me. "She's not a bad person, she's just different and really wants success. Luckily, she has found it so she leaves the rest of us to live our lives." Mom licked her lips. "What do you say we get pizza for dinner?"

Shep came bounding back into the room.

We both smiled. "I swear sometimes he understands us," I said. "And pizza sounds great."

While waiting for the pizza, a text popped in from Jason.

JASON>Nice work with the board!
LIA>Thanks.
JASON>You okay?
LIA>Of course. Like u said, I got what we needed.
JASON>Walking home u seemed.... preoccupied.

My first thought was to type. Of course I was. I'm Super Teen. I always have something on my mind. Plus, I don't love seeing you, my BFF, being with one of my other friends. But I have to deal with that. Instead, I decided to tell Jason about the Mores. I probably should have mentioned it on the way home but I had to digest the info. At least that's what I told myself.

LIA>I learned something weird...
JASON>Okay what could possibly be weird these days????
LIA>There is another super powered family. The Mores!
LIA>But they mostly keep their powers secret
LIA>They are our third cousins
LIA>But they don't trust my dad.
JASON>Well that makes sense
LIA>??????!!!!
JASON>U know I love ur dad
JASON>He's a gr8 mind and a gr8 guy
JASON>But 2 others he might seem...

LIA>Evil mad scientist???

JASON>Well mad scientist

LIA>Thanks

JASON>So you can't blame supers for being worried.

LIA>Got it.

JASON>So u r cool with Tanya and Me?

My first response was going to be, No, No, No times 1000. Of course, I am not cool. Sure, I should be, but I'm not. Just because bullets don't hurt me doesn't mean my feelings can't be crushed. But that was selfish of me. I wanted to have my cake and eat it too. It occurred to me that with Tanya's time control powers she could have her cake and eat it too, over and over if she wanted. For some reason that made me smile.

LIA>I'm cool

JASON>Phew

JASON>You'll always be my BFF!

LIA>Ditto ☺

JASON>Need help with any homework?

LIA>I'm good. C U in the morning

JASON>Night BFF!

LIA>Night BFF!!!

Dear Diary: Short entry. Wow! So one of the biggest teen movie stars in the world, Kara Star is my super powered third cousin. That's neat and freaky at the same time. I am also slowly coming to terms with the idea of Jason being with Tanya. I am!!

More Surprises

When I arrived at school, Wendi and Patti met me at the door.

"So how bad did you fail with the school board?" Wendi mocked.

Patti just giggled then added. "Yeah!"

Wendi's boyfriend, the super cute Brandon actually stuck up for me. "Come on Wendi, I'm sure Lia did her best. That school board is so old and set in their ways, I don't think anybody can get them to change."

"Actually, Lia did," Jason said proudly.

"What?" Wendi and Patti gulped, mouths wide open. I kind of hoped a fly would fly in. No such luck though.

"Lia got them to offer more green and healthy choices!" Jason said.

Tanya, Marie, and Lori overheard our conversation and joined in. "Really?" Lori asked.

I nodded. "Yes. I can be very persuasive at times!"

Wendi put her hands on her hips and leaned into me. "I'll believe it when I get proof."

On cue, VP Macadoo made an announcement to the school. "Great news, kids. Starting today, there will be new fresh, green and healthy choices available in the cafeteria. In other news, whoever ran their underwear up the flagpole, please take it down. It's quite gross. Class starts in three minutes. Have a great day!"

I smiled. It felt good to be me. I had done it. I had used my brain (and my powers) to get the board of education to make a change. A change that would help the entire school. My body tingled with a mix of pride and excitement. For once, I couldn't wait for lunch.

When lunch rolled around, I entered the cafeteria twitching with anticipation. Man, I had to give Tina More credit. She did move fast. The middle of the cafeteria was now dominated by a brand new shining salad bar. The salad bar featured three kinds of lettuce. As well, every color vegetable or fruit you could think of was there…tomatoes, carrots, broccoli, cauliflower, beets, blueberries, celery, four kinds of peppers, watermelon, and corn. Pretty much, if it was plant-based it was on this salad bar. There were over eight salad dressings available, one of them fat-free, another gluten-free. There were even some mixed salads prepared in bowls ready to be served.

The end of the bar also had fresh bread and a variety of cheeses. Finally, there was a spot for fresh soup of the day.

"This is so nice!" Krista said.

"I might even eat more salads!" Tim offered.

The fresh food didn't stop with the salad bar. There were also more hot veggies available in the lunch line. Plus, there was a veggie option main course. Even the pizza now came with pepperoni and veggies.

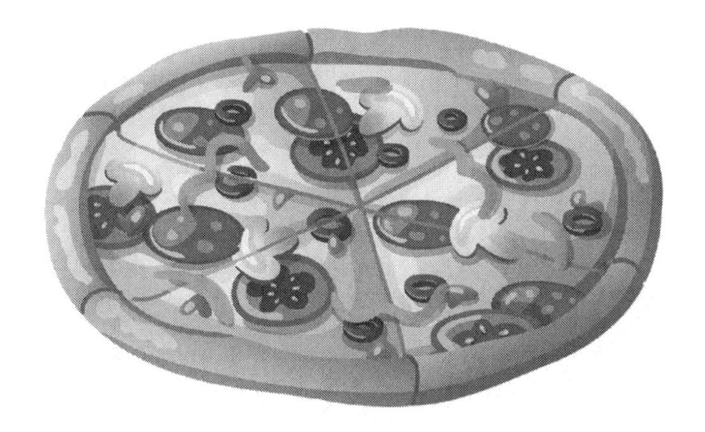

I watched Patti and Wendi and Brandon eying the salad bar. Wendi, Brandon, and Patti pranced up to me.

Brandon gave me a high-five. "Wow, excellent job, Lia!"

"I gotta admit this does look good," Patti told me.

"I think we could use a couple more veggie choices," Wendi moaned.

Brandon rolled his eyes. "Come on, Wendi, what more could you possibly want on this salad bar?" he asked.

"Ah, kale," she said defiantly.

"You hate kale!" Patti and Brandon both said.

"I know, but I still want to give other people choices," Wendi said.

Before I could counter Wendi's remark, everybody in the room stopped moving. I looked over at Tanya. "Why'd you do that?"

"I'm getting a really bad vibe from BMS labs, we'd better get there pronto!" she said, sweat beading up on her forehead.

"Ah, we can't just all leave school in the middle of the day!" Jason told her. "That would be noticed and draw attention to us!"

"Then let's fix that," Tanya said, flicking her hands in the air like she was flipping through an iPad book. But instead of changing pages she flipped forward in time.

We all stood there, our mouths popped open watching time pass in front of us…lunch ended with a wave of Tanya's hand. People and events moved in front of us as if they were in fast-forward mode, which they were. Only none of them knew that. No one noticed the hands of the clock in the cafeteria shooting from 12 to 1, to 2 to 3.

"Okay, day over, let's get there!" Tanya said. "Hopefully, Kayla didn't figure out what was going on and cause even more damage when I sped up time!" She looked at me. "You're the fastest, get there now! Try to keep her distracted. I'll drive the others there."

"Wait, do you have a license yet? Where will you get a car?" I asked.

"Look, we're dealing with my time controlling berserk little sister, I think me bending a law or two isn't really the problem!" Tanya said.

"Right," I agreed. I shot out of the school at super speed. I jumped into the air towards BMS Labs. I didn't even bother trying to have MAC activate my costume because when I looked at his interface, all I saw was a big ☹. That wasn't good!

As BMS labs came into sight, I felt the world around me grow heavy; like I was floating through thick jello. I'd experienced this before when Kayla stopped time, except my super speed kept me going, just not quite at super speed.

The good news was that all the buildings were still there this time. The weird news was, there were no people to be found. The freaky news was, a little wind-up toy creaked its way towards me. The super-duper weird news was that I realized the wind-up toy was Hana.

"Go back, go back! You cannot defeat Kayla," the toy said mechanically. Then it wound down and fell to the ground.

"Oh, so creepy," I said.

A slick red car pulled up and raced through the gates.

The car came to a stop. Tanya rolled out. She pointed towards the quad. "Come on, everybody is there. She has them all gathered together…"

"Whose car?" I asked.

"Janitor Jan's," Tanya said. "She let me borrow it the second before she froze in time."

We walked slowly towards the quad. I didn't really want to walk slowly but I didn't have much choice. It felt as though my entire body had a 10,000-ton weight on it.

"It's taking a lot of energy for me to move," I told Tanya.

She nodded. "Yeah, and if Kayla concentrates on you that will take even more of your energy. Or she could revert you into a baby. Or worse…"

"What's worse?"

"Ah, nothing…." Tanya said.

"So, nothing is worse than her reverting me into a baby?"

"No, I mean she could revert you into nothing. Make you not exist."

I suppressed a gulp. "Yeah, that would be worse." I looked at her. "So, what's the plan? I mean, she is your sister!"

"Reverse of last time, you distract her while I freeze her in time. We keep her that way until your dad's team can find a way to control her powers. She's so young it's hard to control." Then Tanya pointed up. "You get to the air, you have a better chance up there."

"Right!" I said, leaping up. It was slow going and felt like I was pushing my way through deep water. The pressure kept growing. I knew we needed to stop Kayla soon. From the air, I could see the quad's well-groomed courtyard. Kayla stood in the middle, surrounded by about a hundred babies in white lab coats. They actually looked adorable.

"Kayla," I called. "Please turn those people back. Now!"

Kayla tickled one of the babies. "I like them like this, they're nice and quiet. And don't tell me what to do." Kayla looked at me and grinned. "I think I'd like you better like this too!" Her eyes were locked on me. My body felt as though it was stuck in quicksand.

I concentrated on heat and focused next to her feet. Beams of heat ray fired from my eyes. The grass next to Kayla's feet caught fire. "Hey!" she screamed as she darted back.

My body became free. I dove down at her, hitting her with my last bursts of heat vision.

"Ouch! Ouch! Ouch!" she shouted.

Darting behind her at super speed, I hit her in the behind with a couple of quick heat bursts.

"Ouch!" she shouted, turning and rubbing her butt at the same time. A bit of smoke rose from her behind. I noticed I had burnt a hole in the back of her pants. Looking down over her shoulder at her smoldering butt, Kayla cried, "These are my favorite pants!"

I hovered above her and shrugged. "Sorry. But I did give you a chance to turn those people back!" I thought, *"Come on Tanya! I can't keep this up much longer!"*

Sooner rather than later I was bound to get hit by Kayla's time power.

Kayla started spinning her hands quickly. "Time for a time tornado!" she screamed.

Little pieces of time twisted and popped open with each movement of her hand. The world around her became a cracked puzzle, with each separate piece holding a moment in time and space, spinning and spinning. It looked awesome and weird and scary all at once.

The pieces of time spun towards me in a cyclone shape, bigger pieces on top, and smaller pieces on the bottom.

Not knowing what else to do, I focused my freeze breath on the approaching time cyclone. Each fragment of time and space became covered with ice, but they kept spinning towards me except at a slower rate. I could easily dodge them.

Kayla stomped her foot. "I want you to stand sti—"

Kayla stood frozen in mid-sentence.

"No, you're the one who will be standing still, little sister," Tanya said. She looked up at me. "Good job, holding her off."

All the scientists and staff popped back to full grown size. We had done it. We had stopped Kayla!

Dear Diary: Amazing!! We did it. We stopped Kayla. Wow! OMG! OMG! Her powers really are awesome. Watching pieces of time crack and come towards me like that was both awe-inspiring and totally freaky. Man! And the kid isn't even ten. Imagine what she'll be capable of when she's older and has full control of her powers. Yikes! Oh wait, I don't have to imagine. I can see that already with Tanya.

Great! My BFF's GF has cool awesome powers. I mean, come on, she can control time and turn people into babies. Or turn them into younger than babies which is like way scary.

The good news about Tanya is, she is older and has far better control of her powers than Kayla. Which, if I think about it, means my BFF's GF can turn me into a baby (or worse) if she gets angry with me.

The very good news is, Tanya is pretty sane and we get along great. Plus, I have some awesome power myself. I could drop her in her tracks with a fart! But I have to remember, this really isn't a contest. I feel a bit bad that I have to remind myself of that.

On a more down to earth but just as frustrating in its own way note, man, that Wendi is never ever happy. I did a great thing and got the school to give kids way more choices with our foods. Yet, Wendi still isn't happy. I guess you just can't ever please some people. I really shouldn't worry about her, then. She will most likely never change!

The Plan

After a couple of minutes to collect themselves, my dad, Hana and the rest of the staff at BMS Labs began to take charge of the situation.

"That was certainly an interesting experience," Dad said. "Though truthfully, my baby brain didn't remember much of it. I can't wait to see the security video."

That's my dad, always the scientist eager to learn from any experience. Jason, Lori, and Marie stood by in amazement. Jason, like dad, was in awe of what had gone on.

Jason looked at Tanya, "Wow, what amazing power you and your sister have!"

Tanya grinned. She pointed at her sister, now frozen in time. "The problem is…at her age this power is almost impossible to control."

Dad stepped forward and nodded. "True. We'll figure out some way to inhibit her powers." He looked to Tanya, "How long can you hold her like this?"

Tanya shrugged. "Maybe forever. Maybe until tomorrow? No idea."

Dad turned to his team. "Well then people, we'd better get cracking."

"Right!" they all said. I'm surprised they didn't salute.

I had to admit, Dad's team was dedicated. I wasn't sure what they could do. But if anybody could help Kayla, it had to be Dad's team. They were good people who wanted to make the world better for supers and non-supers alike. They put Kayla on a drone stretcher and moved her into one of the research buildings.

One of Dad's red-shirted security people came up and whispered something into Dad's ear. I assumed it was something about Kayla. I heard Dad say, "Oh that's not right, not right at all."

"What's wrong?" I asked Dad.

"It can't be my sister. Can it?" Tanya frowned.

Dad shook his head. "Not directly," he replied. "But, she may indirectly be the cause…"

"Dad, I'm so confused," I said.

"Me too!" Jason said.

"I'm like always confused when it comes to this stuff!" Marie said.

"It's the K-9 comet," Dad said, looking up to the sky.

"What about it," Jason asked. "It's going to swing close to Earth but miss."

Dad stood there in silence.

"Dad? Say something!" I said.

Hana spoke up. "Somehow, the comet has changed its trajectory. It is now on a collision course with Earth. In fact, it is on course to crash into Starlight City."

"Oh, that's so bad…" Lori said.

"Oh, that's such an understatement," Jason said.

"Has the government figured this out yet?" Dad asked.

Hana pulled a tablet out of her side. "Here's a local broadcast."

We all saw Oscar Oranga appear on the screen. "Greetings. I have some fairly terrible news. For some strange reason, the K-9 comet has changed course. The comet is now on a collision course with Earth; Starlight City to be exact. No use trying to run, because if this comet hits, it will destroy a good portion of the Earth. We now need a miracle."

Dad looked at Lori, Marie, Jason, Tanya and me. "Luckily, I'm looking at a whole bunch of miracles!" he said. He pointed. "To our satellite command center room."

"So cool!" Jason said.

The satellite command center room was filled with way cool high-tech scanning devices covering many big screens. There was a map of the earth, a map of satellite paths, and a complete outer space view.

"How the heck are you getting the view from space?" Jason asked.

Dad stood at one of the many control panels that lined the room. "We've launched a couple of our satellites and we have hooked into all the high powered telescopes on Earth." Dad turned to a technician looking at one of the screens. "How long until the comet strikes Earth?" he asked.

The technician pointed to the screen. A countdown appeared in big numbers: 2:20:59, 2:20:58, 2:20:57…

"I don't suppose that's two months and twenty days," I said.

"Two hours and twenty minutes," the technician said.

I looked at the screen. I looked up at the see-through ceiling that I had just noticed. I can leap up into space and smash it!" I said.

Hana shook her head. "No, you can't."

"I'm pretty strong!" I insisted.

Jason stepped in. "True, but the problem with smashing a comet the size of a city block is that Earth and Starlight city will get hit with a bunch of comet pieces instead of one big one. The damage to the area will be pretty much the same…"

Dad looked at Tanya. "Can you slow that thing down?"

Now Tanya looked up to the sky. "I've never tried stopping time from a distance before…. I have no idea…"

Marie put her hand on Tanya's shoulder. "You can do it, I know you can!"

Lori shook her head. "Yeah, come on T-girl. This could help a lot."

I gazed at Tanya. For the first time since I have known her, she seemed unsure of herself. She stood there for a couple of moments in silence. I actually have to admit that made me feel kind of good. Not the fact that Tanya was worried, but the fact that Tanya wasn't totally perfect.

I stepped forward. "Tanya, come on. You have awesome power and constant coolness; you can do this." I nodded towards Jason. "Come on, if this guy likes you, you have to be pretty great."

Tanya smiled at me. She let out a little sigh. "My sister did this; I have to help stop this." She shuddered. "It's just that I'm worried I can't.

Now Jason stepped up. He put both of his hands on Tanya's shoulders and locked eyes with her. "You can do this! You are one of the four most amazing people I know! Not because of your powers, but because of your personality and how you use those powers."

"Four people?" Tanya said with a grin.

"You, Lia and my mom and dad," he said.

"Good enough for me," Tanya grinned. Tanya looked at me.

I found it good enough for me too.

"Gee, what are *we*?" Lori asked. "Artichokes?"

"I like artichokes!" Jason said. "You guys are amazing, too. He looked at everybody around the room. "You all do great jobs!"

"Okay, speaking of which," Dad said. "We need to get back to the business of saving the world."

"I can't just leave time frozen," Tanya said. "That wouldn't be much of a solution."

"No, it wouldn't," Dad agreed. "But if you slow it down enough, that will give us time to crunch the numbers and do the math." He looked over at me. "Then we will send Lia up to stop that comet."

"Wait, I thought I couldn't just smash it?" I said.

"You can't, but you can deflect it," Jason said.

Tanya looked up into the air. She took a deep breath. She inhaled and held it. She pointed in the general direction of where she thought the comet was.

"Well?" she asked.

The counter moved backward to 2:53:59.

The room exploded with applause. "Not a lot of time, but every bit helps," Dad said.

"Okay, team, crunch numbers, and let's come up with the angle and force Lia will need to hit that thing so she can deflect it," Dad said.

"I got it," Hana said.

"Okay, great!" Dad said.

An image of the comet appeared on the screen.

A red arrow suddenly appeared showing the path of the comet.

Hana spoke, "If the comet continues on its current path unabated, it will make a sharp turn and crash into Earth here."

The map zoomed in on Starlight city.

Hana continued, "At the comet's current speed, it will destroy Starlight city and a good portion of the surrounding area. Plus, it will create a nasty dust cloud that could affect weather all over the planet."

"Okay, so how do I stop it?" I asked.

Hana rolled her eyes, literally, which was weird. "As stated, you cannot stop it, you must deflect it by 33 or more degrees. That will cause it to zoom past Earth."

The screen showed an image of me flying towards the comet. I approached at a slight angle. I exhaled on the meteor. My breath forced the big giant frost covered rock off course.

The projected path of the comet now showed it missing Earth with a big green arrow. The screen flashed.

"Good job! Game not over for Starlight City!"

"Okay, easy!" I said.

"Actually, it won't be at all," Hana said. "You'll have to hold your breath and then let it out at exactly the right moment. The force of your breath will cause you to turn course and then propel yourself in the opposite direction, to get back to Earth."

"If I need to pick up speed in space how do I do it?" I asked.

"You fart!" Jason said.

"That will do it!" Dad said.

"Is that it?" I asked.

"Yes, just remember, your reentry into Earth will cause quite a hole, but still far less damage than being hit by a 5-mile wide comet…" Hana said.

Dear Diary: Okay, so we had a plan. It involved me holding my breath, leaping into space, farting, blowing a giant space rock off course, turning around, and then crashing back to Earth. Maybe not the best plan in the world but it was a plan that could work. A plan that had to work. Of course, it would involve me needing to know what a 30-degree angle was. Which I did! Who would have ever thought that math could help save the world!

Outer Space

We all headed quickly outside. Dad and his team gave me an earpiece to wear so I could hear their instructions even when I was in space. Of course, I wouldn't be able to talk back to them since I was going to be in space. Once up there, I was on my own; me against a huge frozen rock. I knew that rock didn't stand a chance!

"While we won't be able to directly communicate back with you, MAC will be able to relay back to us information about you. Plus, you can use his GPS to help close in on the K-9 comet," Hana told me.

Jason walked up and hugged me. "Good luck!" he said.

I smiled at him.

I took a deep breath. I bent down and then pushed myself up into the air.

I felt exhilarated, flying through the sky going higher and higher.

"Okay, Lia," I heard Dad from my ear phone, "you're about to escape the earth's atmosphere, so hold your breath on three, two, one, now."

I drew a deep strong breath, letting my lungs fill with air. Suddenly, the blue sky disappeared and I found myself in the deep blackness of space. I felt myself gaining speed as I escaped the last pull of Earth's gravity. I was now a missile.

"Great, honey!" Dad called into my ear. I heard Hana say something to him. "Okay, Lia, you need to speed up your approach. Time to release a fart!"

That was, of course, easier said than done. I actually didn't really need to fart but I had learned something by watching almost every boy at school...

it was usually pretty easy to force out a fart if needed.

I squeezed my butt cheeks together and then pushed out with my butt. I felt ridiculous. But I also felt a little blast of something come from my behind. I propelled forward fast. Never before had I been so proud of a fart!

I felt a cool rush as I sped nearer to the huge flying frozen space rock. Zooming in closer and closer, I could see the comet without using super vision. The comet had more of a blue color in it than I imagined. I actually found it to be a pretty mix of cold blue with a fiery white ice tail. I found it to be quite striking, but of course, I knew I couldn't let it strike my home city.

I heard Dad in my ear. "Honey, you're coming in at a thirty-six-degree angle. You need to come in a bit lower."

Oh, just lovely. I certainly couldn't let this big rock hit my planet because of a math error. My head started to pound. I needed a way to correct my course and fast. I couldn't hold my breath much longer.

Pointing my arms downward, I let out a little fart. My body changed direction. I let myself drift for a minute.

"Okay, change course now!" Jason said in my ear.

I raised my arms back up and let out a slightly more powerful fart. I shot forward towards the big comet. I wanted to let out a sigh of relief but I couldn't spare the air.

I lined the comet up. I now sped directly at it. I also had silence from the ground. I couldn't feel the earphone in my ear any longer. My fast turn must have caused it to fall.

Oh well, luckily I was good at math and thought I was coming into the comet at pretty near a 30-degree angle. Yeah, I understand I'm using the word "pretty" a lot. This wasn't going according to my exact science. So I needed to use overwhelming force to make sure I blew this big burning ball away from Earth.

I drew closer and closer and closer. Soon, I saw all the nicks and holes on the comet. It looked like it had a bad, bad case of acne.

I glanced at MAC but all his screen said was: U CAN DO IT!!! Great, my high-tech computer had become an inspirational greeting card.

Even though I was still holding my breath, I tightened my chest. When the big comet dominated my vision, I exhaled, pushing the air out with all my might. If I hadn't been in space I would have screamed!

My breath hit the comet pushing it back, way back! Wow, I had changed the comet's course. Now, of course, I was out of air and had to change my course back to Earth. With no gravity to stop me, I would drift forever if I couldn't turn around.

I lowered my hands thrusting them down. My body turned around, but I kept seeing Earth grow smaller and smaller. Not good. *Please let me get a fart to rip,* I thought. I pushed my butt cheeks with all my might. I thought I felt a fart rush. I jolted forward. Earth now came closer and closer.

I had done it. I fell towards the Earth.
Of course, I had to be way off-target. I blacked out, ecstatic I had saved the planet.

Dear Diary: Well, wow! I did it! It took all I had. It took the work of my entire team, but I did it. I stopped a huge comet from crashing into Earth. My team and I did it. Super Breath saved the Earth and a fart or two saved me. Yeah, life is weird sometimes. Life does take funny turns and ups and downs. I now know I just have to ride them out. Not much I can't do if I work at it. Sure, Jason is with Tanya now. I'm not totally sure what I think of that. But they are both great people and they deserve each other. Jason is my BFF. Will we be more someday? I have no idea. What I do know is that he'll always be there for me and I'll always be there for him. That's what being BFF's mean. You are there for each other no matter what. Yeah, I know it sounds silly but there may not be a greater power than love and friendship. Though my farts and foot odor do pack quite the punch! ☺

Feels Good to Be Me

I came to. I found myself lying face first in a giant crater of what felt like chocolate pudding. I stood up. I had to be at least 30 feet deep in a big chocolate pudding crater. Looking up, I saw a bunch of town people, Oscar Oranga and his camera crew. Dad and his team of scientists were there. Of course, my team of Tanya, Marie, Lori, Jason, and Jess were there. I leaped out of the hole, shaking off the chocolate pudding.

I heard Oscar say, "That's right, good people of Starlight City, our very own superhero, Super Teen, saved the day by blowing the K-9 comet out of Earth's path. Then she came crashing back down to Earth, here at Starlight City Lake Park. How this part of the park was transformed into pudding, we may never know. The good news is, we and Super Teen are safe!"

The crowd roared with approval. Oscar ran up to me and put his microphone in my face. "Super Teen, how did you do this?"

I pointed to my dad. "The good scientists at BMS Labs gave me the proper coordinates and a game plan. I just jumped into space and blew," I said as if I was talking about taking a stroll down the street.

"How did you propel yourself back to Earth?" Oscar asked.

"I turned my head and burped!" Sure it was a little white lie, but I figured I'd rather be known as the girl who burped her way back to earth than the one who farted.

I walked over to my friends. They all raced up and hugged me. "How?" I asked. "How did I end up crashing into an area of pudding in the park?"

Jess leaned into me and whispered. "I used a bit of magic to change your course. It seemed to be the least I could do."

Marie leaned into me and whispered. "And once Jason and your dad's team gave me your new landing spot, I did my thing and turned things into pudding."

"Thanks!" I said to everybody.

I heard the sounds of emergency vehicles coming towards us. A police car drove right up next to us. Police Chief Michaels got out of the driver's side. Of course, Kalie Hanson got out as well. Kalie walked up to me.

"Super Teen, I appreciate all you have done for the city. I truly do!" she told me.

"Thanks," I told her. "Now, I hope you see that I can do good."

Kalie nodded. "Yes, but even doing this good, you caused a lot of damage to the city. Plus, this still doesn't mean you are allowed to fight crime. But being the good citizen that I am, I am prepared to let you off with a warning and to drop my charges if you swear never to fight crime again."

I shook my head. "Nope. Sorry. Not going to happen. I mean, I'll try to let the police and other officials handle most things, but there are some things that just call for Super Teen. When those matters call, I will answer!"

Most of the crowd cheered. A few jeered.

Jason ran up to us. "Besides, we have an online poll with over 20 thousand signatures from people who want Super Teen to be deputized."

Kalie shook her head. "Sorry, we don't govern by online polls." She turned to Police Chief Michaels, "Chief, please arrest Super Teen." She looked at me. "I am truly sorry about this."

Police Chief Michaels stood there, arms crossed for a moment. He walked up to me. He put his hand on my shoulder.

"Super Teen, as police chief of this city, I now officially deputize you! You have proven you are ready to fight crime."

"What?" I said.

"What?" Kalie said.

The chief turned to Kalie. "My officers and I consider her to be a valuable asset."

Kalie pulled out her warrant. She shook her head. "Well, I'm a lawyer who likes to listen to the people on the street. I can't believe I am saying this, but Super Teen, if the police want you then I will drop my charges." She tore the warrant in half.

Pretty much all the crowd started to roar.

My mom came rushing up to me. "Super Teen, I'm a doctor, can I check you over to make sure you are okay?"

"Sure, be my guest, Ma'am," I said. "But it takes more than a fall from space into a pile of pudding to stop me!"

The crowd roared again. It felt good to be me.

The Biggest Surprise of All

The next morning, I sat on my porch talking to Jason about the events of the day before. We both felt great about saving Starlight City (and more). Just as I was starting to forget that Jason and Tanya were a thing now, I saw Tanya walking towards us. Tanya wasn't alone. Walking beside her was another girl who looked like a slightly different version of Tanya.

Actually, something about the girl reminded me of Kayla, except Kayla was only eight. This girl was much older.

"Hey, guys," Tanya said. "You know how Kayla had too much power for an eight-year-old to control?"

"Yep," I said.

"Yes," Jason said.

Tanya smiled. "Well, I found a solution. Meet the new 16-year-old Kayla."

Kayla held out a hand to me. "This is certainly going to be interesting from now on!" Kayla said.

Man, was that the understatement of the century, or what?

The end for now.

***

Find out what happens next in
Diary of a Super Girl - Book 7
OUT NOW!

We hope you enjoyed Diary of a Super Girl - Book 6!
If you did, can you please leave a review?
We would be really grateful if you can spare some time and
we can't wait to hear what you think!
Thanks so much!
Katrina and John ☺

Many of the following books can also be purchased as a collection that includes a number of books in the series. Rather than buying each book individually, you can read the entire collection at a DISCOUNTED PRICE! Just search for the titles on Amazon or your favorite online book retailer to see what is available...

I SHRUNK
MY
BEST
FRIEND
BOOK 1
OOOPS!
KATRINA KAHLER & JOHN SAKOUR

I SHRUNK
MY
BEST
FRIEND
ALL
3
BOOKS
KATRINA KAHLER & JOHN ZAKOUR

Diary of a Ghost Buster – Book 1

Zara the Ghost Zapper

This is another fun and exciting story of a girl with special powers. Her powers are very different to Lia Strong's but you'll be amazed at what she discovers she is capable of! Find out what Zara gets up to in this fabulous new series…

Diary of an
ALMOST COOL WITCH
Book 1
Bill & Kaz Campbell

JULIA JONES'
DIARY
BOOK 1
MY
Worst
DAY
EVER!
Katrina Kahler

Body Swap
Catastrophe
ZAP!
Book 1
Katrina Kahler

Witch School
Book 1
Katrina Kahler

MIND READER
BOOK 1
MY NEW LIFE
KATRINA KAHLER

THE SECRET
Mind Magic
BOOK 1

About the Authors

John Zakour is a humor / SF/ fantasy writer with a Master's degree in Human Behavior. He has written thousands of gags for syndicated comics, comedians and TV shows (including Simpsons and Rugrats and, Joan River's old TV show.) John has written seven humorous SF novels for Daw books (the first The Plutonium Blonde was named the funniest SF book of 2001 by The Chronicle of Science Fiction). John has also written three YA books, four humorous self-help books and three books on HTML. John has also optioned two TV shows and three movies.

His books may be found here:
http://www.amazon.com/John-Zakour/e/B000APS2F0

Katrina Kahler is the Best Selling Author of several series of books, including Julia Jones' Diary, Mind Reader, The Secret, Diary of a Horse Mad Girl, Twins, Angel, Slave to a Vampire and numerous Learn to Read Books for young children. Katrina lives in beautiful Noosa on the Australian coastline.

You can find all of Katrina's books here:
Best Selling Books for Kids.com

Follow Katrina on Instagram
@katrinakahler
@freebooksforkids

Made in the USA
San Bernardino, CA
04 December 2017